Praise for Amy Clipston

"This series is an enjoyable treat to those who enjoy the genre and will keep readers wanting more to see what happens next at the Marketplace."

—*Parkersburg News and Sentinel* on *The Farm Stand*

"Amy Clipston's characters are always so endearing and well-developed, and Salina and Will in *The Farm Stand* are some of my favorites. I enjoyed how their business relationship melded into a close friendship, and then eventually turned into so much more. *The Farm Stand* honors the Amish community in the very best of ways. I loved it."

—Shelley Shepard Gray, *New York Times* and *USA TODAY* bestselling author

"Clipston begins her Amish Marketplace series with this pleasing story of love and competition . . . This sweet tale will please fans of Clipston's wholesome Amish romances."

—*Publishers Weekly* on *The Bake Shop*

"Fans of Amish fiction will love Amy Clipston's latest, *The Bake Shop*. It's filled with warm and cozy moments as Jeff and Christiana find their way from strangers to friendship to love."

—Robin Lee Hatcher, bestselling author of *Who I Am with You* and *Cross My Heart*

"Clipston closes out this heartrending series with a thoughtful consideration of how Amish rules can tear families apart, as well as a reminder that God's path is not always what one might expect. Readers old and new will find the novel's issues intriguing and its hard-won resolution reassuring."

—*Hope by the Book*, BOOKMARKED review, on *A Welcome at Our Door*

"A sweet romance with an endearing heroine, this is a good wrap-up of the series."

—*Parkersburg News and Sentinel* on *A Welcome at Our Door*

"*Seasons of an Amish Garden* follows the year through short stories as friends create a memorial garden to celebrate a life. Revealing the underbelly of main characters, a trademark talent of Amy Clipston, makes them relatable and endearing. One story slides into the next, woven together effortlessly with the author's knowledge of the Amish life. Once started, you can't put this book down."

      —Suzanne Woods Fisher, bestselling
      author of *The Devoted*

"With endearing characters that readers will want to get a happily ever after, this is a story of romance and family to savor."

      —*Parkersburg News and Sentinel* on *A Seat by the Hearth*

"[*A Seat by the Hearth*] is a moving portrait of a disgraced woman attempting to reenter her childhood community . . . This will please Clipston's fans and also win over newcomers to Lancaster County."

      —*Publishers Weekly*

"This story shares the power of forgiveness and hope and, above all, faith in God's Word and His promises."

      —*Hope by the Book*, BOOKMARKED
      review, on *A Seat by the Hearth*

"This story of profound loss and deep friendship will leave readers with the certain knowledge that hope exists and love grows through faith in our God of second chances."

      —Kelly Irvin, author of *The Beekeeper's Son* and
      Upon a Spring Breeze, on *Room on the Porch Swing*

"This heartbreaking series continues to take a fearlessly honest look at grief, as hopelessness threatens to steal what happiness Allen has treasured within his marriage and recent fatherhood. Clipston takes these feelings seriously without sugarcoating any aspect of the mourning process, allowing her characters to make their painful but ultimately joyous journey back to love and faith. Readers who have made this tough and ongoing pilgrimage themselves will appreciate the author's realistic portrayal of coming to terms with loss in order to continue living with hope and happiness."

—*RT Book Reviews*, 4 stars, on *Room on the Porch Swing*

"A story of grief as well as new beginnings, this is a lovely Amish tale and the start of a great new series."

—*Parkersburg News and Sentinel* on *A Place at Our Table*

"Themes of family, forgiveness, love, and strength are woven throughout the story . . . a great choice for all readers of Amish fiction."

—*CBA Market Magazine* on *A Place at Our Table*

"This debut title in a new series offers an emotionally charged and engaging read headed by sympathetically drawn and believable protagonists. The meaty issues of trust and faith make this a solid book group choice."

—*Library Journal* on *A Place at Our Table*

"These sweet, tender novellas from one of the genre's best make the perfect sampler for new readers curious about Amish romances."

—*Library Journal* on *Amish Sweethearts*

"Clipston is as reliable as her character, giving Emily a difficult and intense romance worthy of Emily's ability to shine the light of Christ into the hearts of those she loves."

—*RT Book Reviews*, 4^1/2 stars, TOP PICK! on *The Cherished Quilt*

"Clipston's heartfelt writing and engaging characters make her a fan favorite. Her latest Amish tale combines a spiritual message of accepting God's blessings as they are given with a sweet romance."

—*Library Journal* on *The Cherished Quilt*

"Clipston delivers another enchanting series starter with a tasty premise, family secrets, and sweet-as-pie romance, offering assurance that true love can happen more than once and second chances are worth fighting for."

—*RT Book Reviews*, 4^1/2 stars, TOP PICK! on *The Forgotten Recipe*

"In the first book in her Amish Heirloom series, Clipston takes readers on a roller-coaster ride through grief, guilt, and anxiety."

—*Booklist* on *The Forgotten Recipe*

"Clipston is well versed in Amish culture and does a good job creating the world of Lancaster County, Penn. . . . Amish fiction fans will enjoy this story—and want a taste of Veronica's raspberry pie!"

—*Publishers Weekly* on *The Forgotten Recipe*

"[Clipston] does an excellent job of wrapping up her story while setting the stage for the sequel."

—*CBA Retailers + Resources* on *The Forgotten Recipe*

"Clipston brings this engaging series to an end with two emotional family reunions, a prodigal son parable, a sweet but hard-won romance, and a happy ending for characters readers have grown to love. Once again, she gives us all we could possibly want from a talented storyteller."

—*RT Book Reviews*, 4 1/2 stars, TOP
PICK! on *A Simple Prayer*

". . . will leave readers craving more."

—*RT Book Reviews*, 4 1/2 stars, TOP
PICK! on *A Mother's Secret*

"Clipston's series starter has a compelling drama involving faith, family, and romance . . . [an] absorbing series."

—*RT Book Reviews*, 4 1/2 stars, TOP
PICK! on *A Hopeful Heart*

"Authentic characters, delectable recipes, and faith abound in Clipston's second Kauffman Amish Bakery story."

—*RT Book Reviews*, 4 stars, on *A Promise of Hope*

". . . an entertaining story of Amish life, loss, love, and family."

—*RT Book Reviews*, 4 stars, on *A Place of Peace*

"This fifth and final installment in the Kauffman Amish Bakery series is sure to please fans who have waited for Katie's story."

—*Library Journal* on *A Season of Love*

"[The Kauffman Amish Bakery] series' wide popularity is sure to attract readers to this novella, and they won't be disappointed by the excellent writing and the story's wholesome goodness."

—*Library Journal* on *A Plain and Simple Christmas*

"[*A Plain and Simple Christmas*] is inspiring and a perfect fit for the holiday season."

—*RT Book Reviews*, 4 stars

The Coffee Corner

Other Books by Amy Clipston

The Coffee Corner

AN AMISH MARKETPLACE NOVEL

AMY CLIPSTON

ZONDERVAN

The Coffee Corner

Copyright © 2020 by Amy Clipston

Requests for information should be addressed to:

Zondervan, 3900 Sparks Dr. SE, Grand Rapids, Michigan 49546

Library of Congress Cataloging-in-Publication Data
Names: Clipston, Amy, author.
Title: The coffee corner : an Amish marketplace novel / Amy Clipston.
Description: Grand Rapids, Michigan : Zondervan, [2020] | Series: Amish
  marketplace ; 3 | Summary: "In this third installment of Amy Clipston's
  Amish Marketplace series, an acquaintance grows into love over a few
  well-timed cups of coffee"-- Provided by publisher.
Identifiers: LCCN 2020030285 (print) | LCCN 2020030286 (ebook) | ISBN
  9780310356509 (paperback) | ISBN 9780310360919 (library binding) | ISBN
  9780310356493 (epub) | ISBN 9780310356523 (downloadable audio)
Subjects: GSAFD: Christian fiction. | Love stories.
Classification: LCC PS3603.L58 C64 2020 (print) | LCC PS3603.L58 (ebook)
  | DDC 813/.6--dc23
LC record available at https://lccn.loc.gov/2020030285
LC ebook record available at https://lccn.loc.gov/2020030286

Zondervan titles may be purchased in bulk for educational, business, fundraising, or sales promotional use. For information, please email SpecialMarkets@Zondervan.com.

Printed in the United States of America

20 21 22 23 24   LSC   10 9 8 7 6 5 4 3 2 1

For my super-awesome roller-coaster sisters,
DeeDee and Kris, with love.

Glossary

ach: oh
aenti: aunt
appeditlich: delicious
Ausbund: Amish hymnal
bedauerlich: sad
Ban: shunning
boppli: baby
bopplin: babies
brot: bread
bruder: brother
bruderskind: niece/nephew
bruderskinner: nieces/nephews
bu: boy
buwe: boys
daadi: granddad
daed: father
danki: thank you
dat: dad
Dietsch: Pennsylvania Dutch, the Amish language (a German dialect)
dochder: daughter
dochdern: daughters

Dummle!: hurry!

dummkopp: moron

Englisher: a non-Amish person

faul: lazy

faulenzer: lazy person

fraa: wife

freind: friend

freinden: friends

froh: happy

gegisch: silly

gern gschehne: you're welcome

grossdaadi: grandfather

grossdochder: granddaughter

grossdochdern: granddaughters

grossmammi: grandmother

gross-sohn: grandson

Gude mariye: Good morning

gut: good

Gut nacht: Good night

haus: house

Hoi!: Get back here!

Ich liebe dich: I love you

kaffi: coffee

kapp: prayer covering or cap

kichli: cookie

kichlin: cookies

kind: child

kinner: children

krank: sick

kuche: cake

kuchen: cakes

kumm: come

liewe: love, a term of endearment

maed: young women, girls

maedel: young woman

mamm: mom

mammi: grandma

mei: my

Meiding: shunning

mutter: mother

naerfich: nervous

narrisch: crazy

onkel: uncle

Ordnung: the oral tradition of practices required and forbidden in the Amish faith

rumspringa: period of "running around" for Amish youth before they decide whether they want to be baptized into the Amish faith

schee: pretty

schmaert: smart

schtupp: family room

schweschder: sister

schweschdere: sisters

sohn: son

Was iss letz?: What's wrong?

Willkumm: welcome

Wie geht's: How do you do? or Good day!

wunderbaar: wonderful

ya: yes

zwillingbopplin: twins

The Amish Marketplace
Series Family Trees

Grandparents
Erma m. Sylvan Gingerich
|
Lynn m. Freeman Kurtz
Mary m. Lamar Petersheim
Walter m. Rachelle
Harvey m. Darlene

SECOND GENERATION PARENTS AND CHILDREN
Lynn m. Freeman Kurtz
Christiana m. __|__ Phoebe
Jeffrey Stoltzfus

Lamar m. Mary Petersheim
Cornelius (Neil) __|__ Salina

Neil m. Ellen Petersheim
Betsy Kay __|__ Jayne

Darlene m. Harvey Gingerich
Bethany __|__ Anthony

Rachelle m. Walter Gingerich
|
Leanna m. Marlin Wengerd (deceased)
|
Chester

Bertha (deceased) m. Enos Zook
|
Richard m. Magdalena

Magdalena m. Richard Zook
Laverne m. Alvin Bontrager —|— Micah

Laverne m. Alvin (Al) Bontrager
|
Kristine

Joyce m. Merle Stoltzfus
Jeffrey m. —|— Nicholas
Christiana Stoltzfus

Note to the Reader

While this novel is set against the real backdrop of Lancaster County, Pennsylvania, the characters are fictional. There is no intended resemblance between the characters in this book and any real members of the Amish and Mennonite communities. As with any work of fiction, I've taken license in some areas of research as a means of creating the necessary circumstances for my characters. My research was thorough; however, it would be impossible to be completely accurate in details and description since each and every community differs. Therefore, any inaccuracies in the Amish and Mennonite lifestyles portrayed in this book are completely due to fictional license.

Chapter 1

Bethany Gingerich smoothed her hands down her peacock-colored dress as she sat on a bench just outside the doorway of her aunt and uncle's kitchen. She glanced toward the front door and took in a deep breath as excitement bubbled up inside of her.

After months of planning and preparing, the first Thursday in November was finally here. Bethany's cousin Salina Petersheim was going to marry her fiancé, Will Zimmerman, whom she'd started dating nearly a year ago.

Bethany was honored Salina had asked her to be her attendant, and Bethany's brother, Anthony, was just as excited to be Will's. She and her brother would walk down the aisle ahead of the bride and groom in Salina's father's largest barn and then sit in a place of honor at the front of the congregation during the service.

For now Bethany sat with Salina, Anthony, and Will waiting to greet the hundreds of guests who would attend the wedding. The Petersheim and Zimmerman families had invited members of Salina's Old Order Amish community as well as the Old Order Mennonite community in which Will had been raised. About an hour ago, some members of Salina's church district had arrived to help with the festivities. The smells of baked chicken and freshly baked bread floated on the air, along with the voices of the community women who cooked in the kitchen behind them.

Bethany turned toward her cousin, who looked beautiful clad in a dress identical to Bethany's. Salina had taken care when she'd chosen the color of their dresses, and it was a beautiful complement to Salina's dark hair and baby-blue eyes. The bride-to-be looked radiant, but her nerves were obvious as she fiddled with her white apron.

"Are you ready?" Will Zimmerman also turned toward his bride, his blue eyes sparkling as he leaned over and took her hand in his. "It's seven thirty, nearly time for our guests to arrive."

"I think so." Salina's smile seemed forced.

Bethany placed her fingers on Salina's free hand and gave her best encouraging smile. "Everything will be fine. Before you know it, we'll be eating cookies and celebrating with the congregation."

Salina blew out a deep breath. "Right."

"We'll celebrate until we can't stand up straight from exhaustion," Will quipped, and they all laughed.

Both Anthony and Will looked handsome dressed in their Sunday black-and-white suits, complete with crisp white shirts, black vests, and black trousers. At the opposite end of the bench from Bethany sat Anthony. At twenty, he was four years younger than his sister, and although his hair was light brown rather than Bethany's golden blond, they both shared the same bright-blue eyes as their mother.

Bethany was certain to the depth of her bones that Salina and Will's relationship had been blessed by God. They'd met when Will visited Salina's Farm Stand at the Bird-in-Hand Marketplace.

He'd come to buy produce for his business, Zimmerman's Family Restaurant, across the street from the marketplace. Both Will and Salina had been dating other people when they met, and Will had been a member of the Old Order Mennonite church. But they'd realized they belonged together, and before long, they'd fallen in love.

After they both endured emotional breakups, Will had talked to Salina's father, Lamar, who was the bishop in their Older Order Amish district, and had been invited to join the Amish church. Will met with *Onkel* Lamar for three baptism classes in the spring before becoming a member of the church. Soon after, he'd proposed to Salina.

The back door opened, and the crisp early-November morning air wafted in, bringing with it the aroma of moist earth and horses. Bethany and the others stood up and smiled as members of the congregation drifted in, the women dressed in black shawls and bonnets and the men in black coats and hats.

"*Gude mariye.*" Bethany nodded as she shook hands with an older guest who then moved down the line. She worked to keep her expression bright as she continued welcoming congregation members. After each woman greeted Bethany and the rest of the wedding party, she headed upstairs to deposit her bonnet and shawl on Salina's bed while the men went outside to gather by the barn.

Christiana Stoltzfus pulled Bethany into a hug. "Bethany, you look so *schee!*" She gasped as she looked from Bethany to Salina. "The dresses look even more beautiful on you two. I love the color." Christina was twenty-seven and only six months older than Salina.

"*Danki.*" Bethany smiled at her cousin, who seemed to glow.

Although she had always considered Christiana to be beautiful, with her striking blue-green eyes and bright-red hair, she was even more attractive lately. She was now in her seventh month of pregnancy with her first child, and her happiness shone from within.

Salina pulled Christiana into her arms. "I can't believe I'm getting married today," she said, her voice sounding thick.

Christiana sighed. "How are you feeling?"

"*Froh* but nervous." Salina worried her lower lip.

Bethany beamed as she watched her cousins grin at each other. Christiana and Salina were more than Bethany's cousins; they were her best friends. The three of them, along with their cousin Leanna, ran booths at the Bird-in-Hand market. Bethany ran the Coffee Corner, Salina had her Farm Stand, Christiana had her Bake Shop, and Leanna kept her Jam and Jelly Nook. Leanna had been widowed several years ago but she had a son, and now Salina and Christiana would both be married—something that had more than once lately made Bethany feel a bit left behind. Aside from Leanna, she would be the last single member of their friend group. Bethany hadn't had a boyfriend since she briefly dated a member of her youth group when she was nineteen. And as of now, she had no prospects.

She pushed those thoughts away. Today was Salina's day! And Bethany needed to celebrate with her, not wallow in self-pity over her lack of dates.

Bethany looked up and saw Christiana's husband. Jeff and Christiana had met when she opened her Bake Shop booth next to his Unique Leather and Wood Gifts booth at the marketplace.

"*Gude mariye*, Jeff." She reached out to shake his hand and was met by a cold touch.

"Sorry about that." His dark eyes sparkled as a sheepish chuckle escaped his lips. "It's chilly out there." He pushed his hand through his dark hair, which matched his beard, and the curl that always hung over his forehead bounced back into place.

"That is true." Bethany laughed, then turned to the next person in line. "*Gude mariye*, Leanna!"

Leanna reached around and hugged Bethany. "*Gude mariye!* I'm grateful to see you—and that it's nice and warm in here." She rubbed her hands together.

Leanna was her oldest cousin as well as the shortest. She had the same lovely shade of dark-brown hair as Salina, but what Bethany most admired about Leanna was the kind of woman she was. Leanna had been only thirty-one when she lost her husband, Marlin Wengerd, in an accident. Five years later, she was still raising her son alone, although they did live with her parents. With an unwavering positivity, Leanna always remembered to count her blessings, including the success of her Jam and Jelly Nook booth at the marketplace.

"*Ya*, it is cold outside," Chester, her son, chimed in. At fourteen he already towered over his mother by nearly five inches. He shared Leanna's bright smile and chocolate eyes, but his hair was a lighter shade of brown, almost blond, resembling his late father's. He hugged Bethany.

"Hey, Chester." Bethany smiled, patting his shoulder.

"You look beautiful," Leanna said, her eyes misting over. "I can't believe our Salina is getting married." She sniffed as she turned to greet the bride. "You are gorgeous today and always."

Salina blushed, and Bethany felt a tug at her heart as her cousins embraced.

"They're so mushy," Chester quipped, and Bethany gave a

bark of laughter. She cupped her mouth with her hand to stifle the sound.

Leanna and Chester moved on down the line, shaking hands with Anthony and Will before disappearing into the knot of people gathered by the stairs. Bethany shook a few more hands, greeting members of her congregation and also Will's Older Order Mennonite family members and friends. When she spotted Micah Zook and his grandfather, Enos, standing near the end of the line, her heart turned over in her chest. She tried her best to continue greeting the guests moving past her, but her eyes were drawn to Micah. As he moved closer, she sneaked peek after peek.

One of the older men in the congregation paused in front of her and began talking about the cold weather. Down the line, Micah was saying something to his grandfather beside him. She took in his stature, as he stood nearly a foot taller than her own height. His brown hair was hidden by his black hat, but she enjoyed the sight of his intelligent brown eyes, which reminded her of her favorite dark-roast coffee. With his strong jaw and intense demeanor, he was the handsomest man she'd ever met. And he looked even handsomer than usual dressed in his Sunday best. Or perhaps she was seeing him through new eyes lately. His black winter coat was unzipped, and she admired his traditional black-and-white suit as it accentuated his trim waist, broad shoulders, and wide chest.

While she didn't know him well, she cherished their brief encounters each Saturday morning when he and his grandfather came to visit her at her Coffee Corner to purchase coffee and a few donuts. Their visits had become a routine during the past year, and she could count on their arrival soon after the marketplace opened each Saturday. They had become the highlight of her week, and she found herself often wondering about Micah.

If only she could take their relationship from acquaintance to something more . . .

"Don't you agree?"

Bethany's gaze snapped to the older member of her congregation who stood in front of her, obviously waiting for an answer. "I'm sorry?"

The elderly man blinked. "I said we might be getting some snow earlier than usual this year."

"*Ya*, maybe so." Bethany smiled and nodded, then turned to the next person in line, the man's wife. "*Gude mariye*, Fannie."

"It's a *schee* day for a wedding," Fannie said.

Bethany's mouth dried when Micah finally approached her. She looked up at him towering over her, and felt as if her heart might beat out of her chest as she held her hand out to him. "*Gude mariye*, Micah."

"Hi, Bethany." He took her hand and gave it a gentle squeeze. She enjoyed the feel of his cool skin against hers, and a shiver of pleasure trilled along her spine. Oh, how she hoped he couldn't see how his touch affected her, sending her nerves jangling to life.

"How are you today?" She prayed her voice wasn't too perky.

Micah pulled his hand back and nodded. "*Gut, gut.*"

She grasped for something—anything else—to say. "It's awfully cold out there, isn't it?"

Micah glanced at his grandfather. "We were just discussing how the temperature dropped last night."

"*Ya*, it sure did." Enos reached over and shook her hand. Although the wrinkles on his face told he was close to his mideighties, the sparkle in his brown eyes was a clue to his youthful spirit.

Bethany opened her mouth to say something more to Micah, but he had already moved on to greeting Salina and Will.

"I look forward to having your *kaffi* on Saturday," Enos told Bethany. "It's the highlight of my week."

"*Danki.*" *And Micah's visit to my booth is the highlight of mine.*

Enos moved along, and Bethany swallowed a sigh. If only she could figure out how to get to know Micah better. Though friendly, their short Saturday-morning chats weren't enough to forge a relationship.

With Enos and Micah gone, the line of greeters dissipated for a moment. Salina leaned over to Bethany. "*Gern gschehne,*" she whispered.

Bethany felt her brow furrow. "What do you mean, 'you're welcome'?"

"I invited Micah and Enos to the wedding."

Bethany blinked at her. "Why?"

Salina gave a knowing smile. "Because I'm tired of watching you flirt with Micah on Saturdays in your booth and not ever getting further than that. You never have time to talk to him at church services, so I thought maybe you'd have a better opportunity today."

Bethany stared at Salina and her cousin laughed.

"Did you think we all hadn't noticed how you act with Micah?" Salina leaned closer. "We'd love to see you date again. It's been a long time, and he would be a great match for you."

Before Bethany could respond, another line of guests came in the door, bringing with them a blast of cold air. As Bethany greeted the visitors, her mind swirled with what Salina had told her. Was there a possibility that she and Micah could be more than acquaintances?

She shook her head. For years she'd witnessed men in the community asking her cousins out on dates while they walked past Bethany. Most men found her to be cute and silly. They didn't take her seriously or see her as someone with whom they'd share a meaningful relationship.

A few minutes before eight o'clock, Salina leaned over to Bethany. "It's time for Will and me to meet with *mei dat* and the ministers," she whispered, her voice quavering.

Bethany gave her hand a gentle squeeze. "Everything will be fine." She walked with Salina and Will to the family room. When she glanced out the window, she spotted members of their community filing into the barn where the service would be held.

The back door opened, and *Onkel* Lamar, the bishop, walked into the house. With him were Salina's brother, Neil, who was the deacon, and the minister.

"Are you two ready to be married?" Lamar asked his daughter and Will.

Will and Salina nodded before following the three men upstairs. The sound of their footsteps echoed in the stairwell as voices and rattling pots and pans flowed from the kitchen where women from the church district continued preparing for the noon meal. Bethany hugged her arms to her middle. She glanced around the family room as her mind jumbled thoughts of Micah with questions about how her life would change after Salina was married.

"I feel like it was just yesterday that Will asked me to be his attendant."

Bethany turned toward Anthony. She'd almost forgotten her brother was standing beside her. "I know. The wedding came so quickly."

Anthony tilted his head. "You okay?"

"*Ya*, of course." Bethany smiled. "I'm so *froh* for Salina. She and Will make a great couple, and I know they will be happy together."

It seemed like minutes before footfalls again sounded in the stairwell. "Sounds like it's time," said Anthony.

Bethany followed him to the bottom of the steps where they met Will and Salina.

Excitement filled Salina's pretty face as she looked up at Will. "I'm ready."

Will gazed down at her adoringly. "I am too."

And Bethany's heart turned over in her chest.

Chapter 2

When they reached the barn, Bethany's legs wobbled as she and Anthony walked down the narrow aisle together. The congregation sang a slow hymn as the attendants made their way to four matching cane chairs that sat at the front of the barn. Once there, Bethany stood facing Anthony and folded her hands in front of her. She held her breath, waiting for Salina and Will to join them. Then the bride and groom made their way down the aisle, and everyone sat in unison as the wedding service began.

Bethany did her best to focus on the ceremony, but she couldn't stop her mind from wandering as *Onkel* Lamar spoke. She glanced beside her and silently marveled at how mature and beautiful Salina looked. She peered over at Will and found him gazing at her cousin with a look in his eyes that could only be love.

She turned back to *Onkel* Lamar as he lectured concerning the apostle Paul's instructions for marriage included in 1 Corinthians and Ephesians. She couldn't help imagining what it would feel like to sit up in front of this congregation for her own wedding. Would she ever have the chance to be a bride, a wife, a mother?

Would she ever meet a man who took her seriously and wanted to spend the rest of his life with her?

She glanced over toward the married women's section of the congregation and found Christiana resting her hands on her abdomen. Although Leanna was a widow, she still sat with the other married women, right next to Christiana. Bethany smiled as she imagined Christiana holding her first child.

Then an unexpected pang of sadness hit her. After the wedding, Salina would join Christiana and Leanna in the married section of the congregation, and Bethany would be left to find someone else to sit with among the unmarried women. She imagined herself sitting with Phoebe, Christiana's younger sister. Although she loved her younger cousin, she would still miss being with her favorite cousins during the service.

She knew more than just their seating arrangements at church would have to change soon. When Christiana had her baby, she would most likely stop running her Bake Shop at the marketplace. That would mean Bethany wouldn't see her Thursdays, Fridays, and Saturdays. Jeff would probably build Christiana a stand at their house for her to sell baked goods when her baby was older. And when Salina had her first child, she, too, would close her booth at the market—if she didn't close it sooner to help Will run his restaurant.

Bethany felt her emotions reel as she contemplated losing her close relationships with her cousins. She would miss them desperately!

Her gaze moved to Leanna, and she felt a glimmer of hope. At least she would still have Leanna at the market.

Pushing her selfish worries away, she looked over toward the unmarried men's section. As Micah studied his lap, Bethany tried to imagine what it would be like to date him. Could a man like Micah Zook care for someone like her?

He suddenly looked up, and when his gaze tangled with hers, heat infused her cheeks. She smiled, and to her surprise, the corner of his lips turned up, sending her heart into a wild gallop.

How she longed to befriend Micah and get to know him. Did he already have a girlfriend? She'd never seen him with a woman when he and Enos visited her booth on Saturdays, but of course, she'd never asked.

Breaking their gaze, Bethany looked down at her hands. *Onkel* Lamar instructed Salina and Will on how to run a godly household before moving on to a sermon on the story of Sarah and Tobias from the intertestamental book of Tobit. The sermon took forty-five minutes, and when it was over, *Onkel* Lamar looked back and forth between Salina and Will. "Now here are two in one faith—Salina Marie Petersheim and William Martin Zimmerman."

Bethany held back happy tears when *Onkel* Lamar turned to the congregation. "Do any of you know any scriptural reason for the couple to not be married?" he asked, waiting a beat before looking at the couple again. "If it is your desire to be married, you may in the name of the Lord come forth."

Will took Salina's hand in his, and they stood before *Onkel* Lamar to take their vows.

Onkel Lamar addressed Will first. "Can you confess, brother, that you accept this, our sister, as your wife, and that you will not leave her until death separates you? And do you believe that this is from the Lord and that you have come thus far by your faith and prayers?"

"*Ya,*" Will said.

Then *Onkel* Lamar looked at Salina. "Can you confess, sister, that you accept this, our brother, as your husband, and that you will not leave him until death separates you? And do you believe that this is from the Lord and that you have come thus far by your faith and prayers?"

"*Ya*," Salina said.

Bethany looked down at her lap and sniffed, then felt someone watching her. She tilted her head up and found Micah still staring at her, which sent her senses whirling. Was he thinking about her? No, he couldn't be. After all, they hardly knew each other.

Onkel Lamar looked at Will again. "Because you have confessed, brother, that you want to take this, our sister, for your wife, do you promise to be loyal to her and care for her if she may have adversity, affliction, sickness, weakness, or faintheartedness—which are many infirmities that are among poor mankind—as is appropriate for a Christian, God-fearing husband?"

"*Ya*," Will said.

Onkel Lamar asked the same of Salina and she responded with a strong, "*Ya*."

While Will and Salina joined hands, *Onkel* Lamar read "A Prayer for Those About to Be Married" from an Amish prayer book called the *Christenpflict*. Then he announced, "Go forth in the name of the Lord. You are now man and wife."

Tears trailed down Bethany's cheeks, and she was grateful she'd stuck a handful of tissues in her pocket. Weddings always pulled at her heartstrings. She wiped her eyes and glanced at Christiana and Leanna, finding her cousins wiping their own tears as well.

Salina and Will sat down for another sermon and another

prayer, and Bethany forced herself not to look at Micah again and instead listen to *Onkel* Lamar. After he recited the Lord's Prayer, the congregation stood, and the three-hour service ended with the singing of another hymn.

And then it was official—Salina and Will were married. Her cousin was now Will's wife, and Bethany thought she might choke on the lump forming in her throat. She was so happy for them.

Keeping with tradition, younger members of the congregation filed out of the barn first, followed by the wedding party. Anthony nodded at Bethany, and she smiled at him as they walked together to the barn exit with Will and Salina close behind them.

Micah couldn't take his eyes off of Bethany as she stood surrounded by her cousins. In the warm yellow glow of the lanterns, her eyes seemed a lighter shade of blue than they did in the fluorescent lights at the marketplace. She looked beautiful in her bluish-green dress with her sunshine-blond hair peeking out from under her prayer covering. Something so sweet and innocent about her seemed to lure him in.

Micah had noticed Bethany the first time he'd attended church with his grandfather. That had been two years ago when Micah made the decision to move in with *Daadi* and help him run his custom outdoor-furniture business after *Daadi's* helper left to move to Indiana. It had been the perfect opportunity for Micah to leave his father's farm, his father's castigation, and his community behind. Micah had been certain the change would be good after he'd lost his fiancée, Dawn, following a short battle with leukemia—especially when he received no sympathy or support from his father. His heart had been in shambles, and he'd needed a new start. How else could he escape the memories and give his soul room to heal? After all, he'd known Dawn nearly his whole life, and they were going to be married. They had hoped to have a family and grow old together. He had proposed to her, and they'd been planning for the special day. But then she didn't feel well, and the diagnosis came.

Six months later she was gone.

Micah swallowed back the grief that threatened to choke him even now. He had to be strong. After all, it had been two years since he'd lost her. Still, weddings were difficult for him. Such joyful occasions also reminded him of everything he'd lost when Dawn passed away.

He was certain he'd never meet anyone who would warm his heart the way Dawn had, and he still believed he'd never find another woman he would love the way he'd loved Dawn. And he couldn't bear any possibility of facing that kind of loss again.

But there was something about Bethany Gingerich. It wasn't that he longed to replace Dawn. And Bethany couldn't anyway. Bethany didn't look a thing like Dawn, and while Dawn had been outgoing and sociable, Bethany was even more talkative and friendly, not seeming to have a shy bone in her petite body.

Still, as much as Micah craved solitude to spare his heart from more tragedy and sadness, he felt Bethany's charisma pulling him in. At the very least, Micah longed for a friendship with this cheerful young woman.

He hadn't planned on attending the wedding today when Salina invited him. But he was grateful he'd come. It gave him an excuse to see Bethany outside of church and the marketplace.

When he'd felt like his grief was going to overcome him

during the service, he had looked up and found Bethany smiling at him. And to his surprise, her pretty gaze had been just the balm his broken heart needed in that moment. There was something special about Bethany that soothed his spirit.

"What are you looking at?" *Daadi* asked from across the table where they sat eating their roasted-chicken lunch. *Daadi* craned his neck to look over his shoulder at where Bethany stood talking and laughing with her cousins. Turning back to Micah, he waggled his eyebrows. "Oh, I see."

"It's nothing," Micah muttered, scooping up more mashed potatoes.

"I may be old, but I'm not blind, Micah. I know our visits to the marketplace are about more than *appeditlich kaffi* and donuts."

Micah ignored the comment and forked more chicken into his mouth.

Daadi leaned forward and lowered his voice. "It's okay to fall in love again."

"I'm not in love," Micah hissed through gritted teeth.

Daadi harrumphed and returned his attention to his plate, and Micah felt his shoulders relax. He often wondered how *Daadi* seemed to know what he was thinking. Was it an old man's intuition?

He looked past *Daadi* to where Bethany had turned to speak to another group of young women. Her smile reminded him of the summer sun, and when she laughed, he couldn't help but grin himself.

How he longed to be as outgoing and friendly as she was. Micah often found himself at a loss for words when he was surrounded by a group of people, especially if they were strangers. But he'd never witnessed Bethany struggle for something to say to her customers in her Coffee Corner. Instead, she often commanded conversations with sweetness and grace.

"Would you get me a piece of *kuche* and some *kichlin?*" *Daadi's* question broke through Micah's thoughts.

"*Ya*, of course."

Micah stood and walked over to the dessert tables at the far end of the room. The sweet aroma of cakes and cookies beckoned to him as conversations swirled around him. He filled two plates with pieces of chocolate cake and a mountain of peanut-butter, macadamia-nut, and oatmeal-raisin cookies.

When he turned, he stilled as he found himself face-to-face with Bethany. She raised a blond eyebrow and pointed to his plates. "Are you going to eat all of that yourself, Micah?"

"No." He shook his head, then nodded toward where *Daadi* sat talking to an older couple from their church district. "*Mei daadi* asked me to get him some dessert."

"A likely story." Bethany folded her arms over her chest as her pretty pink lips twitched. "I bet you're going to eat it all yourself and then come back for more."

Micah studied her, taking in her beautiful smile and the ease with which she teased him. He wished he could make conversation the way she did.

She picked up a plate for herself and began filling it with peanut-butter cookies. "I'm just kidding. The desserts are for everyone. Don't they look fantastic?"

"*Ya*. They smell fantastic too."

She added a piece of cheesecake before she turned toward him. "Will you be at the market for your usual *kaffi* and donut Saturday?"

"Of course." He shifted his weight on his feet. "*Daadi* likes to start every Saturday morning with our trip to the market." *And I do too.*

"*Gut.*" She smiled and reached for a piece of pumpkin pie. "I don't think I'll be at the market tomorrow. I'll be over here early to help Salina and Will clean up."

"But you'll be there for sure Saturday, right?" He wondered if she heard the hope in his voice.

"Oh, *ya.*" She turned back to the table and added a chocolate-chip cookie to her plate. "I missed today, and I'll miss tomorrow too. I can't go all week without opening my booth."

"How long have you had it now?"

She looked over her shoulder at him. "My booth?"

"*Ya.*"

She stood up straight and twisted her lips as if contemplating the question. "I think it's four years now."

"What inspired you to open it?"

"Well, my cousin Leanna had opened her Jam and Jelly Nook to make some extra income after her husband passed away. I went to visit her one day, and I saw that the booth near hers had become available. I'd been playing around with flavored *kaffi*, and my family enjoyed it. Also, *mei mammi* had taught me how to make donuts. So I asked my parents if I could open the booth as a way to make some money and also spend more time with Leanna. To my surprise, *mei dat* said yes, and the Coffee Corner was born." She laughed lightly. "I didn't think it would last that long, really."

"Why not?"

"Oh, I don't know. I suppose I didn't think the *kaffi* was *gut* enough. And I wasn't sure I'd have enough customers to make a profit."

"But the customers are lined up whenever *mei daadi* and I come to see you."

She shrugged. "I'm grateful the Lord has blessed me with success."

He studied her. She was humble, but obviously gifted with good business sense and a strong work ethic. An admirable combination.

"Bethany!"

Bethany turned toward the table in the corner where Salina, Will, and Anthony sat. She lifted the plate toward Anthony. "I'm coming!"

She looked back at Micah. "*Mei bruder* is waiting for his snacks." Her smile was warm. "It was *gut* talking to you."

"You too."

Micah watched Bethany walk toward her brother and not for the first time wished for more conversations like the one they'd just had.

Chapter 3

Bethany hummed to herself as the warm and delectable aroma of bananas Foster–flavored coffee filled her booth Saturday morning. She flipped donuts in oil on her stove. Once they were golden brown, she set them on the cooling rack and glanced over at her row of coffeepots.

This was her favorite time of the morning—before her customers came in and while the donuts were frying. Anthony always dropped her off a few hours before the rest of the booth owners so she could prepare her donuts and set up the booth well in advance of when the marketplace doors opened and the customers arrived.

She glazed the donuts, then set them on shelves behind her, smiling as she took in the different flavors—cinnamon-sugar, chocolate, strawberry-iced, chocolate-iced with sprinkles, vanilla-iced with sprinkles, and plain glazed. How she loved baking donuts for her customers! She was grateful *Dat* had agreed to allow her to open her booth four years ago.

Ever since she was little, she had enjoyed meeting people. Her *mammi* had always called Bethany a social butterfly, and it was true. Bethany never felt uneasy in a crowd. Instead, she enjoyed talking to people and learning their stories. While Salina would shut down at youth gatherings with other groups, Bethany would take charge, finding out everyone's names and where they were from. Salina called it Bethany's gift, but Bethany just found entertainment in talking to people she had never met before.

When the timer went off indicating it was time to add the vanilla icing to the dozen waiting on the cooling racks, she set to work, humming and glazing while thoughts of Micah filled her mind. The market would open soon, and he and his grandfather would stop by for their usual Saturday-morning snack. Her heartbeat ticked up at the thought of seeing Micah's handsome face and gorgeous smile.

When she heard a meow and a peep, she looked down. Daisy and Lily, the two resident market cats, blinked up at her.

"*Gude mariye, mei freinden.*" Squatting down, Bethany rubbed Lily's chin and touched Daisy's nose. While Daisy was a rotund gray tabby, her daughter, Lily, was a sleek brown tabby. "I suppose you're looking for breakfast. *Ya?*"

The cats responded with a chorus of meows, and Bethany laughed as she motioned for the animals to follow her to the corner where she kept the cat food and their bowls. She filled two bowls with dry food and the third with water.

"Enjoy," she told the cats as the sound of their crunching overtook the booth.

"Do I smell banana-flavored *kaffi?*"

Bethany looked up as Leanna and Christiana stepped into the booth. "*Ya.*" She pointed to the blackboard where she'd written today's specials—coconut-almond, bananas Foster, butter-pecan, regular, and decaf. Just a few months ago, she'd decided to start adding three flavored coffees to her daily specials in order to add more variety for her customers. "Do you want to give it a try? I have regular if it doesn't sound appetizing to you."

"*Ya*, I'll take a cup," Leanna said.

"It smells amazing, but I have to stick with decaf," Christiana said as she gingerly sat on one of the stools at a nearby high-top table.

Bethany cringed at Christiana's effort. "Do you want me to get you a regular chair?"

Christiana glared at her. "You sound like Jeff. I'm fine."

"Okay, okay. I'm sorry." Bethany held her hand up and tried to stop her snicker.

Leanna gave a little snort as she walked over to the table at the far end of the booth where Bethany stocked the creamers, stirrers, powdered flavorings, and sweeteners. She gathered up some coffee fixings and carried them to the table while Bethany poured two cups of coffee for her cousins. Bethany then poured herself a cup of coconut-almond coffee before joining them at the table.

"This *kaffi* is fantastic," Leanna said, holding up her cup.

Christiana nodded. "The decaf is great too."

"*Danki.*" Bethany sipped her own drink. Today's flavors were good, but not her best. "So, how are you both doing this morning?"

Christiana cupped her hand to her mouth to stifle a yawn. "Still tired from the wedding."

Leanna chuckled. "*Ya*, I am, too, but it was lovely."

"It was." Bethany nodded. "I had fun helping clean up yesterday too."

"I wanted to help, but Jeff insisted I rest." Christiana rolled her eyes and laughed. "I appreciate that he cares, but he must think I'm a weakling. My back does hurt, though. And my feet." She paused, then shrugged. "He was right." She looked behind her toward the entrance to the booth and then back at them. "But don't tell him I said that."

"Where is he?" Bethany asked.

"He'll be here soon. We unloaded my baked goods, and he ran to the hardware store for some supplies for his booth." Christiana sipped more coffee. "It will be strange to look across at Salina's booth and see it closed today, even though it was closed last week too. It's not the same when she's not here."

Bethany sighed. "*Ya*, I know. I miss her too."

"But she said she'll be back next week." Leanna stirred more creamer into her coffee. "That's if she's done settling into her new *haus*."

"It's so great that Will found them that four-bedroom *haus* to buy near her parents so they didn't have to stay in that little *daadihaus* he'd been renting," Christiana said. "Salina said Will was concerned about finding her the 'perfect *haus*.'" She made air quotes as she shook her head. "He's so sweet to her."

Leanna held up her cup toward Christiana. "Just like Jeff is to you."

Christiana smiled fondly and gazed down at her abdomen. "I'm very blessed." Then she looked up again. "Now Salina will have to replant her garden in the spring. Her parents said she can still use her original garden, but she'd like to have her new garden going as soon as she can. She said she still has some canned goods to sell this winter, but she'll run out before long and have to close."

Bethany cradled her coffee in her hands as she considered Salina's new life. "I know she's mentioned that she might close down the booth for good and work at the restaurant instead. Do you think she will?"

Leanna nodded. "She told me again that she might. It would give her more time with her husband."

"True," Bethany said, and that familiar sadness crept into her heart. She would miss Salina if she closed up her Farm Stand. Why did everything have to change so quickly?

"Oh." Christiana chuckled as she placed her hand on her belly. "The *boppli* is kicking again." She divided a look between Bethany and Leanna. "Do you want to feel?"

"*Ya*." Leanna scooted her stool over and set her hand on Christiana's abdomen. She nodded at the movement there. "I remember that feeling. Chester had the hiccups every morning when I was pregnant with him. I loved it."

Bethany carefully placed her hand on Christiana's belly and sucked in a breath when she felt the little *bump-bump* of a kick. She giggled. "Hello, little one!"

Christiana laughed too. "I can't wait to meet this little person."

"I know you're excited." Leanna touched her arm. "We're all excited."

"*Ya*." Bethany lifted her cup and once again found herself contemplating if she would ever be as fortunate as her cousins. Would God lead her to a man who would want to marry her, to care for her and make her a home? If so, would God bless them with children?

The buzzer rang, indicating the dough had risen and was ready for Bethany to prepare another dozen donuts for frying. She jumped up and rushed across the creaky, worn wooden floors to her stoves, where she began punching the dough. While she worked, she heard the doors at the front of the market *whoosh* open and voices bouncing off the walls. The marketplace was open for business.

"It's time to get to work," Christiana said as she climbed down from the stool. "I'm not sure how much longer I'll be able to get on your stools, Bethany."

"That's why your husband worries about you," Leanna teased.

Christiana sighed and rolled her eyes.

"You two have a *gut* day," Bethany called to them. "I'll see you at lunchtime."

She busied herself cutting out donuts and began frying them in the oil. Then she finished glazing the last batch. She looked up just as her first customers, Micah and Enos, walked into the booth. Warmth curled in her chest.

Micah had kept his promise from the wedding. He was here to see her. And he looked handsome clad in the gray shirt she could see under his unzipped black coat. A straw hat covered his head, and his eyes were bright and focused on her, sending a ripple through her.

She smoothed her hands down her black apron and stood up straighter. "*Gude mariye.*"

"Hi." Micah nodded toward her row of coffeepots behind the counter. "Do I smell banana *kaffi?*"

"*Ya.*" She shrugged, suddenly feeling self-conscious with her choice of coffee flavors. "I had read about it in a magazine, and I thought I might try it. But maybe it wasn't the best choice."

She pointed to the list of specials on the blackboard beside him. "I also have coconut-almond and butter-pecan. They seem to be popular." Her cheeks heated when she realized she was babbling, but she couldn't stop her mouth from moving. "I sell the most when I stick with almond, caramel, or cinnamon."

"Bananas Foster sounds great." Micah pulled his wallet out of his back pocket and turned toward Enos. "You want a cup, *Daadi?*"

Enos's smile was wide. "Of course I do." He pointed toward the shelf of donuts. "And two of those cinnamon donuts."

"I'll take two donuts as well." Micah set the money on the counter.

"Okay." Bethany poured the coffee and slipped the tops on the cups. She set them on the counter and then put donuts into a small box. After handing the box to Micah, she took his money and set the bills in her cash register before giving him his change. "*Danki.*" She set a pile of sweeteners and a pitcher of cream on the counter beside the cups.

"Thank *you.*" Micah added cream and a few packets of sweetener to the cup before he took a sip.

"Do you like it?" Bethany held her breath.

"It's different." Micah took another sip. "I like it." He looked at his grandfather. "What do you think?"

Enos also added sweetener and cream before he took a sip. "Fantastic."

"I'm so glad you like it." Bethany racked her brain for something else to say to Micah besides the regular pleasantries. Behind him, she spotted customers filing into her booth, and she wished she could ask them to wait until she was done talking to him. "Did you enjoy the wedding?"

"*Ya.*" He nodded. "How did the cleanup go yesterday?"

"It was okay. I had fun, but it took all day."

"I'm sure it did," Enos said. "There had to be three hundred people there."

Bethany nodded. "That's true."

Enos glanced over his shoulder. "Looks like you have a line already. I think your booth is the most popular in the marketplace." He leaned in as a hint of a smirk danced across his face. "Don't tell your cousins I said that, though."

"I won't." Bethany looked up at Micah, wishing she could ask him to stay and chat with her while she served her customers. "I hope you have a great day."

"You too." Micah picked up the box of donuts and lingered for a moment. "I think you'll be busy today. The *kaffi* is great."

"*Danki*." Bethany leaned over the counter as Micah and Enos started toward the booth exit. She tried to imagine how it would feel to spend more time with Micah, get to know him, or even date him. But she quickly dismissed the idea. Surely Micah had better prospects for women in the community. She was just the perky *maedel* who served his Saturday-morning flavored coffee and donuts.

Pushing herself upright, Bethany smiled at her next customer in line, a woman who looked to be in her early twenties, dressed in jeans, a pink coat, and a purple knitted cap. "Good morning. How may I help you?"

The young woman held up her wallet. "I'd love a cup of that bananas Foster coffee and a vanilla-sprinkled donut."

"Coming right up," Bethany said as she shoved thoughts of Micah from her mind and turned her attention back to the workday ahead of her.

Micah followed *Daadi* through the knot of customers clogging the aisles of the marketplace as they made their way to the exit.

The scents of wood and leather wafted around them as they moved past Jeff Stoltzfus's Unique Leather and Wood Gifts booth. Micah glanced into the booth and spotted shelves filled with wooden trains that spelled out names, leather key chains, belts, and personalized bracelets.

The delicious smells of baked goods overwhelmed him as they next walked past Christiana's Bake Shop, which displayed a variety of cakes, pies, and cookies. He spotted the candy, handbags, and lunch meat booths before they reached the exit.

The large glass doors opened with a *whoosh*, and Micah stepped outside behind his grandfather. The crisp air greeted him and seeped through his coat. He glanced around at the parking lot, finding nearly all of the spaces clogged with cars. A line of horses and buggies stood at the hitching post.

Micah climbed into his own buggy and grabbed the reins as *Daadi* took a seat beside him.

"It's another busy day at the marketplace," *Daadi* quipped.

"That's true. I don't think I've ever seen this parking lot empty, except during the dead of winter when the tourist season slows down." Micah guided the horse toward the exit and waited as cars rolled by on busy Old Philadelphia Pike. "And I think you're right that Bethany's booth is the busiest."

Daadi smiled at him. "I still say you're there for more than the *kaffi* and donuts."

Micah shook his head. "You need to stop trying to marry me off. You know I'm not looking."

"You may not be looking, but God always has a plan." *Daadi* opened the box of donuts and held one up. "And God is always in control."

"I know." Micah kept his eyes on the road as he guided his

horse out onto the highway. He set his jaw as he considered the idea of God's plan. He'd never understand why it had been God's plan for Dawn to pass away from leukemia at the age of twenty-three. It would never make sense to him, but he kept those questions to himself. "I'm not interested in falling in love again. I just want to help you run your business."

"We'll just see what God has in store for you. It could be that *schee maedel* with the lovely smile who happens to make the best *kaffi* and donuts in all of Lancaster County."

Micah pressed his lips together. "I'm sure she's nice to all of her customers." He had to change the subject so that *Daadi* would stop nagging him about his nonexistent future wife. "So what are we going to work on today?"

"I thought we'd continue on with our current projects. The winter is the best time to stock up on benches, picnic tables, gliders, and rockers. Then we'll be ahead when the orders show up in February."

Micah halted the horse at a red light while *Daadi* talked on about their plans for the day. He was grateful *Daadi* had accepted his offer two years ago when he asked if he could move to Bird-in-Hand and help him run his business. Getting away from his father and their volatile relationship had been the best choice for him, especially when he no longer had Dawn at his side to keep him calm when things at home got out of control.

Furthermore, Micah enjoyed the hands-on work of building custom outdoor furniture more than helping out on his father's dairy farm. And he'd also longed to take care of his grandparents. Micah and *Daadi* had been devastated when *Mammi* passed away less than a year after Micah moved in. Micah had tried to help *Daadi* through his sadness by keeping him busy with the business and comforting him when the grief threatened to suffocate him.

It seemed God had sent Micah to his grandparents' not only to heal his own broken heart but also to be a comfort to *Daadi*.

Micah steered the horse up the long rock driveway that led to his grandfather's large house, workshop, and barns and guided the animal past the two-story brick farmhouse to the large cinder block workshop. After dropping off *Daadi* and stowing the horse and buggy, he walked toward the shop and the faded sign announcing Zook's Custom Outdoor Furniture. Inside, the large open area was lined with toolboxes, worktables, workbenches, and supplies. The comforting smell of wood and stain welcomed Micah as he walked around the shop and flipped on the overhead propane lights. He spotted the line of benches at the end of the shop and looked over at *Daadi* as he sat down at the desk on the far end of the work area.

For the last couple of months, Micah had suspected that the business was floundering, but *Daadi* never seemed to want to discuss just how bad it was. If Micah brought up the finances, *Daadi* would ignore the question or change the subject.

Micah hung his straw hat on a peg by the door and then turned toward *Daadi*, who was flipping through envelopes. "Are those bills?"

"No." *Daadi* kept staring down at the desk.

"Is there something you want to discuss?" Micah prodded him.

"No, I want you to finish that bench we started yesterday."

Micah walked over to the bench and picked up his sanding block. He looked back over at *Daadi*. "Have you considered maybe advertising in some of the local tourist magazines? Or maybe we can talk to some of the owners of the local home-improvement stores and see if they'll add us to their websites?"

"No." *Daadi*'s voice was stern and insistent. "There's no need to give in to the fancy ways of websites and such. We'll keep running the business like I always have. The orders always pick up in the spring." He looked back down at the desk. "And no matter what, we'll be fine."

Micah felt his jaw tighten as memories of his father lecturing him for doing or saying the wrong thing plagued his mind. He took a deep, shuddering breath, doing his best to settle his nerves and tamp down his temper. He would not allow himself to behave the way his father always had.

"Okay," Micah finally muttered.

Still, as he turned his attention to the bench, he tried to think of a way to convince his grandfather to let him help with the finances and make sure the business truly was fine.

Chapter 4

"Harvey, I just heard the back door! The kids are home! Time for supper!" *Mamm* called later that evening as Bethany walked into the mudroom behind Anthony.

Bethany suppressed a snort as she placed her tote bag and purse on the bench in the mudroom and then entered the kitchen. *Mamm* always announced her children's arrival as if Anthony didn't pick Bethany up and bring her home the same time every day she worked at the marketplace.

"Hi, *Mamm*," Anthony said before continuing through the kitchen toward the bathroom.

"Hi, Anthony. Bethany, how was your day at the marketplace?" *Mamm* asked as she carried a platter of breaded pork chops to the large table in the center of their kitchen. The delicious aroma caused Bethany's stomach to growl. It had been nearly seven hours since she'd eaten her turkey sandwich for lunch.

Bethany crossed the kitchen and set the box of leftover donuts on the counter before washing her hands at the sink. "It was *gut*. *Danki*. Busy as usual. The bananas Foster *kaffi* was a hit."

"I told you it would be." *Mamm* gave her a knowing smile. "You always come up with the most *appeditlich* flavors. You shouldn't doubt yourself."

Mamm was in her early fifties, and Bethany had always found her mother to be so lovely with her rosy cheeks and ivory skin. Although *Dat*'s light-brown hair and beard were threaded with gray, *Mamm*'s butterscotch-blond showed no hint of fading—at least not the locks she could see under the prayer covering. And *Mamm*'s blue eyes still sparkled with youthful mischief.

Dat stepped into the kitchen and grinned as he pointed toward the box on the counter. "Tell me you saved me a few strawberry-glazed donuts."

"Harvey." *Mamm* wagged a finger at him. "You know the doctor told you to watch your blood sugar."

"Bah!" *Dat* waved her off. "I'm sure one donut is okay, Darlene." He reached for the box, and *Mamm* slapped his hand. "Hey!"

"Don't ruin your supper!" *Mamm* ordered.

When *Mamm* carried a basket of rolls to the table, *Dat* opened the box, swiped his finger through a blob of strawberry icing and licked it, then winked at Bethany as he replaced the box top.

Bethany rolled her eyes and grinned before picking up a large bowl of green beans and carrying it to the table. She adored her parents and their silliness. "Supper smells amazing, *Mamm*. How was your day?"

"It was busy but *gut*." *Mamm* pointed toward four drinking glasses on the counter. "Would you please grab those?"

"Of course." Bethany carried the glasses to the table and placed them at each setting. Then she retrieved the water pitcher from the refrigerator and put it in the center of the table.

"I did some dusting and swept the downstairs," *Mamm* said.

Guilt nipped at Bethany. "I told you I would help you clean Monday."

"Don't be *gegisch*, Bethany. You worked all day. Besides, we'll have plenty to do next week to prepare for the church service here next Sunday." *Mamm* glanced around the kitchen. "Where is your *bruder*? Anthony! Supper is ready!"

"I'm coming, *Mamm*," Anthony called from somewhere in the house.

Mamm looked at the counter. "I just need to grab the mashed potatoes."

"I'll get them." Bethany placed the bowl of mashed potatoes and then sat in her usual spot at the long oak table. *Dat* sat down at the head of the table and *Mamm* at the other end. Anthony hurried in and took his seat across from Bethany. After a silent prayer, they all began reaching for the food, filling their plates, and talking at once.

"We got another contract for more gazebos today," *Dat* said.

"I heard from *mei schweschder* Miriam today," *Mamm* shared.

"I think the commode is running in the downstairs bathroom," Anthony announced.

"I believe I'll make bananas Foster–flavored *kaffi* again," Bethany said.

Dat turned to *Mamm*. "How is your *schweschder*?" Then he looked at Anthony. "I'll take a look at the commode after supper."

"I can do it." Anthony sat up straighter. "I fixed the one upstairs last month."

"We can run to the hardware store in the morning if we need to get a rebuild kit," *Dat* said and then looked at *Mamm*. "Is Miriam feeling better?"

"She is." *Mamm* nodded while cutting up her pork chop. "The X-ray showed that her pneumonia is gone. She said she's getting her strength back. So, tell me about this new gazebo contract."

Dat swallowed and took a sip of water. "One of the home-improvement stores in town asked to preorder ten gazebos in preparation for spring. They want to have them in stock for when the orders start in March."

"Oh, that's *wunderbaar*," *Mamm* said.

Bethany scooped mashed potatoes into her mouth. She was certain her family would get to her news soon. This was how suppers went in the Gingerich house—everyone talked at once, commented on one another's news, and talked all at once again. While Bethany loved her family, she sometimes craved a quieter meal with less chaos.

"Did you say the *kaffi* was a hit?" *Dat* asked Bethany, aiming his bright smile and warm blue eyes on her.

Bethany nodded as she swallowed her bite of mashed potatoes. "It was. I expected my customers to prefer the coconut-almond, butter-pecan, or regular *kaffi*, but I ran out of bananas Foster–flavored *kaffi* shortly after lunch. I'll definitely sell it again."

Anthony scrunched his nose as if tasting something foul. "I'm sure it was great, Bethany, but I don't think it sounds appetizing." He held his hands up as if to calm her down. "But that's coming from someone who isn't crazy about bananas."

"It's okay." She shrugged as she picked up her water glass. "I just won't save you any. You stick to building gazebos, and I'll keep making *mei kaffi* and donuts."

She recalled something she'd been meaning to ask her father.

"*Dat*, what do you know about Enos Zook's outdoor furniture business?"

Dat paused as if surprised by the question. "Well, he's been in business for many years. I went to school with his *sohn*, Richard, and I remember Richard telling me how busy they were. At one point Enos was so busy that he had a few seasonal workers helping them. When Richard left to marry his *fraa* in White Horse and take over her *dat's* dairy farm, Enos had to hire a permanent helper to take Richard's place. But Enos has always been known for creating high-quality outdoor furniture."

"I see." Bethany speared a few green beans as she considered the information.

"Are you *really* asking about Micah?" Anthony's voice held a hint of teasing.

Bethany shot her brother a look as annoyance and embarrassment zipped through her. "No, I was just curious."

Anthony pointed his fork at Bethany. "It's okay if you like him. He seems like a nice guy."

She moved the green beans around on her plate. "He's friendly when he and Enos come to see me at the market on Saturdays. I was just wondering about their business." When she looked up, it was to find her family watching her, curiosity sparkling in their eyes. She turned toward her mother. "So, what else did *Aenti* Miriam say, *Mamm*?"

"Oh, she said that she's *froh* to be able to do some chores instead of relying on your cousins to take care of her."

As *Mamm* talked on about her side of the family, Bethany's thoughts once again moved to Micah. Although he'd been a member of their church district for two years, she still didn't know much about him. Why had he chosen to move to Bird-in-Hand and help his grandfather instead of staying in White Horse with his family? Did he prefer working as a carpenter instead of a farmer?

Since White Horse was about ten miles away from Bird-in-Hand, it would take him an hour to visit his family if he took his horse and buggy. Was it a tough decision for him to leave his family and church district? Had he left a girlfriend behind?

Bethany's pulse zinged at the idea of Micah having a girlfriend. What if he did?

But if he had a girlfriend, wouldn't he have brought her to the wedding as his guest? The thought made her stomach sour despite the delicious pork chop.

"Bethany?" *Mamm* asked. "Are you okay?"

"*Ya.*" Bethany forced her lips into a smile. "What were you saying?"

Mamm's brow crinkled, then smoothed. "I was saying that we have a lot to do next week to prepare for the service. This *haus* has to be scrubbed from top to bottom."

"I know." As Bethany pretended to listen to her mother's list of chores, her mind drifted once again. And then the truth hit her: it was time she finally admitted she had developed a crush on Micah.

The thought scared her. Especially because in her secret heart she couldn't imagine a man as handsome and intriguing as Micah being interested in more than a friendship with someone as ordinary as she was.

Bethany stood in front of her mirror. She brushed her hands down her white apron and butter-yellow dress before touching her prayer covering to make sure it was straight. Then she covered her mouth to stifle a yawn. She and her family had been up late last night cleaning and preparing for the service this Sunday morning. While her family enjoyed hosting the service, it was exhausting making certain their house was as close to perfect as possible.

She glanced out her bedroom window and spotted the line of horses and buggies moving up the street and then up the driveway leading to her house. The congregation members were arriving. It was time to prepare her heart for worshipping God.

She rushed down the stairs to the kitchen, where *Mamm* was already greeting women from the church community. In keeping with tradition, the women gathered in the kitchen before the service while the men gathered by the barn.

"*Gude mariye*, Bethany."

Bethany turned and smiled as *Mammi* approached her. "How are you, *Mammi*?" She gave her grandmother a gentle squeeze.

"Oh, you know." *Mammi* gave a little laugh. "I'm as well as I can be for eighty-one. If I'm still upright and here to worship with you, then it's a *schee* day and a gift from the Lord."

"As usual, you're right." Bethany held her grandmother's hand. "It's so *gut* to see you. How's your knee?"

"*Ach*, it hurts." *Mammi* frowned. "I've been trying some new salve, but it's not working." She looked behind her and then leaned in conspiratorially. "But don't tell your *dat* or *daadi*. They'll make me go back to that wretched doctor."

Bethany bit back her grin. "Don't worry, *Mammi*. Your secret is safe with me."

Oh, how she adored her grandmother! Her gray hair and wrinkles gave away her age, but those wrinkles also outlined the same warm, blue eyes she'd given Bethany's father. Although she was a few inches shorter than petite Christiana and walked with a slight limp due to the pain in her knee, she still managed to keep up with her grandchildren and her great-grandchildren— even Leanna's son, Chester.

Mammi also was in tune to her grandchildren's lives. She enjoyed hearing stories of Bethany's adventures at the market-place, and she had taken part in Salina's wedding plans. Best of all, she was never short on good advice. Bethany prayed she'd have *Mammi* by her side for many more years.

"Bethany!" Salina said as she headed toward her with Christiana and Leanna in tow. She approached them and hugged *Mammi*. "I'm *froh* to see you, *Mammi*!"

Mammi took Salina's hands in hers. "How's married life?"

A dreamy smile overtook Salina's face. "It's *gut*. Very *gut*."

"That's *wunderbaar*." *Mammi* touched her cheek and then turned to Christiana. "How are you feeling, *mei liewe*?"

"*Gut*." Christiana palmed her lower back. "Tired. Sore."

"I'm sure." *Mammi* hugged Leanna, who was just about her height. "And you, Leanna?"

"Fine, same as usual." Leanna shrugged. "How's the *haus*?" she asked Salina.

"It's coming together, but taking longer than I expected." Salina's smile was so bright that Bethany was almost certain she glowed. "I'm starting to feel organized enough to come to the market next week."

"*Gut*. We've missed you," Christiana told her.

"We have," Bethany echoed.

Salina looked at Bethany. "I heard about your bananas Foster–flavored *kaffi*. I want a cup when you make it again."

Bethany blinked. "Who told you?"

Christiana held her hand up. "Me. I know I'm supposed to only drink decaf, but I stole a sip from Leanna."

"It sounds spectacular," Salina said. "Will said he wants a cup too."

"I'll make sure to save some for you and Will when I make it again."

Bethany smiled, but a twinge of jealousy nipped at her. Her cousins had obviously been spending time together. She had always known that Christiana and Salina were closer to each other than to her. For some reason they had always shared a deeper connection, and now that connection would grow since they were both married. Once again Bethany felt her favorite cousins leaving her behind, and it sent sadness rushing through her.

"Bananas Foster–flavored *kaffi?*" *Mammi* asked. "Oh my. I want some too!"

The clock in the kitchen chimed nine o'clock, and the women started to file outside toward the large barn where the service was going to be held. The benches had been delivered earlier in the week, and *Dat* and Anthony had set them up yesterday after sweeping the barn.

Bethany lingered behind as her cousins headed toward the back door, pulling their shawls close to their bodies. Today would be the first time she would sit through a church service without at least one of her favorite cousins. She would have to find someone else to sit with her.

Turning, she scanned the kitchen until she found her cousin Phoebe, Christiana's twenty-year-old sister. Phoebe met her gaze and gave her a little wave. With her light-brown hair and blue eyes, Bethany had always thought Phoebe looked more like

Salina's younger sister than Christiana's, since Christiana's hair was fiery red.

Bethany waited for Phoebe and her best friend, Suzanna, to walk over. Then she took a deep breath. "Could I please sit with you two today?"

"Of course." Phoebe looped her arm in Bethany's. "I was going to ask you to join us since Salina will be joining *mei schweschder* and Leanna."

Suzanna grinned at Bethany. "How is the Coffee Corner these days?"

"*Gut.*" Bethany felt her body relax as she walked toward the barn. "It stays busy."

Phoebe glanced over at Suzanna. "We need to stop by there. It's been too long."

Bethany smiled, grateful for her younger cousin and for company to sit with at her first service without Salina.

Chapter 5

Bethany sat on the bench beside Phoebe and pressed a hand to her hymnal as the congregation continued to file in and take their seats. She smiled at Phoebe and Suzanna as they spoke softly, discussing young men in their youth group. While Bethany wished she could participate, she didn't know the men they were talking about.

When the service began, Bethany redirected her thoughts and joined in as the congregation slowly sang the opening hymn. A young man sitting across the barn served as the song leader. He began the first syllable of each line, and then the rest of the congregation joined in to finish the verse.

As the congregation continued to sing, the ministers met in another room for thirty minutes to choose who would preach that day. During the last verse of the second hymn, Bethany's gaze moved to the back of the barn just as the ministers returned. They placed their hats on two hay bales, indicating the sermon was about to begin.

Onkel Lamar began to speak, and she glanced at the unmarried men's section. Her pulse took flight when she found

Micah watching her. He smiled, and she returned the gesture, heat crawling up her neck. Turning back toward the front of the barn where *Onkel* Lamar sat, she tried to force herself to concentrate on the service and not on how Micah's eyes sent her nerve endings into a wild frenzy.

Please, God, she prayed, *please help me focus on worshipping you and not on my growing feelings for Micah. Also, if it's your will, please help me get to know him so that I can be his friend instead of only an acquaintance.*

Then she sat up straighter and focused on her uncle's holy words.

When the service ended, Bethany walked with Phoebe and Suzanna to the kitchen to help serve the noon meal. She found the kitchen was hot and stuffy due to the knot of women already buzzing around, rushing to gather up trays of food to bring back to the barn. *Mamm* stood in the middle of the kitchen, barking orders to the women who looked as if they needed some guidance. When she spotted Bethany, she pointed to a nearby coffee carafe. "Bethany. Please take that *kaffi* and go fill cups."

"*Ya, Mamm*." Bethany picked up the carafe and sniffed the warm scent of the coffee. It was the typical, bland dark-roast they always served at church service. She smiled as she imagined sneaking in one of her flavored coffees at a future service. How would the congregation react if they sipped their cups and their taste buds were greeted with blueberry- or chocolate-flavored coffees instead of this bitter dark-roast?

She chased the idea from her mind and breathed in the crisp

morning air as she made her way toward the barn where the men had converted the benches into tables and seated themselves to eat. She started toward the first table and held up the carafe.

"*Kaffi?*" she asked before moving down the bench, filling cups.

When she reached the end of the table, she stilled as she spotted her father sitting across from Enos and Micah. *Dat* was speaking while Enos and Micah looked over at him and grinned. Squaring her shoulders, she approached Micah and tried to stop her hand from shaking.

"*Kaffi?*" she asked.

Micah looked up at her, and a smile turned up his lips. "*Ya*, please."

She took the cup from his hand, and when their fingers brushed, she felt a spark dance up her arm, causing her fingers to shake even more. She tried her best to keep her eyes focused on the cup and not spill any of the hot liquid on him.

"Is it bananas Foster—flavored?"

Her eyes darted to his. "Unfortunately, no."

"What is it, then?" His lips twitched.

Was he flirting with her? The idea sent excitement buzzing through her.

"It's a bland dark-roast, but I've always wondered how the congregation would react if I secretly replaced it with something else."

"I'd vote for your peppermint mocha. That's my favorite."

"Really?" She made a mental note to make him some as she handed him the cup.

"*Danki*." He took a sip. "Definitely not one of yours."

Bethany couldn't stop her smile before she turned toward his grandfather. "Would you like some *kaffi?*"

"Of course." Enos held out his cup. "And I agree with Micah. There's no way it will be as *gut* as yours."

"You'd better stop with the compliments or *mei dochder* will become prideful," *Dat* teased from across the table.

"We're just telling the truth, Harvey." Enos pointed toward Micah. "Just ask Micah. Going to get *kaffi* and a donut from Bethany on Saturdays is the highlight of our week. Right, Micah?"

Bethany handed Enos his filled cup and then looked over at Micah as he nodded.

"That is the truth," Micah said.

Bethany pursed her lips. Was seeing her truly the highlight of his week? Surely not! He looked forward to the coffee and donut, not seeing her. He had to have more important things to anticipate than spending a few minutes chatting with her at the market.

She took her father's cup and filled it.

"I know my Bethany is successful with her Coffee Corner. Darlene and I are very proud of her." *Dat* winked at Bethany, and her cheeks heated as her heart swelled with love for her father.

If only she could find a man who was as proud of her as her father was. She longed for someone who would look at her the way Will looked at Salina or how Jeff looked at Christiana. But perhaps there wasn't a man who would ever love her like that. She would have to wait and see what God had in store for her future.

She shook herself from those thoughts and lifted the carafe higher.

"*Danki.*" She nodded at *Dat* and snuck one last glance at Micah before continuing down the table with the coffee carafe. She couldn't help but hope that later she could get a few minutes to talk to him—if he'd be interested in talking to her outside of the Coffee Corner.

Micah watched Bethany as she moved on to the next table, her smile almost as bright as her sunshine-colored dress. She looked radiant today. Her eyes seemed to be bluer, and her face was even more beautiful. Was Micah imagining the change? Was he possibly seeing her in a new light?

He studied her as she laughed at something the middle-aged man sitting at the end of the table said and then filled the man's cup. Micah silently marveled at how Bethany always seemed upbeat and positive. Was it exhausting for her to constantly be so outgoing and friendly? He had the feeling it wasn't; it seemed natural for her. And it intrigued him.

"It sounds like you're staying busy," Harvey said.

Micah turned back toward Bethany's father. He'd been surprised when Harvey had greeted *Daadi* and him and asked if he could sit with them. While Harvey had always seemed to go out of his way to talk to *Daadi* and him, Micah still didn't know him very well. Maybe it was Micah's fault for being so shy and reserved, but he'd never been comfortable making conversation with folks he didn't know well.

If only he could be more like Bethany . . .

"*Ya*, we are just fine," *Daadi* said. "I'm sure things will pick up in the spring like it always does." He picked up a pretzel and popped it into his mouth.

Micah felt a muscle in his jaw flex as he studied his grandfather. Why couldn't *Daadi* just admit the business wasn't as busy as this time last year or the year before? In fact, it was slower than ever.

Turning to Harvey, Micah racked his brain for something to say that might encourage *Daadi* to tell the truth. "How is your gazebo business going?"

"*Gut.*" Harvey began to smother a piece of bread with peanut butter spread. "We just got an order for ten gazebos."

"Really?" Micah asked. "From whom?"

"One of the local home-improvement stores. They like to offer the gazebos along with their other furniture. I'm talking to a few of the pool and deck places as well. I'd like to get some more stores on board before February so that we have plenty of work going into the spring."

"That's a great idea." Micah angled his body toward *Daadi*. "We should think about that too. Maybe I could go to visit some of the pool places and see if they'd be interested in offering custom furniture along with their pools and gazebos."

"Nah." *Daadi* waved him off. "We're fine doing with what we've always done. It's worked for me for years, and it will continue to work."

"Times are changing, *Daadi*."

Daadi's expression was suddenly fierce. "But we *aren't*. We're Amish, and we don't change with the times."

Micah turned toward Harvey and found an intrigued look on his face. Micah wished he could be honest with Harvey and ask for his advice, but he couldn't betray his grandfather that way. Instead, he just had to be patient and work to find other ways to convince *Daadi* to try new options to increase sales.

"How is Richard doing?" Harvey asked after a pause.

At the mention of his father's name, Micah's body went

rigid. He pressed his lips together, hoping to maintain a neutral expression.

"I believe he's doing well," *Daadi* said, his words measured. "We don't hear from him much since he's busy with his farm."

"Did you know that your *dat* and I were *freinden* when we were younger?" Harvey asked Micah. He picked up his piece of peanut butter bread and took a bite.

"No, I didn't." Micah piled lunch meat and cheese on a piece of bread and folded it in half. He tried to imagine his father and Harvey spending time together as boys. Why would someone as kind and friendly as Harvey want to be friends with a domineering, quick-tempered man like *Dat*?

"Oh, *ya*. We grew up together and were in the same youth group."

Daadi chuckled. "That was a long time ago."

Micah felt his body relax, grateful to see his grandfather's pleasant mood return.

"Well, we're not spring chickens anymore, are we, Enos?" Harvey joked. "I remember a time when we went camping. Your *dat* used to love to camp. But there was this one time when we should have checked the weather report before we headed out. We didn't realize a big rainstorm was coming. About that time your *dat* realized he had holes in his tent."

Micah was intrigued as Harvey talked on about times spent with his father. He tried to imagine his *dat* as a fun-loving young man who would laugh and joke with his friends. This sounded like a man Micah had never had the pleasure of knowing. Was there truly a time when his father wasn't so quick to criticize, the way he always criticized Micah?

When lunch was over, Micah and *Daadi* stood.

"Enos! How are you doing?" Lamar, the bishop, called to *Daadi*.

"I'm well. And you?" *Daadi* walked over to where Lamar waited with his son, Neil, who was the deacon.

Micah pivoted as Harvey rose. He longed to have an honest conversation with Harvey about his grandfather's business, but he had to find a way to get him alone. "Harvey, could I possibly get a quick tour of your shop?"

Harvey seemed surprised by the question, but he smiled. "*Ya*. Come with me."

"*Danki*." Micah walked with Harvey toward the open barn doors. To his right, he spotted Bethany serving plates of lunch meat at a table where some of the women in the congregation had sat down to eat. He took in her bright smile and moved along, hoping for a chance to talk with her again later.

Micah and Harvey stepped out of the barn and into the cool November afternoon as they walked toward a large cinder block building near the pasture. When they went inside, Micah took in the sweet aroma of cedarwood and stain, reminding him of his grandfather's shop. Harvey flipped on a few of the overhead propane lights, and they hissed to life.

Micah surveyed the rows of toolboxes and workbenches, peppered with tools and paperwork. He spotted pieces of a gazebo in the corner and walked over to them, marveling at Harvey's talent. He turned toward diagrams on the wall and studied the different designs, stunned by the beauty of the work.

Micah looked back at Harvey. "How long have you been working with wood?"

Harvey held up his hands. "I suppose since I was about four. *Mei dat* was a carpenter. He built sheds. I was originally going to follow him into his business, but my older *bruders* did. I worked one summer with a man who built gazebos, and I was inspired to start up a similar business."

"You do incredible work." Micah pointed to the posters on the wall. "Which is your most popular gazebo?"

Harvey pointed to a twelve-foot cedar octagon. "I would say that's our most popular design."

"Wow." Micah folded his arms over his chest and tried to imagine building something so large and intricate. How he would enjoy the challenge of learning to create something new with his hands! He'd always found joy in building things out of wood. While he worked, he prayed and spent time talking to God.

"Micah, is there something else you wanted to discuss?"

Micah faced Harvey. "What do you mean?"

"I could tell something was on your mind during lunch." Harvey pointed to two folding chairs in the corner. "Why don't we sit?"

They walked to the corner where they sat down across from each other on the cool metal chairs. Micah tried to gather his thoughts as Harvey watched him with a relaxed expression. He wished his father would treat him this way—with patience and respect. But he'd given up that hope years ago.

"You seemed uneasy as Enos was talking. Is he all right?" Harvey asked.

"Oh, *ya.*" Micah nodded. "He's healthy, but I don't think the business is."

"What do you mean?" Harvey's smile melted into a concerned frown.

"Last year we stayed busier later into the year, but this year we were finished with our orders by October. Most of our customers have either found another supplier or have closed. Whenever I try to talk with him about the decline in orders, he either changes the subject or tells me that we're fine. I honestly don't know if we are. We could be, but what if we're not? I'm worried we'll go bankrupt." Saying the words out loud squeezed the air from Micah's lungs.

"Hmm." Harvey crossed his arms over his chest and touched his long, graying beard. "It sounds like you need to find a way to have an honest discussion with your grandfather."

"I know." Micah pushed his hand through his thick hair. "I just don't know how. I suggested running ads in the tourist newspapers, since the tourists love buying Amish-made goods. He said no. Then I suggested we ask some of the local home-improvement stores to include us on their websites, and he got very upset with me for even bringing it up." He threw his hands up in the air. "I have no idea what to do. I thought maybe you could give me some advice."

Harvey nodded slowly. "I can see the challenge. I understand and agree with his conviction to stay Plain, but we also need to find ways to keep our businesses alive without breaking the rules of the *Ordnung*."

"Exactly."

"I think your ideas for advertising and making connections with local home-improvement shops are the way to go. If your customer base is running low, then you need to find a way to reach some new ones."

"I just don't know how to convince him to listen to me. I understand that his current methods used to work, but the world is changing."

"The business is out there. Your *daadi's* furniture has a great reputation."

"*Danki.*" Micah rested his hands on his thighs and glanced around the enormous shop before looking back at Harvey. "Would you please think about how I can get through to him without being disrespectful?"

"I'd be glad to."

"*Danki.*" Micah smiled. Bethany was truly blessed with a wonderful father. If only his own father treated him with the same easy and approachable demeanor. Once again he wondered how his father and Harvey had ever been friends. Maybe Micah was somehow to blame for the problems he and his father could never resolve between them. His stomach tied itself in a knot at the thought.

The shop door suddenly opened, and Bethany stood in the doorway, hugging a black sweater against her lithe body. Micah swallowed as he took in her beautiful face. She looked back and forth between Harvey and Micah, then stepped into the shop.

"Bethany." Harvey stood and walked over to her. "Is everything all right?"

"*Ya. Mamm* is looking for you." She jammed her thumb toward the door.

"Oh. Micah and I were just talking business." Harvey started toward the door, looking over his shoulder at Micah. "We'll talk again soon."

"Thanks." Micah lifted his hand at him.

Harvey walked out of the shop, and when the door clicked shut behind him, Micah was alone with Bethany for the first time since he'd met her.

Chapter 6

Micah walked over to where Bethany stood near the line of workbenches. Warmth sizzled in his chest as he watched her fiddle with the zipper on her sweater and smile at him. He searched for something to say to her, but he drew a blank.

If only he could start conversations as easily as she did. Surely she took him for an awkward *dummkopp*, or possibly a mute snob, as he stared at her.

"When I was little, *mei dat* would bring me in here and let me sit on a stool and watch him work." She gestured toward the pieces of gazebos over in the corner as her pretty voice echoed throughout the large shop. "I always tried to imagine what the gazeboes would look like when they were put together."

She pointed toward the posters in the corner. "I would look at the poster, and since I couldn't read, I'd ask *mei dat* which gazebo the pieces would become. Then when he built them, I'd ask if I could go with him for delivery. But he explained that a man with a truck would come to get the gazebos and deliver them for him."

She walked over to the poster. Micah came up behind her and

breathed in the dizzying flowery scent of her shampoo. "Which one is your favorite?"

She turned to him, and when she gave him a shy smile, he suddenly felt an achy longing to know her better. Was he losing his mind?

"I'm embarrassed to tell you."

"Why?" He tilted his head.

"It's *gegisch*."

"How can it be silly?" He stepped closer to her, and her nearness sent his senses spinning.

"Well . . ." She pointed to a white gazebo with a red roof. "I've always loved the wedding gazebo. When I was little, I used to imagine what it would be like to have my own wedding there."

When she shook her head, he spotted a pink tinge on her cheeks. She was blushing, and she was adorable! She faced the poster as she continued to talk, as if she was too embarrassed to face Micah while sharing her childhood memories.

"I know it's ridiculous since we don't have elaborate, outdoor weddings like the *Englishers*, but I used to have a fantasy about getting married in the middle of a lush green field. The gazebo would be there, and I'd stand inside of it with my groom. *Onkel* Lamar would perform the service, and my two cousins, Salina and Christiana, would be my attendants, and of course my groom would have his attendants as well. The congregation would sit on the benches outside of the gazebo, and it would be a warm and *schee* spring or summer day without a cloud in the azure sky." She pointed up toward the ceiling as if they were standing outside.

Micah grinned, enjoying her creative description as she continued.

"After the ceremony, we would walk out of the gazebo, and

then the men would set up the tables there for the food. We'd spend the rest of the day singing hymns, and my wedding gazebo would be the *schee* backdrop. Maybe at the end of the evening when everyone had gone, I'd sit in my gazebo with my new husband and we'd talk."

Silence overtook the workshop, and when he looked over at her, her expression had become hesitant. Or maybe ashamed.

"I know what you're thinking," she said, her voice soft. "Why would an Amish *maedel* dream of having a fancy outdoor wedding? It's outrageous and *gegisch*. You think I'm ridiculous, right?"

"No." He shook his head. "I'm just marveling at your creativity. You've painted a beautiful picture in your head."

"Really?" Her brow puckered, and then her eyes narrowed. "You're teasing me, right?"

"Why would I tease you?"

"I don't know." She looked back at the poster. "Which one is your favorite?"

"That one." He pointed to the twelve-foot cedar octagon. "Your *dat* told me it was his most popular."

"It is. Is that why it's your favorite?"

He shook his head. "No. I just have always loved cedar."

Bethany's face lit up. "The aroma, right?"

"Exactly."

"*Mei dat* made me a cedar chest when I turned sixteen, and I love to open it and smell it." She studied him. "Have you always liked to work with wood? Is that why you decided to work for your *daadi* instead of your *dat*?"

Micah crossed his arms over his chest and considered his response. He wasn't ready to tell her about Dawn or his volatile relationship with his father, but he didn't want to lie to her either.

"I'm sorry. That question was too personal."

"No, it's okay." He leaned back on a nearby workbench. "I never wanted to be a dairy farmer, and *mei dat* had hired a farmhand. I always enjoyed working on furniture projects when I visited *mei daadi*. He used to take me out to his workshop and teach me how to build things when I was little. I liked bonding with him, and I discovered my love of carpentry when I was very young. When I heard *Daadi*'s helper had quit to move to Indiana, I asked if I could come and help him."

She suddenly smiled. "Did you know our *dats* were *freinden* when they were younger?"

"*Ya.*" Micah nodded. "Your *dat* was sharing some camping stories during lunch."

"I bet they were amusing."

"They were."

They stared at each other for a moment, and he felt as if something shifted between them. It was as if an invisible magnet were tugging him toward her. Had she felt it too? No, she couldn't have. They didn't know each other well enough for that. And he wasn't looking for a relationship that could lead to another debilitating heartache.

"What's your favorite piece of furniture to make?" she asked.

"Oh," he said, surprised by the question. "Probably gliders and rockers."

"That's nice. You'll have to show me your furniture sometime."

"Sure." He glanced toward the door as a brick of worry formed in his stomach. How long had they been talking in the workshop? They had been alone together for what felt like a long time. Would her father be upset if he found out they were still in there? What would the other congregants say?

He looked at her, and something in her face changed. Her smile wobbled as if she sensed his apprehension.

"I should probably check on *mei daadi* and see if he's ready to leave yet," Micah said.

"Oh, of course. I'm sorry for keeping you." Bethany fiddled with the zipper on her sweater again and started for the door. He held it open for her and shivered as a cold wind greeted them. They walked side by side toward where *Daadi* stood talking to Lamar.

"There he is," *Daadi* announced as they approached. "I thought you might have gone home without me."

"I'm right here." Micah glanced at Bethany, but her expression seemed to have lost some of its sparkle. Had he done something wrong? Maybe he shouldn't have ended their talk so abruptly, but he was concerned for her reputation. He wanted nothing more than more time with her, but it was risky doing that at church.

"It's chilly out here. I should get inside." Bethany looked up at Micah. "I guess I'll see you Saturday."

"*Ya.*" Micah nodded. "Have a *gut* week."

"You too." Bethany smiled at *Daadi*. "Take care." She nodded at her uncle, then headed toward the house.

"See you soon, Lamar," *Daadi* told the bishop.

"*Ya.* Be safe going home," Lamar replied.

Micah glanced over his shoulder toward Bethany's house. When he saw her standing on the porch, he lifted his hand in a wave. She returned the gesture before he looked away.

Bethany leaned forward on the back porch railing as she watched Micah and Enos walk toward the waiting buggies. Resting her elbow on the cold railing, she dropped her chin to her palm as she recalled their conversation in the workshop. She swallowed a sigh of regret as she tried to comprehend why Micah had ended their conversation in such an abrupt way.

Had she bored him by going on and on about her stupid childish fantasy about the wedding gazebo? Or worse, scared him off? She moaned and covered her face with her hands. Why had she shared that secret with him? She'd never told anyone about how she'd dreamed of getting married in that gazebo. Of course that was what had driven him away! Surely he now considered her to be an immature and ridiculous *maedel*, just as the other men in the community did. Why couldn't she have kept her big mouth shut?

But still, he had seemed to like her for a while. When he talked about his love of woodworking, he'd seemed genuine. And when he looked at her, she'd felt something sincere and intense, which she'd never felt with any other young man. His stare set a thousand hummingbirds free inside her. It was a sensation she enjoyed and wanted to keep feeling.

But then he'd all but run out of the workshop.

"Are you going to the youth gathering?"

Bethany jumped with a start and turned toward Leanna, who stood behind her. "You scared me."

"I'm sorry." Leanna held up her hands as a smile played at the corners of her mouth. "I thought you heard me come outside. I was surprised you were still here."

"Why?"

"I thought you'd go to the youth gathering with Phoebe and Suzanna."

"No." Bethany turned back toward where a line of horses and

buggies moved down the driveway, the *clip-clop* of hooves and the whir of buggy wheels filling the air. "I would feel strange there without Salina or Christiana."

"You could have invited Micah to go."

Bethany looked over at her cousin as she leaned on the railing beside her. "I don't think he would've gone."

Leanna chuckled. "You're underestimating yourself."

"I'm not. He's twenty-seven, so why would he want to hang out with a bunch of kids in their early twenties? Besides, I don't think he likes me that way."

"You won't know unless you ask him."

Bethany felt her eyebrows shoot up with surprise. "Don't you think that would be awfully forward of me?"

"Maybe." Leanna shrugged. "Maybe not. What have you got to lose?"

"His respect."

Leanna twisted her lips. "What if you asked him as a *freind?*"

Bethany couldn't stop her eyes from rolling.

"What was that for?" Leanna laughed. "Am I that old-fashioned since I've been married and have a *sohn?*"

"No, no, no." Bethany pivoted toward her cousin. "It's not that." She sighed and looked down at the toes of her black shoes. "It's just that none of the guys in the community take me seriously. I've watched Salina and Christiana date, fall in love, and marry, but I'm still alone. I don't think I'll ever find anyone who loves me for me."

Bethany hated the vibration in her voice. She looked out toward her father's vast pasture to avoid Leanna's gaze, taking in the rolling patchwork of land that had gone from lush shades of green to dull browns as winter set in. She breathed in the crisp air, inhaling the scent of animals, crumbling leaves, and burning fireplaces.

"Oh, Bethany." Leanna looped an arm over her shoulders. "You are way too hard on yourself. You are *schee*, sweet, funny, bubbly, and outgoing. You're the life of the party. I've always struggled with meeting new people and talking to them, but I could count on you to take over and introduce me to everyone."

Leanna gave her arm a gentle squeeze. "There is a man out there whom God has chosen to love you and cherish you for the rest of your life. You just have to trust God's perfect timing."

"You're right." Bethany sniffed. Why was she so emotional today?

"Hey. *Was iss letz?*" Leanna placed her hands on Bethany's shoulders and turned her so that they were facing each other. "This isn't like you."

Bethany looked down at her shoes again. "Micah and I talked in *mei dat*'s shop for a while. It was going well, and then he suddenly said that he had to go. I feel like I shouldn't have been so talkative. Maybe if I had been quiet and let him talk, he would have wanted to spend more time with me. But instead I scared him off."

Leanna's expression was warm. "I'm sure you didn't say or do anything wrong."

"But what if I came on too strong?"

"No, *mei liewe*." Leanna touched her cheek. "If he doesn't like you for who you are, then he's not the one God has chosen for you."

"But I . . . care about him, and rejection hurts."

Leanna shook her head. "Just keep praying and asking God to send you down the right path. You'll find the man who's meant for you."

Bethany nodded, but Leanna's words didn't shrink the pit in her stomach.

The back door opened, and Salina stuck her head out. "Are you two going to stand out in the cold all afternoon?" She beckoned them to come in. "We're having tea with *Mammi*. Come join us."

"We're coming." Leanna looked at Bethany. "I imagine some time with our favorite cousins and *Mammi* will make you feel better."

"Sure it will." As Bethany allowed Leanna to steer her into the kitchen, she tried to concentrate on Leanna's encouraging words instead of the ache that lingered in her heart.

Chapter 7

Micah guided the horse down Gibbons Road toward Old Philadelphia Pike. He gazed out toward the dairy farms, taking in the large pastures dotted with cows as he recalled his conversation with Bethany. His lips turned up in a smile, and he felt his heart tug every time he thought about her sweet story of her childhood fantasy of getting married in one of her father's wedding gazebos.

While she had worried that her story was ridiculous, he had found it endearing and sweet. She was the most charming and outgoing *maedel* he had ever met—even more so than Dawn. But the way that she had captured his attention scared him. While he feared spending the rest of his life alone, he was more terrified of falling in love and then losing his beloved in a tragic way. The easiest alternative was living with *Daadi* and not allowing himself to get attached to anyone. It somehow seemed to solve all of his problems.

But still—he felt himself being drawn to Bethany as if some invisible force were pulling him to her. Could it be God?

"When are you going to ask out that *schee maedel?*"

"What?" Micah glanced over at his grandfather.

Daadi gave him a look of disbelief. "Bethany, of course. How long are you going to make her wait for you to ask her out?"

Micah opened his mouth but was rendered speechless for a few moments. "How did you know?"

"Please, Micah." *Daadi* gave a bark of laughter. "You've always been a quiet young man, but I know you better than anyone. I can tell when you're interested in a *maedel*, and I haven't seen that sparkle in your eyes since—" He stopped, and his expression darkened slightly. "For a long time."

Micah swallowed as his familiar baggage weighed heavily on him—the grief, regret, and sadness. He tried in vain to shake it off as he turned his attention back to the road ahead.

"I remember when I met my sweet Bertha." *Daadi* looked over at Micah, and a wistfulness clouded his eyes, as if he were reliving the memory. "We had a combined youth group event with some neighboring church districts, and she was the prettiest *maedel* I had ever seen. At first I was too *naerfich* to ask her out, but I was afraid one of the other young men would scoop her up. I asked her if I could give her a ride home, and we talked as if we had known each other forever."

Micah gripped the reins tighter as his heart clenched.

"We dated for about six months, and then I couldn't wait any longer. I asked her *daed* if I could marry her. We were married that fall, and we started praying for *kinner*. After your *dat* was born, we prayed and prayed, but the Lord didn't see fit to give us any more. But we cherished your *dat* and our life together. It was a simple life, but a grand one too."

Micah nodded, hoping *Daadi* wouldn't become more emotional. He wasn't sure he could keep his own grief at bay today.

Daadi tapped Micah's shoulder. "That's what I want for you, *sohn*. I know you're still hurting from losing Dawn, but you're young. I've had the love of my life, and I was blessed. But it's not natural for you to be alone. You should ask Bethany out. She's a sweet *maedel*, and you'd be *froh* with her. You two could take the *haus*, and I'll convert one of my old workshops into a *daadihaus*. And then—"

"Hold on now!" Micah held up his hand. "Slow down there, *Daadi*. I'm not sure Bethany would even considering dating me, so you need to stop planning my wedding and living situation."

"I think she'd be *gut* for you."

"Why?"

"Because she's sweet and outgoing. I always see her smiling. She would be the one to piece your broken heart back together and brighten your day. You need some happiness in your life. I'm afraid you'll spend your days sad and alone. I don't think I've ever seen her without a smile."

Micah was stuck on that detail as well. His grandfather was right. He'd never seen Bethany without a smile either.

"And you're too young to be alone. I know you miss Dawn, but she would want you to move on."

Micah gritted his teeth. He couldn't stand when other people told him what Dawn would want or not want. How did they know what his late fiancée would want? Micah would never disrespect his grandfather, but he needed to change the subject before he got angry.

"I spoke to Harvey about our business," Micah said.

"You *what?*" *Daadi's* voice rose in agitation, sounding like his father's before he lost his temper. "What did you tell him?"

"I told him I'm worried that we're losing customers and that

I'm concerned it's going to keep getting worse." Micah kept his words slow and steady as he felt his grandfather's tension coming off of him in waves. "I told him what I had suggested to you about reaching out to other home-improvement stores, running more ads, and seeing if we can get some ads on websites."

"How could you?" *Daadi* nearly spat the words at him. "This is a personal matter and not something we want spread throughout our church district."

"I know, but I trust Harvey. Also, his business is similar to ours, and it's thriving. I felt he would be the best person to ask for advice."

"We don't need advice, Micah. I've been running this business for nearly sixty years. I know what I'm doing. If I didn't, then I wouldn't be in business anymore."

Micah nodded while keeping his eyes on the road. He steered the horse onto the path that led to their small farm.

"You shouldn't talk to anyone about this except for me. I decide what we do for our future, not you and not Harvey. Do you understand?"

"*Ya, Daadi.*"

"We are going to be fine. You need to trust me and trust God."

"I do." Micah glanced over at him as the horse pulled the buggy up their driveway. "I would never do anything to disrespect you."

"*Gut.*"

Micah halted the horse by the back porch, and *Daadi* pushed the door open. "I'm going to my room to take a nap," he announced before climbing out of the buggy and padding up the path toward the back door.

"Okay." Micah sighed as he pushed himself out of the buggy

and unhitched the horse. As he led the horse toward the barn, he looked up at the gray November sky. Then he opened his heart up to God.

"Lord," he whispered, "I'm confused about a lot of things. I'm grateful that you led me to Bird-in-Hand to take care of my grandparents and to help *Daadi* run the business. Still, I don't understand why I can't convince *Daadi* to respect my opinions. Why would he be so stubborn that he would let things go downhill?"

He stepped into the barn as he continued to pray. "And then there's Bethany. She's sweet and *wunderbaar*. But I'm not sure if my feelings for her are true. And if they are, how do I convince my heart to allow her in and risk losing someone all over again? I don't think I'm strong enough to face another heartbreak." He led the horse to the stall.

"Please guide me toward your plan, Lord. Help me see where you want me to go."

Once the horse and buggy were stowed, he headed into the house to rest.

"It's a *schee* day at the market!" Salina announced as she walked into the Coffee Corner Saturday morning.

"Yes, it is," Bethany agreed. She sat at a high-top table with Leanna and Christiana. "It's been so *wunderbaar* having all of my favorite cousins here at the market this week." She hopped down from the stool and hurried behind the counter to pour Salina a cup of coffee.

"Oooh," Salina cooed as she leaned against the counter. "Do I smell French-vanilla?"

"You do." Bethany handed her the cup, and Salina paid her. Then she pointed to the blackboard by the counter. "The other specials are cookies-and-cream and also cranberry-cream."

"So many *gut* choices." Salina paused and sniffed. "Do I smell peppermint mocha too?"

Bethany hesitated, then nodded. "*Ya*, I made a small pot of it."

"Isn't it early in the season for peppermint mocha?" Leanna called from the table. She pointed to the blackboard. "It's not listed as one of your flavors of the day."

"You're right. It's not." Bethany shrugged as she slipped the money into her cash register. "I just made a small pot." When she looked up, she found Salina watching her. "What?"

"Nothing." Salina bit her lip, and a coy smile appeared. "Did you make the peppermint mocha for a certain someone?"

"Who?" Bethany tried to play dumb.

"Oh, please, Bethany," Christiana chimed in. "Micah, of course."

"Is peppermint mocha his favorite flavor?" Leanna asked, her smile wide.

Bethany was caught, and her cousins wouldn't let it go until she told them everything. She nodded as she gathered up creamers, sweetener, and stirrers and then walked to the table with Salina. She hopped up on the stool between Christiana and Leanna and across from Salina. "It's his favorite."

Leanna clucked her tongue and gave a sweet smile. "Which is why you made a small pot just for him. That's so sweet."

"And romantic," Christiana added before sipping her decaf.

"How did you find out it was his favorite?" Salina asked.

Bethany ran a finger around the lid of her coffee cup as she thought back to Sunday. "He told me on Sunday when I served his *kaffi* after the service. We also talked for a while in *mei dat*'s workshop afterward."

"What?" Salina nearly squeaked. "Why didn't you tell us that you talked to him?"

"Were you alone?" Christiana asked.

Having already heard the details, Leanna smiled.

Bethany held up her hands. "Calm down. I'll tell you." She shared how she had wound up alone with Micah in the workshop and described their short conversation. She left out the details of how she'd told him all about her childish fantasy about the wedding gazebo and also how he suddenly said he had to leave.

"It wasn't a big deal. We talked about gazebos." She looked down at her coffee cup to avoid her cousins' wide-eyed grins. "That was all."

Salina reached across the table and gave Bethany's hand a gentle squeeze. "That's *wunderbaar*, Bethany."

"*Danki*. Maybe it means he at least sees me as a *freind*."

"Absolutely," Christiana said through a yawn.

"Are you okay?" Bethany asked.

"*Ya*. I didn't sleep well last night." Christiana rubbed her abdomen. "This little one decided to do somersaults all night, and I couldn't get comfortable. Jeff tried to convince me to stay home today, but I wanted to come in. After all, I'll be shutting down my booth soon. I need to talk to Kent about it today, so he can start advertising the booth to potential vendors."

"You're getting ready to shut down your booth permanently?" Bethany asked.

"*Ya*, I'll give him a month's notice. I have so much to do at the *haus* to get ready. I told Jeff I'd like to have a bake stand at the *haus* when the *boppli* is older, but we'll see what God has in store for us and our family."

"We'll miss you," Bethany said as sadness squeezed at her chest.

"I'll miss you all too." Christiana glanced around the table. "But you all can come visit me anytime. Maybe we can have a lunch every week."

Leanna tapped the table. "I love that idea."

"I do too." Salina held up her coffee cup. "Let's toast to that."

Bethany smiled as she touched her cup to her cousins'. "How is business going for you this week, Salina?"

"It's okay. I'm running out of canned goods to sell. I might have to close up for the season soon too. Will wants me to help out at the restaurant, so I'll probably just work there on days I don't need to get chores done at the *haus*." She brightened. "But I have my new garden sketched out. I can't wait to get started with the planting in the spring. Will is also going to install a second kitchen for me in the basement. That way I have room to pack and can my produce. I'll have to keep the booth closed until I have enough to sell, but I'm going to tell Kent that I will be back."

"That means we definitely need to institute those weekly lunches," Bethany said. "We have to stay in touch."

"We will," Christiana said. "I need my cousins."

"I do too," Bethany agreed. In fact, she didn't know how she'd cope without them.

Chapter 8

Micah blew on his cold hands as he stepped through the large, glass entrance doors into the Bird-in-Hand market and was greeted by a blast of heat and loud voices chatting, along with the succulent smells of candy, chocolate, baked goods, lunch meat, and coffee.

Coffee.

He couldn't stop the grin that framed his lips. He had looked forward to this day since he'd left Bethany's family's house last Sunday afternoon. As much as he'd tried to put thoughts of Bethany out of his mind, her pretty smile, adorable laugh, and sweet voice had crept into his thoughts throughout the week.

Micah glanced to his left toward the long lunch meat counter as his *daadi* followed him in. The owner of the booth, a middle-aged Amish man, greeted an *English* woman wearing a pink knitted cap before he began slicing roast beef. Across from his counter, a young *English* woman with purple hair perused a display of purses.

"This place is hopping already," *Daadi* commented as they

moved through the crowd, passing *English* and Amish customers moving in and out of other booths.

"I see that," Micah quipped as he narrowly avoided tripping over the wheel of a stroller as a young mother bounded past, pushing a baby through the crowd.

As they rounded the corner past Salina's Farm Stand, passing her colorful displays of ripe produce, *Daadi* stopped in front of the Quilt Shop, located beside it. Colorful quilts were draped around the booth, while a table at the front stood clogged with smaller quilted gifts, including pot holders, oven mitts, dolls, tote bags, coasters, and other homemade items. A young Amish woman with dark hair stood at the back of the booth, folding a large quilt with a gray, blue, and teal pattern that he'd heard his sister Laverne once call the Lone Star pattern.

"Why did you stop?" Micah asked, almost bumping into his grandfather.

"We need to find a birthday gift for Krissy."

Micah swallowed. "So I guess we're going to her party?" His sister had left them a message inviting them to supper at his parents' house to celebrate his niece's birthday.

Daadi gave him a look of disbelief. "Would you truly allow your issues with your *dat* to prevent you from celebrating your only niece's birthday?"

"No." Micah's shoulder slumped with the weight of his guilt. As much as he adored his niece, he still dreaded the thought of having to have supper with his parents for her birthday. Not only that, but he also had to face his father at Thanksgiving before the birthday party. But he knew he had to be a man and handle the situation as best he could.

Daadi gestured toward the booth. "Why don't we get Krissy

a quilt?" He pointed to a smaller quilt decorated with pink, baby-blue, and yellow flowers. "You know Krissy likes anything pink."

Micah hesitated, and the Amish woman walked over, her expression bright and cheery.

"*Gude mariye*," she said, her voice a little too loud. "*Wie geht's?*" She held out her hand to them.

"Hello," *Daadi* said, shaking her hand. "I'm well. How are you?"

"I'm fantastic." The young woman turned her gaze on Micah, and her smile widened as she looked him up and down, reminding him of a lioness stalking her prey.

Micah shifted his weight on his feet.

"Hi. I'm Sara Ann King, but you can call me simply Sara Ann." She laughed as she shook Micah's hand, and he noticed she had lovely gray eyes.

"Nice to meet you. I'm Micah Zook, and this is *mei daadi*, Enos."

"You look familiar." She tapped her chin. "I've seen you around the market before."

"We come in every Saturday to visit the Coffee Corner," *Daadi* said.

"That's right." Sara Ann snapped her fingers. "I've seen you in Bethany's booth."

"Her *kaffi* is the best," *Daadi* said.

"That's true." Sara Ann kept her eyes focused on Micah. "I see you looking at my quilts. Is there anything I can help you find today?"

"We were looking to buy a birthday gift for my great-granddaughter." *Daadi* answered her question even though Sara Ann acted as if Micah were the only person there.

"Oh. How old is she?" Sara Ann asked Micah.

"She's turning four in a few weeks," Micah said.

Sara Ann gave him a strange expression. "Is she your *dochder*?"

"No." Micah shook his head. "She's *mei bruderskind*."

Sara Ann laughed. "Oh, of course!" She pointed to his clean-shaven face. "How could you have a *dochder* when you're not married?" She walked into the booth and motioned for them to follow. "Let's find her the perfect quilt. What's her favorite color?"

"She loves pink," *Daadi* said. "I was looking at this pretty quilt over here." He pointed to the flowered one he'd been eyeing. "I think she'd love this one."

"Oh, *ya*." Sara Ann picked it up. "It is lovely, isn't it? I made this one a few months ago. I had a little girl in mind too." She held it out to Micah. "Touch it. The fabric is very soft. I imagine she'd love to hug it when she takes her afternoon nap."

Micah ran his finger over the fabric as Sara Ann studied him. The intensity of her stare made his skin itch. Why was she so focused on him? Was this her way of flirting? He resisted the urge to leave the booth and head straight for the Coffee Corner to find some relief.

"The quilt is nice," Micah said as he turned to *Daadi*. "I think she'll like it."

"Great." Sara Ann showed him the price tag, and Micah cringed. She must have seen his reaction because she quickly added, "I'll give you twenty percent off since you are regular visitors to the market."

"Oh." Micah felt his brow knit. "Okay. Then we'll take it."

"*Wunderbaar.* Do you know Bethany well?" Sara Ann asked as they walked over to the counter at the back of the booth.

"She's a member of my church district."

"Is that so?" Sara Ann seemed stuck on that detail. "She's a lovely *maedel*."

"She is." Micah pulled his wallet out of his back pocket. He had the distinct impression that she was digging for information, and it irritated him.

Sara Ann told them the total, and they each pitched in half of the money. She slipped the money into her register and folded up the quilt before dropping it into a large, brown-paper shopping bag. "You'll have to let me know how your niece enjoys the quilt."

"We will," *Daadi* said.

"What's her name?" Sara Ann asked.

"Kristine, but we call her Krissy."

Micah winced. For some reason, he didn't want his grandfather sharing any more information with Sara Ann. His intuition told him she wasn't to be trusted. He put his wallet into his back pocket and then glanced toward the booth exit. He was ready to get out of this shop and get some coffee from Bethany.

She held out the bag to Micah. "Have a great day."

"You too." As he reached for the handles, she held on to the bag too long, as if deliberately letting her fingers brush his. What was she trying to prove?

Micah took the bag and stepped out into the knot of shoppers, making his way through to the Coffee Corner.

"Wait up," *Daadi* said from behind him.

When he walked into the Coffee Corner, Micah breathed a sigh of relief as his eyes found Bethany standing behind her counter and chatting with a customer. The booth was buzzing with customers sitting at high-top tables drinking coffee and eating donuts. The delicious smells of cinnamon donuts and French-vanilla coffee made his stomach gurgle with delight.

Bethany looked beautiful clad in a black apron and a pale-blue dress that complemented her sky-blue eyes. Her cheeks were pink, and her smile was wide as she laughed at something the young *English* woman in front of him said. Micah enjoyed the sound of her laugh, and he wanted to hear it more often.

The woman paid for her coffee and donut and slipped past him.

Bethany looked over at him, and her expression brightened when she met his gaze. "Hi there. How are you two doing this morning?" She smiled at *Daadi* and then looked back at Micah.

"I'm fine." Micah set the large shopping bag on the floor at his feet.

Bethany pointed toward it. "What's in the bag?"

"We bought a gift for my niece's birthday." Micah gestured. "We got her a quilt from the Quilt Shop."

"How nice." Bethany nodded.

"That Sara Ann is a talker," *Daadi* quipped.

"You have no idea," Bethany muttered.

Micah snorted, and Bethany's cheeks reddened.

Daadi leaned on the counter. "Do I smell French-vanilla?"

"You do." Bethany's smile seemed almost mischievous as she turned to *Daadi*. "Do you like French-vanilla?"

Daadi rested his elbows on the counter. "*Ya*, very much."

"*Wunderbaar.*" She poured a cup of coffee and handed it to *Daadi*. Then she turned to Micah and grinned. "I have something special for you."

Micah felt his eyebrows shoot up. "What is it?"

"You'll see." She sang the response as she moved to a smaller coffeepot on a burner and filled up a coffee cup. When she carried it over to him, the delicious scent swarmed his nostrils.

"Is that peppermint mocha?" he asked. "I didn't see it listed on your flavors of the day."

"It is peppermint mocha. And you're right. It's not listed up there." She lifted her chin, which was adorable. "Here." She handed him the cup, along with sweetener and cream, and after he added them, he took a sip.

"It's amazing." He grinned. "You remembered it was my favorite."

"How could I forget?" The gleam in her blue eyes sent warmth radiating through his veins.

Bethany divided a look between Micah and *Daadi*. "How about some donuts?"

"I'll take two strawberry-glazed," *Daadi* said.

"And I'll take two cinnamon." Micah pulled out his wallet and paid for the coffee and donuts. As she handed him his change, he felt the overwhelming urge to stay and talk to her. Although his mind kept telling him to keep his distance, his heart longed to know her better.

Bethany loaded the donuts into a box and set them on the counter. "*Danki* for stopping by today. Enjoy your *kaffi* and donuts." She smiled at them before her eyes focused past Micah toward the middle-aged *English* couple behind him. "Good morning. How may I help you?"

Micah felt disappointment curl through him as he watched Bethany turn her attention to the next customer. How could he imagine he was someone special to her when she clearly treated all of her customers with equal warmth?

Then again, she had made a special pot of peppermint mocha just for him.

Micah sipped his delicious coffee and grinned as he headed

toward the booth exit behind *Daadi*, who had his coffee balanced in one hand and the box of donuts in the other.

"Micah! Micah!"

He spun toward Sara Ann King as she rushed toward him waving a small piece of paper in her hand.

"I forgot to give you your receipt. I'm so sorry." She laughed and seemed to make a spectacle of trying to catch her breath as she caught up to him. "I asked one of the *maed* in the candy booth to watch my quilts so I could hurry after you."

"*Danki*." Micah took the receipt from her and dropped it into the bag as he studied her. "You really didn't need to come after us. We weren't planning on returning the quilt."

"I know, but I'm supposed to always give a receipt. You never know which customer will need it, right?" She laughed again and glanced toward Bethany's counter, giving her a little wave.

When Micah looked over at Bethany, she quickly looked back at her customer. He turned toward Sara Ann again and eyed her with suspicion. She gave him an eerie feeling.

"Do you have plans for Thanksgiving next week?" Sara Ann asked him.

"We're eating at *mei schweschder's haus* in White Horse."

"Oh, how nice." Her voice dripped with saccharine. "*Mei mammi* has our family over to her *haus* in Bird-in-Hand. All of my cousins will be there, and it's so much fun. We always eat too much and then laugh until our bellies hurt." She gave another chuckle that seemed too loud.

Why did she laugh so much? Did she think he might find it attractive? Instead of being alluring, it just seemed forced. It was as if she wanted everyone in the market to look at her.

"Great." He took a step back.

"I hope you have a nice Thanksgiving."

"You too. *Danki* again for the receipt." Micah started toward the exit, spotting *Daadi* waiting for him with an impatient scowl outside the Jam and Jelly Nook.

"Micah." Sara Ann caught up with him once again. "Did you say you're a member of Bethany's church district?"

He hesitated as he took in her eagerness. "That's right."

"My cousin Fern is a member of their church district too. Maybe I'll see you at a service sometime."

"Great." He smiled flatly, and a feeling of foreboding overtook him. "I need to get going to work. You take care."

"You too."

As Micah turned back toward *Daadi*, he was tempted to sprint out of the marketplace to get away from Sara Ann once and for all.

Anger rumbled deep inside of Bethany as she glanced toward the exit to her booth and watched Simply Sara Ann full-on flirt with Micah. The nerve of her! The woman batted her pretty eyelashes, tossed the tie from her prayer covering over her shoulder, and grinned at Micah as if he was the most handsome man she'd ever seen.

Simply Sara Ann. Bethany knew she wasn't being entirely kind with that name. But she and her cousins had started calling Sara Ann that behind her back because she always introduced herself with a coy glance as "I'm Sara Ann King, but you can call me simply Sara Ann." And although it seemed immature, they had begun to resent her since she was known as the marketplace gossip, always meddling in everyone's business.

Simply Sara Ann had even waved at Bethany as if to brag that Micah was talking to her and paying attention to her right in front of Bethany! The thought of that woman stealing him away and dating him made Bethany even more nauseated.

But Bethany had no right to feel any ownership over Micah. He didn't belong to her. He wasn't her boyfriend.

But oh, how she wished she could call him that!

Not for the first time, Bethany wished Simply Sara Ann would go back to her booth and mind her own business.

"Excuse me?"

"What?" Bethany looked over at her customer, a middle-aged woman who was staring at her, holding out her hand.

The woman raised her dark eyebrows. "My change?"

"Oh, right. I'm so sorry." Bethany fumbled with the register and then counted the money. "Forgive me." She quickly loaded a dozen assorted donuts into a box for the woman and handed them to her. "Thank you so much. You have a nice day."

When the customer walked away, Bethany looked toward the aisle and found that Micah was gone, but Sara Ann was walking right toward her. Bethany grasped the counter and took a deep breath. Now was the perfect time for a line of customers to walk into the Coffee Corner, but Bethany had served them all. The line was gone, and the high-top tables were clogged with customers already drinking coffee and eating donuts while chatting.

Sara Ann sashayed over to the counter and leaned forward, her smile wide and haughty. "Isn't that Micah Zook the most handsome man you've ever seen?"

Bethany gave a slight nod as she clutched the counter with such force that her fingers ached.

"He came into my booth and bought the prettiest quilt for

his niece. He said her birthday is in December, and she's going to be four. Her name is Krissy. She likes the color pink, so we picked the perfect quilt for her. I gave him a deal on the quilt since I've seen him around the market so much."

Sara Ann took a dramatic breath. "Anyway, he was just so nice and kind to me that I couldn't let him leave without his receipt. I asked Marilyn from the Candy Stand to watch my booth so I could run after him and give it to him. He said he's a member of your church district. You know that my cousin Fern is a member, so I told him I might see him."

Her expression became secretive, and her pretty gray eyes narrowed. "I just might have to start attending church with her so I can see him more. After all, I just love a tall man. He seems like the strong-and-silent type, you know? He doesn't seem to have much to say, but I can tell he's thinking a lot by the way he looks at me."

Bethany was almost certain she was going to be sick. The eggs and bacon she'd eaten before she headed to the market turned sour and curdled in her belly. She picked at a nick on the edge of the counter to stop herself from screaming at Sara Ann to leave.

"Well, I better get back to work. You have a great day now. Sell lots of *kaffi*." Sara Ann gave her a little wave. "Bye, now!"

As Simply Sara Ann sauntered from the booth, Bethany worked to keep her breathing even. Anthony had once commented that Sara Ann tended to come on too strong, which wasn't always appealing to men. Perhaps Micah would not appreciate how boldly she had been flirting with him.

Still, there was one detail Bethany couldn't shake: Micah had shared more information about his family with Simply Sara Ann than he had ever shared with her. Did that mean he felt more comfortable with Sara Ann than with Bethany?

If that were true, then she was certain Micah would break her heart. And the only way to prevent that would be to concentrate on being his friend. As difficult as it would be, Bethany might have to give up her dreams of being his girlfriend.

Chapter 9

Daadi chuckled to himself as Micah guided the horse onto Old Philadelphia Pike and toward their house. They had quickly exited the marketplace and then rushed across the cold parking lot to their waiting horse and buggy.

"What's so funny?" Micah couldn't stop his own smile as he turned toward his grandfather sitting beside him.

"I was just thinking about how those *maed* were night and day."

"What do you mean?"

"Well, that Sara Ann never stopped talking and barely let you get a word in edgewise. She seemed awfully aggressive. And then there's Bethany, who is sweet and bubbly. She even made your favorite *kaffi* without your asking. That's special." *Daadi* sipped his coffee.

"*Ya*, it is special." Very special, indeed. Did it mean she cared for him?

"I think Bethany is genuine, but Sara Ann seemed more like she just wanted to flirt with you so everyone else could watch."

Micah nodded slowly. "I would agree that is an accurate observation." He kept his eyes on the road as he contemplated how sweet Bethany had been. If only he'd had more time to talk to her.

And he definitely agreed with *Daadi*. Not only was Sara Ann aggressive, but she made him feel uncomfortable. He didn't look forward to seeing her at church.

"I can't wait until you settle down." *Daadi* shifted in the seat. "I'd like to see you married and with a family before I pass away. I need another great-grandchild."

Micah responded with a nervous chuckle. "Uh, I think you're rushing things. I've told you I'm not looking for a *fraa* right now."

"You should be. I'm not going to be around forever."

"*Ya*, you are." Micah gave him a grin. "You're going to live on well into your hundreds, so you can sit on a stool and tell me what I'm doing wrong when I build the furniture."

Daadi's laugh was loud, and Micah's smile widened. He adored his grandfather. He'd always been a balm to Micah's soul when things were out of control with his father. *Daadi* was the best friend he could always count on.

He hoped *Daadi* did live for a long, long time.

A week and a half later, on the Tuesday after Thanksgiving, Bethany struggled to lift another heavy bag of flour from the shelf in the bulk-foods store to her large cart. She stuck out her tongue and grunted as she heaved. Just as she felt herself teeter and start to lose her balance, a strong arm swooped in and grabbed the bag from her.

"Whoa. Let me get that from you."

She looked up and swallowed a gasp as Micah picked up the large bag with ease and set it into her cart. Her pulse kicked up into high gear as she took in his handsome face.

"Micah. Hi."

"Hey." He pointed. "I thought for sure you were going to wind up on the shelf beside those bags."

She laughed. "It wouldn't have been the first time."

He looked around. "Where's Anthony?"

"He and *mei dat* had a meeting with a supplier. They're going to pick me up on their way back home." She brushed her hands down her black apron and green dress, hoping she didn't look as disheveled as she felt.

An Amish woman who looked to be in her early thirties moved past them with three children in her shopping cart and two walking beside her. Micah nodded at her and stepped closer to the shelves of flour to give her room to pass.

"How was your Thanksgiving?" Bethany asked when he faced her again.

"It was *gut*." Micah leaned his elbow on the shelf beside him. "*Mei daadi* and I ate at *mei schweschder* Laverne's *haus*. My parents were there too." Something unreadable flashed in his expression.

"Oh." Bethany longed to know more about his family. "Where does your *schweschder* live?"

"In White Horse near where I grew up."

"Really?" She hoped he'd share more so that she didn't have to pry.

"*Ya*. They're just a few miles away from my parents. Her husband breeds horses. Their *dochder* is turning four in a couple of weeks."

"That's nice. Is Laverne older or younger than you?"

"Older. She's thirty-two." He touched the edge of her cart. "How was your Thanksgiving?"

"*Gut. Mei mammi* hosted us all." She shrugged. "Actually, we eat at Leanna's parents' house, but *mei mammi* likes to do the bulk of the cooking. My grandparents live in the *daadihaus* at their farm. All of my cousins were there, and we enjoy getting together." She touched her abdomen. "I just always eat too much."

"Don't we all?" He laughed, then pointed to the flour. "I guess you're stocking up on supplies for the market."

"*Ya*, I am." She felt her cheeks heat. "I always struggle with those large bags, but I go through so many for the donuts."

"Do you want another one?"

"How about two more?"

He loaded the bags as if they were weightless, and she tried not to stare at his muscular biceps. Then she looked at his basket and found bags of peanuts, chocolate-covered pretzels, trail mix, and gummy worms.

"I guess you like your snacks, huh?"

His expression became sheepish. "Believe it or not, it's for *mei daadi*."

"A likely story," she teased, and he chuckled.

"He likes his candy, so he asked me to stop by here on my way home from the hardware store." He nodded at her cart. "Do you buy your *kaffi* supplies here too?"

"Some of them." She held up her list. "I'm still working on it."

"Do you need company while you shop?"

Her heart warmed. "That would be nice."

They moved through the aisles together, weaving past Amish families and chatting about items as Micah loaded them into Bethany's cart. Conversation with him was easy as they joked and laughed together. Was that how Salina felt with Will and Christiana felt with Jeff?

She tried to drive the question away. Micah was her friend and nothing more.

Disappointment filled Bethany when she crossed the last item off her list and they walked toward the cashiers together. Why wasn't her list twice as long?

She paid for her items and he paid for his before she zipped up her black coat and they stepped out into the parking lot together. The early-December breeze nipped at her nose, making her shiver. She glanced around the parking lot, taking in the line of horses and buggies at the hitching post along with the row of sedans in the parking spaces.

"Are you sure you don't need a ride?" he offered, gesturing toward a waiting horse and buggy.

She nibbled her lip. If only she had a cellular phone and her brother had one too. Then she could call him and tell him she'd found another way home. "Anthony is supposed to pick me up soon."

"Oh. Okay." His expression seemed as disappointed as she felt. "It was nice seeing you." He picked up his shopping bag full of snacks. "You have a *gut* afternoon."

"You too." She gave him a wave, and he started toward his buggy. Then an idea hit her. "Micah!"

He turned toward her, his expression bright. "*Ya?*"

"Do you and Enos like chili?"

He nodded. "We do."

"Do you have plans for supper?"

He took a step toward her. "No."

"*Mei mamm* and I made chili last night, and we always make

87

too much. Would you and Enos like to join us for supper tonight?" She held her breath, hoping he wouldn't reject her.

A warm smile lit up his handsome face. "That sounds nice. I'll ask *Daadi*, but I imagine he would love to come. Today is the perfect day for chili."

Excitement buzzed through her veins. "It always is when it's cold. How does six sound?"

"Sounds *gut*. I'll talk to *Daadi* and leave a message for you."

"Okay."

He started walking backward and pointed toward his horse and buggy. "I don't like the idea of leaving you standing out here in the cold. You sure you don't want a ride?"

"*Danki*, but I have to wait for *mei dat* and Anthony."

"Okay." He lifted his hand. "Hopefully I'll see you later."

She waved as anticipation she couldn't quell twirled through her. Maybe she would have her first family supper with Micah and Enos. She just hoped he and Enos would come.

Later that afternoon Bethany stood at the counter and iced a lemon cake she had baked just in case they had company for supper.

"That smells *appeditlich*." *Mamm* stepped into the kitchen. "Enos and Micah will enjoy it tonight."

"*Danki*. That's if they join us tonight for supper."

The back door opened and then clicked shut before Anthony appeared in the doorway that led to the mudroom. "I just got a message from Micah."

"And . . ." Bethany's heart thumped at the sound of his name.

"He and Enos are coming for supper tonight." Anthony tilted his head. "You really like him, don't you?"

"We're just *freinden*."

Anthony smirked. "Sure you are."

Bethany bit back a groan. Was her younger brother really going to tease her about this again?

"He sounded excited," Anthony added. "He said they'll be here at six." He turned and disappeared, the back door clicking shut behind him.

Bethany looked up at the clock. "Six o'clock . . . That only gives me an hour and a half to get ready. I need to bake some corn bread to go with the chili and—"

"Bethany," *Mamm* interrupted her. "You're getting awfully worked up about this." She studied her, and Bethany shifted her weight on her feet. "He must mean a lot to you."

"I don't think he wants to be more than *freinden*."

"Why would you say that?"

"It's just a feeling I have." She took a deep breath, deciding to be truthful about her feelings. "I saw him talking to Sara Ann King at the marketplace, and he also cut off our conversation when I saw him at church. Also, there haven't been many men who were interested in me. Why would Micah be any different?"

Mamm tutted in disagreement. "I had only dated one other man before I met your *dat*. You only have to find the one God has chosen for you."

"I know, but Micah is so special. And handsome. Why would he want me when he could have any of the *maed* in the community? I'm not *schee* like Christiana or *schmaert* and sophisticated like Salina. I'm just awkward, *gegisch* Bethany." Her voice sounded thick.

"*Ach, mei liewe.*" *Mamm*'s expression clouded with a sad frown as she crossed the kitchen and touched Bethany's cheek. "Why would you put yourself down like that? You're *schee*, sweet, and funny. When you were in school, I once watched you leave a softball game to talk to a *bu* who was sitting all alone. You have a kind heart and a gentle spirit, and if Micah can't see that, then he's not the one meant for you."

Bethany didn't want her dear *mamm* to see the tears forming in the corners of her eyes, so she spun away and headed toward the pantry. "I'm going to see if we have any corn bread mix. I'll need two boxes."

Her mother's words floated through her mind as she focused on preparing for the meal. While her mother might have considered her to be worthy of someone like Micah, Bethany had a difficult time believing he could care for her as more than a friend.

But wouldn't it be a blessing if he did?

Chapter 10

Micah halted the horse by the Gingerichs' back porch later that evening. He glanced up at the dark sky and admired the puffy clouds and the streaks of orange and yellow as the sun started to set.

He glanced over at the porch and took in the warm glow of the lanterns in the kitchen windows as a smile curved his mouth. He had hoped *Daadi* would agree to come to supper tonight, and thankfully, *Daadi* had jumped at the chance to spend an evening with the Gingerich family.

But now, as he imagined spending time with Bethany and her loved ones, Micah felt a flutter of nerves. Would he be able to sustain an entire evening of conversation that was as easy as their chat at the bulk-foods store?

"Why are we still sitting here like two stones? There's chili waiting for us in that *haus*." *Daadi* pushed open the buggy door and climbed out of the passenger side.

Micah reached behind him and picked up the apple pie he had purchased at the grocery store on the way over and then climbed out of the buggy. After tying up the horse, he followed *Daadi* up the porch steps and knocked on the door.

"Coming!" Bethany's muffled voice sang from somewhere inside the house.

The bolt clicked and the door opened, revealing Bethany standing behind the storm door. She looked beautiful clad in a plum-colored dress and a black apron. With a warm smile, she pushed open the storm door. The tantalizing aroma of chili filled his senses, along with loud voices from the kitchen.

"Hi." She looked down at the apple pie in his hand. "Oh, how nice of you to bring dessert. I made a lemon cake too."

"Oh. I didn't know." He fidgeted with the pie as warmth crept up his neck.

"It's *wunderbaar*. We'll have plenty. Come in." Holding the door open with one hand, she beckoned for them to enter the house.

"It smells *appeditlich* in here," *Daadi* announced as he stepped into the mudroom and began removing his hat and coat.

"It does." Micah handed Bethany the pie and then took off his hat and shucked his coat.

"*Danki* again for the pie. I'll turn on the oven so we can warm it up for dessert."

Micah followed *Daadi* into the kitchen, where Harvey, Anthony, and Darlene were gathered. The long kitchen table was set for six. Two pans of corn bread sat in the center, along with a large pot of chili.

"Enos!" Harvey shook his grandfather's hand. "We're so glad you could join us for supper tonight." Then he turned to welcome Micah.

Micah shook Anthony's hand and greeted Darlene, then walked over to the sink and washed his hands with *Daadi* in tow.

When they finished, Darlene made a sweeping gesture toward the table. "We're ready to eat, so please have a seat."

Micah hesitated, waiting to see where Bethany planned to sit. Then he slipped into the chair beside her. She glanced over at him, and her sweet smile made his pulse tick up.

After a silent prayer, voices broke out around the table as everyone began reaching for the food.

"So, how was your day, Enos?" Harvey asked.

"Micah, isn't it funny that you ran into Bethany at the bulk-foods store?" Darlene commented. "What were you buying?"

"How was your day, Micah?" Anthony asked from across the table. "What are you and Enos working on?"

Micah looked back and forth from Anthony to Darlene, not sure whom to respond to first. Then Bethany gave his arm a gentle bump and held out the pan of corn bread.

"Would you like a piece?" she asked.

"Sure," Micah said, taking the pan. He looked at Anthony and then Darlene, preparing to respond to their questions, but they had both moved on to another conversation, looking at Harvey as he spoke. Anthony cut in, adding commentary.

Micah's mind spun as Bethany's father and brother continued to talk, their voices so loud they were nearly startling. He scooped the corn bread onto his plate just as Bethany nudged him again. When he turned toward her, she pointed to the bowl on his plate.

"Would you like some chili?" she asked.

"*Ya. Danki.*"

"So then we went to talk to the owner of that shed dealer out on Lincoln Highway," Harvey was saying, speaking so stridently Micah was certain the horses could hear him in the barn.

"And when we got out of the van, the owner came out to greet us. He said he was looking for Amish folks to build gazebos because the customers don't want gazebos built by *Englishers*. They're convinced ours are better quality."

"Just because we're Amish," Anthony chimed in. "Not because they've seen our products."

Harvey nodded. "They think our craftsmanship is superior, and he said he's going to cancel his contract with his current supplier."

"Isn't that something, Micah?" Anthony asked.

"So what were you getting in the bulk-foods store, Micah?" Darlene queried.

"What?" Micah turned toward Darlene.

Darlene's smile was warm. "I asked what you were buying at the bulk-food store when you ran into Bethany."

"What do you think of that, Micah?" Anthony asked again. "We got a contract simply because we're Amish. He didn't even ask to see our gazebos first."

Micah thought his head might explode. He couldn't keep up with the conversations. He glanced over at *Daadi*, sitting across from him and beside Anthony. *Daadi* just grinned as he scooped chili into his mouth and looked at Harvey.

"Micah was getting snacks for Enos," Bethany told her mother. "He had peanuts, trail mix, gummy worms, and chocolate-covered pretzels in his basket." Her voice took on a teasing tone. "At least he *claimed* it was for Enos."

"Micah," Anthony said, his voice loud enough to be heard over his father. "Maybe you should talk to the shed dealer about your outdoor furniture. If the customers only want Amish-made products, then you and Enos could sell a lot there."

Micah opened his mouth to respond, but Harvey cut him off. "That's what I was going to tell Enos. It's a great idea to get more orders for spring." Harvey lifted his eyebrows as if he were responding to an unspoken question.

Micah could tell he was trying to offer solutions to Micah's conundrum for their business. His shoulders tightened as he awaited his grandfather's protest. However, when he turned toward *Daadi*, he found him studying his chili. At least he wasn't arguing with Harvey. While both his father and grandfather had similar short tempers, he was grateful his grandfather rarely lost his cool in public. If *Daadi* did here, Micah might pass out from embarrassment.

"*Dat*," Bethany began, speaking loudly. "Tell Micah about when you went fishing with his *dat*."

"Oh, right." Harvey laughed. "And then we found out the boat had holes in the bottom of it, just like the tent when we were camping."

"That was so funny." Darlene tapped the table. "You have to hear this, Micah."

"I know exactly what you're taking about," *Daadi* piped up, smiling. "That was actually my boat they took fishing."

"I think we were about nineteen or so," Harvey began, "and we were going fishing with a few of our *freinden*."

"Listen, Micah. This is so funny," Anthony said.

"So, when we got to the lake, we all unloaded the boat, gathered up our fishing gear, and headed out on the water. But . . . no one was *schmaert* enough to check if that old boat could still float."

Bethany tapped Micah on the arm. "Are you going to eat?"

"Oh. Right." Micah took a spoonful of chili, enjoying the taste of it.

Harvey continued. "We went to the center of the lake, and I soon realized my shoes felt wet. Needless to say, we didn't last very long. Once the boat started taking on water, we had to find a way to get back to shore before we all ended up at the bottom of the lake."

Micah ate his supper, but he felt as if he were watching a volleyball match as Bethany and her family continued to share stories of his father's youth, all jumping in to outdo one another with details of the story. By the end of the meal, he was as exhausted as if he had run the length of his father's pasture four times. Bethany's family was kind and welcoming, but their energy was draining. He wished he could disappear into a quiet corner to cool down.

After drinking a cup of Bethany's delicious toasted-almond coffee and eating slices of apple pie and lemon cake, Micah sat in the Gingerichs' large family room with Anthony, *Daadi*, and Harvey while they continued to talk about work. Micah tried to relax in the wing chair, but he longed for quiet conversation elsewhere. He was ready for some downtime away from the boisterous Gingerich family. He glanced toward the doorway leading to the kitchen, where Bethany and Darlene cleaned up after the meal.

If only he could make an excuse to get Bethany alone. But how could he do that when her family seemed so eager to spend time with both him and *Daadi*?

"I think Enos and Micah enjoyed supper," *Mamm* said as she scrubbed the large pot that had held the chili.

"*Ya*." Bethany finished drying the bread pans and set them

in the cabinet before looking over toward the doorway leading to the family room. She could hear her father telling a story about the gazebos he had built for a resort located on the Outer Banks of North Carolina. Her shoulders hunched as she recalled how Micah had remained silent and looked uncomfortable during supper.

She turned back to *Mamm*. "I don't think he likes me."

"What?" *Mamm* spun to face her. "Why would you say that?"

"Shh!" Bethany shushed her and pointed to the doorway. "They'll hear you."

"No, they won't. They're not paying any attention to us." *Mamm* waved her off. "Why would you think he doesn't like you? He came over to have supper with us. He could have made up an excuse to stay home."

Bethany nodded as she began drying a bowl. "I know, but he didn't speak much at all during supper and seemed uncomfortable." She finished drying the bowl and grabbed another one.

"Why don't you ask him?"

Bethany's gaze snapped to *Mamm*'s. "What do you mean?"

"I mean, go ask him." *Mamm* pointed to the family room. "Go in there and ask him if he wants to go for a walk. Then grab your coat and a lantern and walk outside where you can talk alone."

Bethany hesitated.

"Go on. I'll finish the dishes."

Bethany bit her lip and looked toward the doorway again. Would she seem too forward if she invited him to walk alone with her?

Mamm waved her off. "*Dummle*! Before he says he's ready to go home. You've never been shy before. What's holding you back now?"

Mamm had a point. Bethany had never shied away from talking to people in the past, so why would she now?

She was strong. She could handle it.

"Okay." Bethany set the dish towel on the counter. "*Danki* for doing the dishes."

"*Gern gschehne*. Now, go get him."

Bethany grinned at her mother's comment as she walked toward the doorway. Then she squared her shoulders and smoothed her hands down her apron. She rested her hand on the wall and peered into the room. *Dat* and Anthony sat side by side in the matching dark-brown recliners while Enos rested on the worn brown sofa. Anthony and Enos nodded and smiled while *Dat* talked on about which of his gazebos was the most popular.

Her eyes settled on Micah, and she found him sitting rigid in the wing chair. His expression was stoic. Was he bored or uncomfortable? Or maybe a little of both? A muscle in his strong jaw flexed as he stared at her father.

Bethany padded into the room, and the conversation stopped as all four pairs of eyes turned to her.

"Excuse me." She glanced over at Micah. "I was wondering if I could speak to Micah for a moment."

"Oh." Micah stood and looked over at *Dat*. "Excuse me, Harvey." His expression relaxed slightly as he met her gaze and walked over to the doorway.

She looked up at him, and her mouth dried as his deep-brown eyes locked on hers. "I was wondering if you would take a walk with me. So we can talk."

He seemed relieved. "That sounds nice."

"Great." She glanced over at her mother, who winked at her, and excitement hummed through Bethany's belly as they walked to the mudroom together. She hoped Micah hadn't seen *Mamm's* gesture. She pushed her feet into a pair of boots and then pulled on a coat and grabbed a lantern.

Micah put on his coat and hat, wrenched open the back door, and held open the storm door for her. Then he lifted his hand and took the lantern from her.

As Bethany stepped out into the cold night air with Micah, she looked up at the dark sky and smiled. She hoped this would be one of many walks she would take with Micah by her side.

Chapter 11

Bethany shivered as she walked down the back steps. The scent of a neighbor's wood-burning fireplace filled her nostrils. She turned toward Micah beside her, his handsome face illuminated by the warm glow of the lantern. "Do you want to walk around the pasture or sit on the porch?"

He held the lantern in one hand and jammed his other hand into the pocket of his black coat before lifting his chin toward the pasture. "We can walk."

"Perfect."

They moved in silence toward the split-rail fence, the only sounds coming from their boots crunching on dead leaves and the hum of traffic out on Old Philadelphia Pike a few blocks away. A dog barked somewhere in the distance. Bethany racked her brain for something to say to him, but for the first time in a long time, she struggled with how to start a conversation. Taking a deep breath, she decided to go with the first subject that came to her mind.

"The pie was delicious," she said. "Where did you get it?"

"The grocery store by the market." He lifted his hand from

his pocket and pointed in the direction of Old Philadelphia Pike.

"Oh." She forced a smile. "It was really *gut*. I'm glad *mei dat* suggested we get out the vanilla ice cream. I love the taste of melted ice cream on pie. Don't you?"

He nodded.

She studied him. What did his silence mean? Worry nipped at her.

She stopped walking and faced him. "Is everything okay?"

One corner of his mouth lifted as he gave her a half shrug. "I'm just not talkative."

She searched his eyes for a sign of a lie, but she found none.

He tapped the back of the worn bench her father had built by the pasture when she was little. "I know the wood is cold, but would you like to sit?"

She took his suggestion as a sign that he might actually like being with her. Relief loosened a few of the knots in her shoulders. "*Ya*."

He sat down, set the lantern on the ground, and patted the spot beside him. "It's not too terribly cold. Or maybe my legs have gone numb."

With a little laugh, she sat down beside him. She glanced out at the pasture for a moment and then turned toward him. "You're close to Enos, aren't you?"

"*Ya*." Micah leaned back on the bench. "He's my best *freind*."

"My cousins are my best *freinden*." She pressed the palms of her hands to the wood of the bench as a small sigh escaped her lips.

"You sounded *bedauerlich* when you said that."

She turned toward him, surprised he was so in tune with her

feelings. She blinked when she found him watching her. The intensity in his eyes sent an unfamiliar tremor through her.

His expression warmed. "Do you want to talk about what's bothering you?"

Something in his kind expression caused the emotions she'd kept bottled up since Salina's wedding to break free.

"Everything is changing, and it scares me." She looked down at the peeling white paint and picked at a few chips. "Christiana got married last year, and now she's expecting a *boppli*. And now Salina is married."

She looked up quickly, needing to explain herself. "It's not that I'm jealous. I'm not. I'm truly *froh* for them, but their new lives mean we won't have much time together. Christiana is closing down her Bake Shop booth at the end of the month, and she won't reopen it since she'll have the *boppli*. Salina has to replant her garden at her new *haus*, and she said she might spend more time helping Will at his restaurant. If she closes her booth, then I'll only have Leanna at the market.

"The four of us used to have *kaffi* together every morning before the market opens. It won't be the same if it's just Leanna and me. Salina and Christiana have always been a part of my life. We've been through everything from dolls to our first boyfriends together. Now I can't even sit with them at church anymore since the three of them are in the married women's section now. I can't imagine my life without them."

"Change is scary, isn't it?"

Her spirit lifted when she found understanding in his eyes. "It is."

He looked out toward the pasture as something unreadable flickered across his face. "Sometimes things happen that we don't expect, and it can turn our lives upside down. When that happens, we have to rely on God to get us through it. But it's not always easy. His plan isn't always what we want or what we hope for. But we have to accept it."

She held her breath, waiting for him to elaborate, but he remained silent.

"You're right," she finally said.

He looked over at her, and his expression relaxed. "I have a feeling you'll always be close to your cousins. Your relationship might change, but you'll always have them in your life."

She nodded. "*Ya*, I hope so."

"So, what is the secret to your amazing *kaffi?*"

She laughed at the change in subject. "I'll never tell."

"Oh, come on. You can trust me."

"Nope. It's a secret." She shrugged. "I use special flavorings."

"Interesting. Tell me how you learned to make those donuts. You mentioned your *mammi*. How old were you when you started cooking?"

Happiness bubbled up in her chest as she fell into an easy conversation with him about her booth.

When they heard the back door open, Bethany and Micah got up and ambled back to the house, where Enos stood on the porch with her family.

"There you two are," Enos announced as Micah and Bethany walked up the path toward the porch. "We were just discussing sending out a search party," he quipped before shaking hands with *Dat*, *Mamm*, and Anthony. "*Danki* for a *wunderbaar* meal."

"We're so glad you could come," *Dat* told him.

"*Gut nacht*." *Mamm* waved at Micah. "I'm going to go back inside. It's cold out here."

Enos pulled a small flashlight out of his pocket and started toward the horse and buggy as *Dat* and Anthony headed toward the barn to check on the animals.

Micah turned to Bethany. "*Danki* for inviting us. I had a nice time." He shook her hand.

"*Gern gschehne.*" She enjoyed the feel of his cold skin against hers as she smiled.

Enos reached the buggy and then waved at Bethany. "I'll see you soon."

As he disappeared into the buggy, Bethany headed up the porch steps, set the lantern on the floor, and stood by the railing as Micah guided the horse down the driveway. The *clip-clop* of the horse's hooves echoed as the buggy's taillights flashed and then disappeared into the pitch-black night.

"How was your talk with Micah?"

Bethany jumped with a start as *Mamm* appeared behind her on the porch wearing a shawl. "I thought you went inside."

"I did, but when you didn't come in, I came out to check on you." *Mamm* sat down on the glider. "Sit with me. Tell me about your walk."

Bethany sank down beside her on the glider and pushed the swing into motion with the toe of her boot. "It was fine."

"Fine?" *Mamm* looked curious. "Can you elaborate?"

"We talked a little bit, but it seems like he doesn't know what to say to me. I asked him if something was wrong, but he said he's not talkative. If he liked me, then he'd had more to say to me, right?"

Mamm shrugged. "Not necessarily. Maybe he just felt like being quiet. He went for a walk with you. Doesn't that mean something?"

"I suppose so." Bethany rested her elbow on the arm of the chair and her chin on her palm. "I think he only likes me as a *freind*."

"But that could be a start, right?"

Bethany smiled at her *mamm*, feeling herself growing more and more attached to Micah despite her best efforts. Would her heart recover from the disappointment if he never reciprocated?

Micah guided the horse down Gibbons Road as his mind spun like his buggy wheels while he considered his evening with the Gingerich family. Although he'd enjoyed his time talking with Bethany alone, he was still feeling overwhelmed by her family.

"Well, that was a fun evening. *Danki* for taking me there." *Daadi* patted his middle as he grinned in the light of the lantern at his feet. "I'm stuffed."

"I enjoyed the *gut* food too."

"And fellowship. Those Gingeriches are funny. I enjoyed their stories."

Micah nodded and contemplated his conversation with Bethany by the pasture. When she'd talked about her cousins and her fear of losing them, he'd almost told her about Dawn. But something had held him back. He just couldn't allow himself to be that honest and vulnerable with her yet. If he let her in, she could hurt him—and he wasn't ready to take such a risk with his heart.

Still, some strange part of him wanted to open up to her. That part craved her friendship and camaraderie. What was it about Bethany that made him feel so comfortable and so on edge all at once?

"I would say Bethany enjoys your company."

Micah glanced over at *Daadi*. "Yeah, I think she does. We had a nice talk by the pasture." He shook his head. "She's not short on words."

"No, she isn't. That's part of what makes her so likable. She's a chatterbox, always eager to talk."

Micah nodded, but a thought struck him: Bethany was his complete opposite. While he was happy to sit on the bench beside her and enjoy the silence, she seemed determined fill the air between them with conversation.

How could two opposites forge a friendship?

Doubt filled Micah as he guided the horse toward the road that led to their house. Even if he and Bethany were to become friends, he worried they might be too different to become anything more.

"How was the market yesterday?" Christiana held a hand to her lower back as she stood with Bethany and their other cousins in the Glick family's kitchen before the church service on Sunday nearly two weeks later.

"It was *gut*," Leanna said. "Busy. I'm selling a lot of jam and jelly gift baskets since Christmas is only two weeks away. I'm going to have to make some more baskets so I have some ready to sell on Thursday."

"That's great," Salina said. "I miss seeing you all at the market, but I've been busy at the restaurant. I feel like we never talk anymore."

Bethany frowned. "I know." She missed having Christiana

and Salina with her and Leanna during their morning coffee and at lunchtime at the marketplace. She rarely saw Jeff at the market nowadays. He seemed to stay in his booth since Christiana wasn't there.

Salina turned to Bethany. "How about you? I bet you've been busy, too, selling your eggnog and peppermint mocha."

Peppermint mocha. Bethany pressed her lips together as her thoughts turned to Micah.

Salina touched Bethany's arm. "Hey. What was that frown for? Are the sales down for the Coffee Corner?"

"No, it's not that." Bethany glanced around the kitchen and then stepped closer to her cousins, lowering her voice. "I was hoping things would change between Micah and me after I invited him and his *daadi* over for supper two weeks ago. But nothing has changed at all. He and Enos stopped by for *kaffi* yesterday, and we had our usual chat about the weather. Then he bought his *kaffi* and donuts and left. We're still just acquaintances who chat for a few minutes every Saturday morning."

Bethany looked down at her black shoes and shook her head. "I know what you're thinking. I'm *gegisch* for believing anything would change. Why would he want to date me?"

"No, no, no." Salina gave Bethany's shoulder a gentle squeeze. "We would never think that. If he didn't like you, he wouldn't have come for supper, and he wouldn't keep coming to see you every Saturday for his *kaffi* and donut. I don't know Micah well, but he seems really shy and quiet. Maybe it will just take him a while to ask you out. Maybe he wants to get to know you better before he takes that step."

"*Ya,*" Christiana chimed in. "That makes sense. Jeff had been hurt, so he was hesitant to ask me out. Maybe Micah has been hurt, and that's why he's a little *naerfich* to jump into another relationship."

Bethany felt herself gape as she looked at Salina. She had never considered that Micah may have dated someone in the past, but it made sense. After all, he was twenty-seven, which was three years older than Bethany. He could have had a long-term relationship before he moved from White Horse to Bird-in-Hand.

If he had dated someone else, would he ever open up to Bethany about it? She felt a tumble of raw emotions at the thought of finding out more about his past.

"Don't give up on him," Leanna said. "Sometimes it takes people a little longer to open up."

Bethany nodded slowly, her mind twirling with questions about his past. "That makes perfect sense."

The clock chimed nine, and Bethany followed her cousins out into the cold. She glanced over to where the unmarried men were walking toward the barn, and her eyes locked on Micah. When he met her gaze, he nodded and gave her a half smile. She returned the gesture, but sadness filled her. Despite the pep talk from her cousins, she just couldn't keep from wondering about his reticence. Maybe he wasn't only shy; maybe he truly just didn't like her enough to ask her to be his girlfriend.

As she caught up with Phoebe and Suzanna and walked with them toward a bench in the unmarried women's section of the congregation, hope and disappointment warred in her heart.

Chapter 12

Micah did his best to keep his gaze and his mind focused on the service while Bishop Lamar lectured on the book of Mark. But as he listened, his eyes kept betraying him, finding their way to Bethany sitting with her younger cousin, Phoebe. His heart had tripped over itself when he'd spotted her walking with her cousins toward the barn before the service. Her bright-blue dress reminded him of the brilliant summer sky.

He had smiled and waved at her, but although she had returned the greeting, she'd seemed less perky than usual. Her lack of enthusiasm had piqued his curiosity, and he hoped to talk to her after the service to find out if she was okay.

Micah worked to keep his thoughts and his heart engaged in the service. Relief flooded him when the fifteen-minute kneeling prayer ended following the second sermon. The congregation stood for the benediction and sang the closing hymn.

Once the service was over, Micah began helping the other men convert the benches into tables for the noon meal. While Anthony took one end of the bench, Micah helped him slip it into a stand so that it would serve as a table. Then they worked together to do the same with another bench.

"How was your week?" Anthony asked him.

"*Gut.* Yours?"

"Busy." Anthony nodded at him. "Did you or your *daadi* talk to that shed dealer we told you about at supper the other night?"

Micah shook his head. "No. *Mei daadi* doesn't agree that it's a *gut* idea, even though I think it is."

"That's a shame." Anthony smiled. "Don't give up on it, though. Maybe Enos will change his mind."

"Maybe so." Micah couldn't help thinking that Anthony was just as friendly as his older sister. The Gingerich family resemblance was uncanny when it came to their personalities. If only Micah could find a way to be that comfortable chatting with folks.

After they had set up the benches, Micah turned to look for *Daadi* and see where he had chosen to sit to eat today.

"Micah!"

He swiveled at the sound of his name and then stilled as Sara Ann King made a beeline toward him. Clad in a yellow dress, her smile was wide, and her gray eyes were bright. He bit back a groan as she approached.

"Micah!" She shook his hand. "It is so great to see you." She jammed her hand on her small hip. "I told you I would come and see you at church."

She pointed toward a young woman with light-brown hair standing in the corner. "That's my cousin Fern. She was so excited when I told her I wanted to come to church with her today. We're really close. We're both twenty-five, so we've been close since we were born. Are you close with any of your cousins?"

"Ah. Not so much. Most of them live in Ohio."

"Really?" She took a step toward him. "That's interesting. I have some relatives in Indiana. I love to go to Shipshewana. It's so fun. Have you ever been there?"

"No, I can't say that I have." Micah glanced around. Now would be the perfect time for *Daadi* to come and announce they needed to sit down for lunch.

"You should really go. It's fantastic. And it's a nice bus ride too."

Micah scanned the barn again as Sara Ann went on about the bus ride to Indiana. He spotted his grandfather in the corner, talking to Lamar, and tried to think of an excuse to go join them.

"Did you give Krissy the quilt?"

Micah looked back at Sara Ann's eager smile. "Not yet. Her birthday is Friday, so *mei daadi* and I are going to *mei schweschder's haus* for a little party."

"Oh, you need to let me know how Krissy likes the quilt."

He nodded.

"I bet she will enjoy it." Sara Ann suddenly snapped her fingers as if an idea had hit her like a bolt of lightning. "Why don't you stop by my booth on Saturday and tell me? I'd love to hear all about the party. Maybe sometime you could bring Krissy by the booth. She might want to pick out another quilt."

"*Ya.* Maybe." Nodding numbly, he looked around the barn again. When his eyes settled on Bethany standing in the barn door holding a tray of food, he felt his body freeze in place.

Bethany's blue eyes were wide as she studied him. Her expression looked deflated, and she turned and suddenly bolted back through the door, almost knocking into Leanna and her coffee carafe. Pivoting, Leanna took off after her.

Micah suppressed the urge to go after Bethany to make sure

she was all right. When he heard shuffling, he turned as the men began to take their seats at the long tables.

"I need to go," he told Sara Ann. "Enjoy your lunch."

"You too." She gave him a little wave. "I'm sure I'll see you soon."

Shaking his head, Micah made his way over to *Daadi*. While he hoped to avoid Sara Ann for the rest of the day, he also longed to get a chance to check on Bethany.

Bethany's lip quivered as she rushed past the line of women carrying food from the Glick family's kitchen to the barn.

"Bethany!"

She felt an arm on her back as she reached the porch, and when she turned, she found Leanna.

"What happened?" Leanna asked, her dark eyes full of concern.

Bethany looked behind her and spotted a sea of curious faces watching them. She held out the tray full of pretzels toward Phoebe. "Would you please take these to the barn for me?"

"Sure." Phoebe's brow puckered. "You okay?"

"*Ya.*" Bethany nodded.

Leanna handed the coffee carafe to Suzanna. "Would you please take this?"

"Of course." Suzanna took the carafe and followed Phoebe toward the barn.

Once the girls had moved off, Leanna took Bethany's arm and steered her around the side of the house, away from the curious stares. "You look like you're about to burst into tears. Tell me what happened."

Bethany took a few deep, shaky breaths and then sniffed. "I saw Simply Sara Ann talking to Micah."

"Oh?" Leanna's brow knitted in confusion. "She's here?"

"*Ya.* I never had a chance to tell you about the day she came to the booth and talked on and on about Micah." She quickly told her the details of the day Micah had bought a quilt from the Quilt Shop and then how Sara Ann had made a big deal about talking to him. She shared how Sara Ann had talked about how handsome he was and how she planned to visit the church district to see him.

"Now she's here, flirting with him." Bethany pointed toward the barn. "She's going after Micah. And . . . even though he's not my boyfriend, I'd still like a chance with him."

Leanna frowned and shook her head. "Sara Ann is a flirt, and she's a busybody and a terrible gossip. Just because she's flirting with him doesn't mean he likes her. You know how she is. She likes to be the center of attention, and from what I've seen of Micah, I don't think he'll find that very attractive."

"But she *is* attractive, Leanna. Sara Ann is beautiful. I've seen men at the market give her second looks when she walks by."

"But then she opens her mouth, and the allure is over."

Bethany looked down and kicked a stone with the toe of her shoe.

"Look at me, Bethany."

She raised her head and tried to clear her throat past the lump swelling there.

"You've been down in the dumps all day. What's going on? Why are you so convinced you have no chance with Micah?"

Bethany hugged her arms to her chest. "I just don't think I do."

"Why? Because of Simply Sara Ann?" Leanna scoffed. "I don't think you have to worry about her." She looped her arm around Bethany's shoulders. "Why don't we go and serve the meal? Don't pay any attention to Sara Ann or Micah. Just focus on lunch. Later, we can visit with our cousins and *Mammi*. I know that will make you *froh*."

Bethany lifted her chin. "Okay. Can I just check my appearance in the mirror first? I don't want anyone to be able to tell I was on the verge of tears."

"We can go in the front door since everyone is in the kitchen."

Bethany let Leanna guide her toward the front door. As they walked up the steps, Bethany sent up a silent prayer:

Lord, please give me strength. Help me figure out how to deal with all of these overwhelming feelings I have for Micah. I wonder if he might be the one you've chosen for me, but then I see him talking to Sara Ann. On one hand, I want to just be his friend, but then I feel this invisible force pulling me to him. Please help me sort through all of my feelings, and please lead me to the path you've chosen for me. I need you to help me understand what you have planned for me.

"Happy birthday, Krissy!" *Daadi* announced as he and Micah walked into Laverne's large, two-story brick home Friday night. The delicious aroma of baked chicken filled Micah's senses and made his stomach gurgle with delight.

Krissy came running toward the front door and squealed. "*Danki!*" His sweet niece jumped up and down, her light-brown braids bouncing off her slight shoulders.

Daadi leaned down, picked her up into his arms, and kissed her cheek. "*Gern gschehne*. We brought you a present." He pointed to the brown shopping bag that Micah held.

"Ooo! What is it?" Krissy reached for the bag.

"You have to wait to open your presents," Laverne said as she walked over. She smiled at Micah and *Daadi* and welcomed them in.

Micah had always thought that Laverne looked just like *Mamm* since they had the same light-brown hair and deep brown eyes.

"How are you?" Micah asked her.

"I'm fine. Just tired." She touched her midriff before she pointed toward the kitchen, which piqued Micah's curiosity. Would he have another niece or nephew soon? "Come join us. We have baked chicken, mashed potatoes, carrots, and rolls." She turned toward Krissy and tapped her little nose. "All of the birthday girl's favorite foods."

"Yay!" Krissy sang, and Micah laughed. Krissy ran toward the kitchen with *Daadi* in tow.

Laverne turned toward Micah. "You okay?"

"*Ya*." He folded his arms over his chest as his shoulders and back stiffened. He had to prepare himself for his father's explosive temper, which seemed to always be directed at him. "How is his mood?"

Laverne grimaced. "It's just about the same as Thanksgiving."

Micah swallowed a groan. He had barely endured his father's judgment of his life choices during Thanksgiving. *Dat* had grilled him about still living with his grandfather and "freeloading" off of him instead of building his own *haus* "like a man." While Micah had tried his best to keep his temper in check, he had finally told his father to mind his own business. His mother had left the family room and hidden in the kitchen, as she always did when *Dat* was on a criticizing tear. And *Daadi* had stepped outside to sit on the porch for a while after saying the house was too warm.

How he longed for his mother to defend him! But Micah had learned as a child that his mother never had his back, and he only felt protected when he was with his grandfather.

Laverne rested her hand on Micah's chest. "Please ignore him. Just put up with him and let his hurtful comments go. Okay? For Krissy's sake."

Irritation plagued him as he looked at his sister's pleading expression. Just like *Mamm*, Laverne never defended him either.

Micah blew out a puff of air and nodded. He could put up with his father for one night—for Krissy. "Fine," he muttered.

"*Danki*," she said.

They walked into the kitchen, where Micah's parents and Laverne's husband, Al, sat at the table with Krissy and *Daadi*. Micah nodded at his parents and washed his hands at the sink before sitting down across from his father, who gave him his usual unimpressed expression. Why had Micah always been such a disappointment to him?

After a silent prayer, they began filling their plates with Krissy's favorite foods.

"So, how's the business?" *Dat* asked *Daadi*. In his early fifties, *Dat* had medium-brown hair, nearly the same shade as Micah's, except for the silver that had recently begun to shimmer on both his head and in his beard. But that was where Micah wanted to believe their similarities ended.

"*Gut*," *Daadi* said.

Micah nodded, not wanting to reveal details of his worries

in front of the entire family. For sure *Dat* would find some-thing to criticize in that. It was best that he kept his concerns to himself.

"Any news on the dating front?" *Mamm* asked.

Micah stopped chewing his chicken as he felt all of the eyes around the table focused on him. "No."

"That's not entirely true," *Daadi* began

Micah shook his head. "*Daadi*, please don't."

Laverne leaned forward as if trying to hear better. "Oh, this sounds interesting."

"Do tell," *Mamm* said with a grin.

"Laverne," *Dat* said to Micah's sister. Then he looked at *Mamm*. "Magdalena. If Micah wanted us to know about his personal life, he would tell us."

"I just want to hear the news, Richard." *Mamm* looked back at Micah. "So you met someone?"

Laverne grinned. "Tell us *all* about her."

"There are two *maed*, actually," *Daadi* said.

"*Daadi*, will you stop?" Micah snapped. He didn't want his family to know anything about his life. For sure and for certain, *Dat* would find fault in that too. After all, he'd never approved of Dawn.

"No, *Daadi*," Laverne said. "Keep going."

"Please don't," Micah said, pushing his hand through his hair with frustration.

Daadi pointed to the brown-paper bag on the floor by the wall. "Well, one of them made Krissy's present."

"My present?" Krissy clapped her hands. "My present!" She pointed to the bag. "My present! My present!"

"Krissy," *Dat* snapped. "You need to be quiet during supper."

Micah gritted his teeth. His father couldn't even allow Krissy to enjoy her birthday. Krissy was a sweet, innocent child—not a subject for judgment! But Micah had promised his sister he would keep his frustration in check today, so he bit back the angry retort that threatened to spill from his mouth.

Al gave *Dat* a look and then turned to Laverne. "Why don't we let her open it?"

Laverne gave in and wiped Krissy's hands before handing her the bag. Krissy pulled the quilt out of the bag and squealed as she hugged it, and *Mamm* and Laverne oohed and ahhed as Laverne moved her hand over the stitching.

"I love it!" Krissy announced as she continued to hold the quilt against her chest.

Micah's heart warmed. He leaned over and kissed his niece on her head. "I'm so glad. Happy birthday, *mei liewe*."

"Who made this?" Laverne looked at Micah. "She's talented."

"Her name is Sara Ann, and she has a booth at the Bird-in-Hand marketplace," *Daadi* volunteered with a smile that seemed to be full of delight. "And that is also where your *bruder* goes to see the other *maedel* every Saturday morning for a cup of *kaffi* and a donut at her Coffee Corner booth."

Micah glowered at his grandfather as he swallowed a mouthful of mashed potatoes. "Thanks, *Daadi*."

"Sara Ann is a very talented quilter," Laverne said, touching the pieced fabric again. "This is lovely stitching." She tried to lift it away from Krissy, who whined in protest. "You need to finish your supper, and I don't want you to get food on it. You can snuggle with it after you eat." She set the quilt in its bag on the floor and looked over at *Daadi*. "Tell me more about her."

"Well, she's *schee*," *Daadi* said.

"And she's very outspoken and aggressive," Micah added before sipping from his glass of water.

"And who is the other *maedel*, the one with the *kaffi* booth?" *Mamm* asked.

"Her name is Bethany." Micah turned to *Dat*. "She's Harvey Gringerich's *dochder*. I heard you two used to be *freinden*."

Dat tilted his head. "Harvey from my school and youth group days?"

"That's right," *Daadi* said as he cut up his chicken. "We had supper at his *haus* a couple of weeks ago."

"I remember him," *Mamm* said. "How is Harvey?"

"He's fine. His family is very loud. They were a bit overwhelming. It was almost too much for me." Micah grimaced.

"Huh." Laverne studied him. "How do you like Bethany?"

"She's very sweet and outgoing." Micah speared a few pieces of carrot with his fork. "She goes out of her way to talk with me while Sara Ann is *too* interested and flirtatious. I think she likes being the center of attention. I'm just not sure about Bethany's family. I don't think I fit in since I'm not that . . . loud."

"But opposites attract." Laverne pointed back and forth between herself and her husband. "Look at us. I'm a chatterbox, and Al is quiet, like you. Most people don't marry someone exactly like them. If they did, they would probably have a very boring life together."

"She's right," *Mamm* added. "Your *dat* and I are different too."

Micah held his hands up. "I'm not looking for a *fraa*. I gave up on that after . . . ." His voice trailed off, and he looked down at his plate.

"You shouldn't stay alone forever," *Mamm* said. "I know you were hurt when you lost Dawn. You'll always miss her. But at some point you need to try to move on. You'd be much happier if you found someone to spend your life with."

"That's right," Laverne seconded.

Micah took a deep breath in hopes of holding back his angry response. His mother and sister made it sound so easy. They had no idea how he felt and how much it hurt to think about even the possibility of losing another person he loved.

"It's definitely time for you to move on," *Dat* added. "Surely you can find someone else."

Micah looked up at his father, anger boiling in his gut. He felt his eyes narrow. Those were almost the exact words his *dat* had said to him after Dawn passed away. *Dat* had never liked her. He had said she was too bold to be a proper Amish *fraa*. And those words were the catalyst that had pushed Micah to move to Bird-in-Hand.

"You're nearly thirty, Micah," *Dat* continued. "It's time for you to build a *haus*, find a *fraa*, and have a family. You need to be a man and support yourself instead of depending upon your grandfather."

"Micah does support himself," *Daadi* chimed in. "He and I share the work, but lately Micah does almost all of the building while I do the supervising."

"Richard." *Mamm*'s words were hesitant. "Please don't start this again."

"*Ya*, please don't," Al chimed in. "We had enough of this argument at Thanksgiving, and this is Krissy's day."

Dat's sneer bounced between *Mamm* and Al. "It's a *daed*'s job to make sure his *sohn* is behaving like a proper man. And Micah is still acting like a *kind*."

Micah pushed back his chair as fury burned through him. "Maybe I should go."

"Please don't." *Mamm's* voice held a hint of desperation. "Stay."

Micah swallowed and nodded before shooting his father a glower. "I'll stay as long as *Dat* leaves me be."

Dat frowned down at his plate.

"Are you all right, *Dat?*" *Mamm* suddenly asked *Daadi.* "You look kind of pale."

Alarmed, Micah turned toward *Daadi.*

"*Ya.*" *Daadi* nodded, and his voice trembled. "I've been a little tired lately, but I think I just need to get to bed earlier." He waved everyone off with a frown. "Quit staring at me. This is my Krissy's day." He smiled over at his great-granddaughter. Then he glanced over at Laverne. "I hope there's *kuche.*"

"*Ya!* Chocolate *kuche!*" Krissy announced.

Micah looked at his beautiful niece. He suddenly found himself wondering what it would be like to have a family of his own. What would such blessings look like in his life?

Though doubt gnawed at him, a tiny glimmer of hope took root in his heart.

Chapter 13

Bethany hummed to herself Saturday morning as she glazed another dozen donuts. The warm and delicious aromas of peppermint mocha, eggnog coffee, and chocolate glaze permeated her senses.

"You're peppy this morning," Leanna said as she leaned on the counter.

"*Ya*, I am." She handed her cousin a cup of peppermint mocha and a strawberry-glazed donut. "I'm tired of feeling sorry for myself. Today is a *schee* day, and I'm going to enjoy it."

"That is a positive outlook!" Leanna handed her the money for the coffee and donut and added sweetener and creamer to the cup.

Bethany returned to glazing the donuts and glanced over her shoulder at her cousin. "How was your evening?"

"It was *gut*." Leanna ran her finger over her coffee cup. "I had to put together some more gift baskets to sell. I can't believe Christmas is next week. I feel like I have so much to do. I considered closing down the booth today, but I can't say I don't need the money. I feel bad that my parents have been supporting Chester and me for five years now, and I want to contribute something." Leanna ran her finger through the strawberry glaze, then licked it. "*Mei dat* said he would buy Chester his first horse and buggy since he's going to start going to youth events. I feel like I should help, you know?"

Bethany nodded.

"That's what I've been trying to save up for." Leanna shook her head. "I can't believe Chester is going to be sixteen in only two years. How did that happen?"

Bethany sighed. "Time moves quickly."

"It does." Leanna sipped her coffee. When two loud meows sounded, she looked down. "Why, hello there, Lily and Daisy. How are you two this morning?"

The kitties screeched in response.

Bethany laughed as she came around the corner. "Are you two hungry?"

The kitties responded with louder meows, and Bethany motioned for them to follow her. She filled two bowls halfway with dry cat food and then gave them fresh water from the sink located beside her oven.

After washing her hands, she returned to glazing her donuts. When she completed the current batch, she pulled a stool over to the counter. "Are you done Christmas shopping?"

"*Ya.*" Leanna took a bite of her donut, swallowed, and wiped her mouth. "I finished last week." She described the gifts she'd bought for her family.

They continued discussing Christmas gifts while Bethany moved between her bar stool and the fryer, slipping more donuts into the oil and flipping them when the dough rounds appeared golden and ready. Soon the marketplace doors opened, and the sound of voices and footsteps filled the air.

Leanna leaned over and touched Bethany's arm. "Be strong today when you see Micah."

"I will." Bethany smiled at her. "Go sell all of your gift baskets of jams and jellies."

Leanna gave her a thumbs-up, then hurried out toward her booth while Bethany finished glazing her last dozen donuts and set them on the shelves behind her. She turned toward the entrance to her booth just as Micah and Enos walked in, and her stomach fluttered.

Micah looked handsome today, as usual. He wore a gray shirt under his black jacket, and a black stocking cap covered his hair. His dark eyes seemed to shine in the fluorescent lights above him.

Act natural!

Bethany smiled as Micah and Enos approached her. "*Gude mariye!* You're my first customers today."

"Is that so?" Micah glanced behind him, where a line had already begun to form in the booth. "I can see we won't be your only customers."

Bethany gave a warm laugh and motioned toward her line of coffeepots behind her. "I've brewed a variety of flavors today. I have peppermint mocha, eggnog, dark-roast, white-chocolate, regular, and decaf."

"Oh my." Enos rubbed his chin. "That's a tough choice, but I think I'll go with the white-chocolate today."

"One white-chocolate coming up!" Bethany looked up at Micah and suddenly felt drawn into his stare. Her heart trilled.

How could she concentrate on being only his friend when her heart craved him? "And you? Let me guess. You'd like peppermint mocha."

"Am I that transparent?" His smile was warm, sending her pulse racing even faster.

"*Ya*, you are." She retrieved two cups and began pouring Enos's coffee. "How was your week?"

"It was *gut*," Micah said. "We were in White Horse for my niece's birthday party last night."

"Oh, *ya*?" She handed Enos his coffee and then returned to the coffeepots to pour Micah's. "How was the party?"

Something flashed in his eyes. "Fine, I suppose. Krissy was excited to turn four."

"That reminds me," Enos said. "We need to tell Sara Ann how much Krissy liked the quilt."

Bethany started at the sound of Sara Ann's name, and the cup in her hand teetered to the right, sending scalding hot coffee splashing over her fingers. She gasped and sucked in a breath as she flipped up the spigot on the coffeepot and turned to the sink. Dropping the cup, she flipped on the cold water. She slammed her eyes shut and leaned forward, taking deep breaths as she let the cold water rush over her stinging skin.

"Bethany!" In a flash, Micah was beside her, touching her arm. "Are you all right?"

"*Ya*." She looked up at him and tried to smile, but she couldn't convince her lips to tip up. Instead, she shook her head as hot humiliation scalded her too. How could she let the mention of Sara Ann's name affect her so deeply that she would injure herself? She was such a moron!

"Do you have an ice pack?" he asked.

She nodded toward the refrigerator and freezer at the far end of the counter. "In there."

He rushed over to the freezer, opened it, and retrieved a blue ice pack before hurrying back over to her. He wrapped the pack in a paper towel and held it out to her. "Here."

Danki." When she removed her hand from the cold water, her stinging skin began to turn red.

"Bethany, use the ice." He gently placed the ice pack on her palm and then put his hand over it. His eyes were full of concern as he looked down at her. He kept his hand on hers, and the sweet gesture made her heart squeeze as she breathed in his scent—spicy aftershave mixed with soap and sandalwood. "Are you okay?"

She cringed. "I feel like a *dummkopp.*"

His bark of laughter startled her. "Not even close. I've hammered my thumb more times than I care to admit."

She glanced over her shoulder at the line of customers and inwardly groaned as her shoulders slumped. Now she had to figure out how to serve people with a burned hand.

If only she could start this day over.

"Let me help you," Micah said.

She looked up at him. "You already have."

"You sit on that stool there, and I'll serve your customers until your hand feels better."

She stared at him, speechless. "But I'm sure you have things to do today."

"I can spare an hour or two." He released her hand, then glanced over at his grandfather. "I'm going to help Bethany until she's able to work again. Okay?"

"*Ya*, that's a *gut* idea." Enos wagged a finger at her. "You sit and keep that ice pack on your hand. Use some salve when you get home too."

She smiled at Enos. "I will. *Danki*."

Enos jammed his thumb toward the high-top tables. "I'm going to sit."

Micah washed his hands in the sink before turning back toward the counter. "Put me to work."

"Okay." Bethany looked up at a group of teenaged girls dressed in matching pink parkas and pink scarves. "I'm so sorry for the wait. What can Micah get you?"

The girls gave their orders, and Micah rushed around, filling coffee cups and handing out donuts. As he worked, Bethany felt herself relax, enjoying herself as she watched him smile at the customers and fumble with the coffee cups and cash register. After nearly an hour the line died down, and her hand had begun to sting less. She stood up from the stool and walked over to where Micah leaned on the counter.

"I hate to keep you here."

"I'll stay as long as you need me." He reached out and gently took her wrist in his hand, careful not to touch the sensitive red skin. His touched weakened her, making her limbs feel like noodles. "How does it feel now?"

"It's better," she managed to say.

He studied her hand. "Does it still sting?"

"*Ya*, a little." She shrugged.

He pursed his lips. "I should stay. This booth is a lot busier than I thought."

"No, no. I can handle it." She reached up to touch his shoulder and froze. Unwilling to appear too forward, she pulled her hand back. "You've helped so much. You should take your *daadi* home. I'll be fine. I can call Leanna to come over if it gets bad."

He lifted a dark eyebrow. "But Leanna is busy too." He pointed at the entrance to her booth across the aisle. There was a line there too.

"Then I'll close up early if the pain gets bad again." She looked up at him, and appreciation for him bubbled up in her. "*Danki* so much. You really were a lifesaver."

"I'm glad I was here to help you." He pulled his wallet from his back pocket. "I never paid you for *mei daadi's kaffi*."

Now it was her turn to raise her eyebrow. "Are you kidding me?" She pointed toward the rows of donuts. "Pick out a dozen to take home."

"A dozen?"

"I owe you more. I'll have to pay you for your time."

"No, you won't." He rubbed his hands together. "But I'll gladly take the donuts."

"And get yourself a cup of *kaffi* too."

While Micah filled a box with donuts, Bethany glanced toward the customers sitting at the high-top tables. She spotted Enos at a table by himself, and she studied his profile. He seemed older today and paler than usual. He looked haggard and worn, his eyes swollen with exhaustion.

The scent of peppermint mocha overwhelmed her as Micah sidled up to her holding a box of donuts in one hand and a cup of coffee in the other. "What are you looking at?"

"Your *daadi*. He looks tired."

Something flashed over Micah's face. It looked like concern or possibly fear, and it sent worry coursing through Bethany.

She swiveled toward Micah. "Is he okay?"

"He's been really tired lately, and I've tried to convince him to see his doctor. But he's stubborn. He refuses to go."

Bethany wished she could think of a way to help him. "Would you like me to talk to him for you?"

Micah seemed struck by that. "No, but *danki* for asking."

"*Gern gschehne.*"

They stared at each other for a moment, and she felt the air in her lungs squeeze. Did he feel that invisible thread pulling them together? Did his heart thump when he saw her too?

"Are you sure you can take over now?" he asked.

"*Ya*, of course." She set the ice pack in the sink. "If it starts throbbing again, I'll just tie a damp rag around my hand."

"Okay." He slipped out from behind the counter. Turning, he smiled at her. "That *kaffi* is dangerous. You be careful now."

She laughed. "I promise I will be."

She leaned on the counter as Micah approached his grandfather. When Enos looked over at her, she waved.

As she watched them leave, she felt as if Micah took a piece of her heart with him.

❦

"Does she need you to stay longer?" *Daadi* asked as he walked beside Micah toward the exit.

They passed the Unique Leather and Wood Gifts booth, and Micah spotted a display of wooden signs, blocks, and letters, as well as leather belts and bracelets. He breathed in the pleasant smells of wood and leather.

"She said she was fine." Micah shook his head. "The burn looked like it really hurt. I hope she takes care of it."

"I do too," *Daadi* said.

"Micah! Enos!"

Suppressing an eye roll, Micah turned toward the Quilt Shop. Why hadn't they walked the other way toward the exit?

"Hi, Sara Ann." Micah lifted his chin and his cup of coffee at the same time.

"How was Krissy's party?" Sara Ann asked as she sauntered toward him.

"It was fine. She loved the quilt. *Danki*." Micah turned to go. "We need to get—"

"Don't rush off. How was your week? I haven't spoken to you since church."

"It was *gut*. Busy." Micah glanced at *Daadi*, who divided a look between them. "I'm sorry, but we really need to go and finish that project. Right, *Daadi*?" He kept his words measured, hoping *Daadi* would go along with him.

Daadi looked confused. Then his eyes lit up as if he'd just understood what Micah was saying. "Right. We need to get those rockers done before our driver comes to pick them up and deliver them to the store."

"Oh, you make furniture?" Sara Ann asked. "What do you make?"

Micah wished again he could make a run for it. "We make custom outdoor furniture. I'll have to tell you some other time. Have a *gut* day."

Before Sara Ann could respond, Micah headed toward the exit, passing the Farm Stand and the Candy Booth, where the aroma of chocolate made his mouth water. As he pushed open the door with the side of his arm and held it open for his grandfather, a realization hit him. While he had longed to stay in the

Coffee Corner all day helping Bethany, he couldn't get away from Sara Ann fast enough.

What did that mean?

Surely he wasn't falling for Bethany. No, he couldn't be. He wasn't ready to give his heart away again.

But what if it was too late and his heart already belonged to her?

The question followed him as he and *Daadi* climbed into his buggy and started toward home.

"I need to apologize to you for something," *Daadi* said as Micah guided the horse onto Old Philadelphia Pike.

Micah gave him a sideways glance. "What do you mean?"

Daadi's face crumpled. "I'm sorry your *dat* is so hard on you. It's my fault. If I had been a better *daed*, he wouldn't treat you that way."

Confusion swamped Micah. "What are you talking about?"

"I was always hard on your *dat* when he was young. I was quick-tempered, impatient, and demanding." *Daadi* stared out the window toward the passing traffic as he spoke. "Your *mammi* tried to tell me to be more patient, but I believed a *daed*'s job was to browbeat his *sohn* into being the best man he could possibly be."

Micah shook his head. "No, *Daadi*. You're not like that at all. You've never treated me that way."

Daadi turned toward Micah, his expression stoic. "I *was* like that. By the time I realized I was wrong, it was too late. I tried to make it right when you came along."

Micah stared at him for a long moment and then turned back toward the road, his mind racing.

"I'm sorry for that." *Daadi* touched Micah's arm. "I hope you can find it in your heart to forgive me and to someday forgive

131

your *daed*. My actions have trickled down to you in a way I never could have imagined. I've tried to talk to your *daed* about how he treats you, but he's just as stubborn as I used to be. He told me to mind my own business. I keep praying he'll realize the terrible rift he's created with you and that he will repair it."

Micah swallowed as his throat dried. He nodded, hoping to keep his emotions at bay. "*Danki*."

"I need to tell you something else."

Micah felt his arms go rigid as he tried to prepare himself for another shocking revelation.

"After your *mammi* died, I rewrote my will. I'm leaving you everything—the *haus*, the land, and the business."

"Why would you do that?"

Daadi sighed. "I feel like I owe it to you after the way your *dat* has treated you. Plus, your *dat* never had any interest in my business, and you do. You've earned it. I told your *dat*, and he wasn't thrilled about it. But it's my business, not his."

Micah swallowed against his suddenly dry throat. "*Danki*," he said again. The word felt inadequate.

"I just wish I had more to give you. That I . . ." *Daadi* began.

"What?" Micah asked.

"Never mind." *Daadi* waved off the thought. "I just hope you can forgive your *dat* someday. Deep down, he has a *gut* heart. Hopefully he'll see his mistakes and try to forge a better relationship with you before it's too late."

Silence stretched between them, filled only by the sounds of their horse and buggy. Micah tried to imagine a close relationship with his father, but the thought seemed preposterous.

But with God all things were possible.

Perhaps someday he'd know what it was like to have a close family like Bethany's. But until that day, Micah would cherish his relationship with his grandfather. It was all he needed to sustain him.

Chapter 14

A little over three weeks later on a Tuesday afternoon, Bethany held a bag of diapers and wipes as she stood on Christiana's front porch between Salina and Leanna. She shivered in the early-January wind as she waited for Christiana to come to the door.

After a few moments, the lock popped, and the door opened, revealing Christiana in a green dress and black apron.

"Hi," Christiana said as she opened the door wide. "It's so *wunderbaar* to see you three."

"How are you?" Salina asked as she hugged Christiana.

"I'm *gut*. Tired." Christiana turned to Bethany and hugged her next. "I can't believe Kaylin is eight days old already."

"It goes quickly," Leanna said as she hugged her chest.

"Come in." Christiana beckoned them to follow. "The *haus* is a mess, but you're not here to see the *haus*, right?"

"We're here to see you," Bethany said as they walked into the large kitchen. She set the bag on the table. "We brought you four packages of diapers and some wipes."

"And a chicken-and-rice casserole." Leanna held up a casserole dish and then slipped it into the refrigerator.

"Oh, *danki*! What a *wunderbaar* help. I appreciate you all so much," Christiana said before hugging each of them again.

"Where is that *boppli*?" Salina asked, rubbing her hands together. "I can't wait to hold her."

Christiana gestured toward the table. "She's napping at the moment in a bassinet in the *schtupp*, so we'll have to enjoy the quiet while we can. I promise you can hold her when she wakes up." She pointed to the stove. "Would you like some tea?"

"Let me make it." Bethany hurried over to the counter. "You sit, and I'll put on the kettle."

"Okay." Christiana sat down.

"Where's Jeff?" Leanna asked as Bethany filled the kettle and set it on a burner.

"He's helping his *dat* with the cows, but he'll be back soon. He comes to check on me periodically. He's been great. He even helps with the feedings at night. We're still trying to settle into a new routine, and he's been so patient." She cupped her hand to her mouth and yawned. "I'm sorry. I'm just surviving on little naps here and there."

She pointed toward a cookie jar. "There are some oatmeal raisin *kichlin* in there if you want to put them on the table, Bethany. Phoebe brought them over." Then she looked at the other cousins. "How are all of you?"

Salina shrugged. "I'm fine. Same as always!"

"Me too," Leanna said.

Bethany brought the cookies to the table.

"How about you, Bethany?" Christiana asked. "How's Micah?"

Bethany leaned on the back of the chair beside Leanna. "I

haven't spoken to him much since the market closed down for Christmas and New Year's. I've only seen him briefly at church, but Simply Sara Ann keeps coming to 'see her cousin.'" She made air quotes with her fingers as frustration built inside her. "Sara Ann monopolizes his time at church, so I assume he's more interested in her than me."

Christiana gaped. "You're kidding."

Leanna pressed her lips into a flat line and shook her head. "Bethany's not telling you everything."

"What do you mean?" Christiana asked.

"Tell them about the burn," Leanna said. "That was a really sweet story."

"What happened?" Salina spun to face them.

Bethany sighed and walked over to the counter. "I need to get out the mugs."

Leanna popped up from her chair. "I'll do that, and you tell the story."

"*Ya*, tell us," Christiana insisted.

Bethany sat down and shared the story of how she had burned her hand when Enos said Sara Ann's name, detailing how Micah not only tended to her burn but also stayed for an hour serving customers. Salina and Christiana listened with their eyes wide.

"You're saying he stayed in the booth, took care of your customers, and wouldn't take any money from you?" Salina asked.

"That's right. I paid him with a dozen donuts and a cup of coffee."

"He definitely cares for you," Christiana said.

Leanna carried four mugs to the table and set them down. "That's what I told her, but she won't listen to me."

Bethany spun to face Leanna. "But if he cares for me, then

why haven't I had a decent conversation with him since that day?"

"You just said that the market has been closed and that Simply Sara Ann has blocked all access to him at church." Salina held up a finger. "There's your answer."

"But he knows where I live," Bethany said. "He could come by and visit me in the evenings like men do when they want to date a *maedel*."

"Maybe he's shy," Christiana said.

Leanna gestured with her palms up. "Or maybe he's not sure you care for him."

"He should ask me, then." Bethany blew out a heavy sigh. "It's making me *narrisch*. I like him so much, but I don't know how he feels. And seeing him with Simply Sara Ann makes me nuts."

The kettle whistled, and Bethany jumped up, grateful for the distraction. While Leanna put teabags in their mugs, Bethany filled the cups and set the kettle on a cold burner.

"Don't give up on him, Bethany," Salina said. "I have a *gut* feeling that God has great things in store for you and Micah."

Bethany nodded, then took a sip of tea.

When a wail sounded, Christiana popped up from her chair. "Duty calls. I'll be right back." She disappeared into the family room. After a few moments the wailing subsided.

"She seems to be doing well," Leanna said. "I'm so happy for her."

"I know." Salina sighed. "I hope I'm next. Will and I are praying to be blessed with *kinner* soon."

Bethany glanced over at Salina's dreamy smile, and something inside of her broke apart. A bittersweet feeling whipped through her. While she was happy for her cousins, she felt an overwhelming longing to be like them. She craved a loving, true relationship with a good Amish man, just like her cousins had.

Could she have that with Micah? Her good sense told her she never would. How else could he go three weeks without talking to her? She'd felt something spark between them when he had touched her hand and tended to her wound that morning in the Coffee Corner. But then at church he'd barely acknowledged her. It just didn't make sense.

Christiana stepped into the kitchen holding her tiny baby wrapped in a pink blanket in her arms. "This is Kaylin Joy."

"Oh, she is just beautiful! And I love that her middle name is the same as yours," Bethany said as she smiled at the baby.

"*Danki*. That was Jeff's idea." Christiana beamed down at her baby. "Kaylin, these are my favorite cousins. They will love you, and you will love them."

"Oh, we already love you, Kaylin." Salina rushed to the sink and began scrubbing her hands. "I want to hold her."

"I do too," Leanna said as she stood and walked over to Christiana. "But I'll wait my turn." She smiled down at the baby. "Hi, Kaylin. It's so nice to meet you."

Bethany joined them and peered down at the infant, taking in her sweet little face, tuft of red hair, and pretty greenish-blue eyes. "Hi, Kaylin. You are a *schee boppli*."

"*Ya*, she is." Salina grinned as she came up and held out her hands. "Could I please hold her?"

"Of course." Christiana nodded to the chair beside her. "You sit, and I'll get her bottle ready."

Salina sat, and Christiana handed her the baby before walking over to the refrigerator and pulling out formula that had been mixed in a plastic pitcher.

"Oh my." Salina's blue eyes sparkled as she stared down at the baby wrapped in a blanket and snuggled in her arms. "She's so tiny and so perfect." She looked up at Leanna. "Do you remember when Chester was this small?"

Leanna laughed. "*Ya*, I do, but it seems like it was a long time ago. Now he's a lot taller than I am."

"I can't believe it. Look at her little nose, her little hands, and her little eyes." Salina shook her head and clucked her tongue. "She's just amazing!"

The excitement in Salina's face and voice was almost palpable. Bethany could imagine Salina holding her own beautiful baby. Jealousy raised its ugly head, and Bethany had to look away. Jealousy was a sin! And Bethany was happy for her cousins. She couldn't allow herself to succumb to the alienation and bitterness that emotion could bring.

She stood and walked over to the counter where Christiana stood by a pot of water, waiting for it to warm up the bottle. "Do you need help with anything?"

Christiana shook her head. "No, but *danki*."

"Can I do any chores for you?" Bethany gestured around the kitchen. "Maybe clean the bathrooms? Sweep the floor? Do a load of laundry?"

"I don't think so, but you're so kind to offer. *Mei mamm* and Phoebe were here yesterday and took care of everything." She studied her cousin. "Is everything okay?"

"*Ya*." Bethany looked over at Salina, who was whispering to Kaylin while Leanna looked on and grinned. *No, I feel like I'm coming apart at the seams because I'm losing my cousins and I'm falling for a man who doesn't seem to care about me.*

"You know you can talk to me, right?"

Bethany took in the dark circles under Christiana's pretty blue-green eyes. Seeing how exhausted her cousin was pierced her with guilt. How could she burden her cousin with petty problems when she was clearly suffering from sleep deprivation?

"*Danki*, but I'm fine." She pointed to the bottle. "Is that ready?"

Christiana turned toward the bottle and nodded as she yawned. "I think so." She turned off the burner and then tested the formula by shaking some onto her wrist. Then she retrieved a burp cloth from a nearby diaper bag and brought them both over to Salina. "Do you want to feed her?"

"Oh, I'd love to," Salina said.

As Christiana got Salina adjusted with the bottle, Bethany felt her heart swell. She wasn't jealous. Instead, she was truly happy for her cousins, and she hoped someday to share similar joys in her own life.

"How was Christiana?" *Mamm* asked as Bethany stepped into the kitchen later that afternoon.

"She's doing well." Bethany set her tote bag and purse on a kitchen chair.

Mamm sat in a chair herself and pointed to one across from her. "Sit and tell me everything."

"She looked tired, but she was upbeat and seemed very happy." Bethany snatched a paper napkin from the holder in the center of the table and began to fold it as she spoke. "I offered to help her with chores, but she said that her *mamm* and *schweschder* came over yesterday to help her. Salina and Leanna took turns holding Kaylin."

"Did you hold her?"

Bethany nodded. "I held her for a few minutes, but then it was time to go." She unfolded the napkin and then folded it up again as her confusing emotions continued to plague her.

"Is there something you want to talk about?" *Mamm*'s voice was warm and comforting.

Bethany shrugged. Her heartache became a dull throb.

Reaching over the table, *Mamm* rested her hand on Bethany's. "Look at me, *mei liewe.*"

Bethany sniffed and looked up, tears and pain threatening to burst through.

"*Was iss letz?*"

"I just feel like my cousins are leaving me behind. I know it sounds *gegisch* and immature, but I always knew that Salina and Christiana were closer to each other than they were to me. They're closer in age, and they always clicked. I tried to ignore it and just accept it. But now they have more than ever in common since they are both married." She paused and took a deep breath. "And when Salina has a *boppli*, I'll have even less in common with them. And then Salina will stop coming to the market altogether. I love Leanna, and I'm grateful for her. But I miss how the four of us would get together and talk in the Coffee Corner before the market opened and then again at lunchtime. That was our special time to get caught up and share our secrets. So much has changed, and things will never be the same again."

Mamm reached over the table and touched her hand. "Change is difficult. I remember when my best *freind* got married two years before I did. I felt the same way, and our friendship definitely had to adapt. We didn't see each other as often, but when we did, we would just pick up from where we left off. That's what happens when you become an adult. Your priorities change, your friendships change, and your life changes. But you'll never lose your cousins. You may not see them as often, but you'll always have church. And you may just have to try harder to make time for each other."

"Right." Bethany nodded.

"You'll be fine, *mei liewe*. Besides, I have a feeling you'll be married soon too."

Bethany's heart thumped. "What do you mean?"

"It's just a feeling I have." *Mamm* shrugged. "God will lead you to someone, and soon you'll be meeting your cousins for lunch and talking about your husbands."

"Maybe so." Bethany let her mother's words roll over her, but she couldn't erase the sadness that plagued her heart.

Chapter 15

Bethany walked toward the Smoker family's house with her family Sunday morning nearly two weeks later. She glanced up at the late-January sky and took in the gray clouds as she breathed in the sweet scent of rain. A cold wind rushed over her, seeping in through her black shawl and sending a shudder through her body.

She stopped moving when she spotted Micah and Enos standing with a couple who looked to be in their midfifties, a younger couple who looked to be in their thirties, and a little girl who looked about four.

She chewed her lip as she watched Micah nod while the woman spoke. Her soul grew heavy as she considered how confusing their friendship had become. Though her feelings grew and morphed every time she saw him, she still had no idea what he thought of her.

"What are you looking at?" Anthony asked.

She tilted her head toward where Micah stood. "I wonder if that's Micah's family."

"Richard!" *Dat* called as he started toward Micah and the family. "Oh my goodness!"

"I guess that *is* Micah's family," Bethany muttered as she followed her *dat* toward the barn.

Richard looked up and laughed. "Harvey!" He started toward *Dat*, and when they met, they shook hands and patted each other on the back. "How long has it been?"

"At least thirty years, right?" *Dat* chuckled.

Enos grinned. "I was so *froh* when Richard said he wanted to attend church with us today. I knew you two would be excited to see each other again."

"This is such an unexpected blessing." *Dat* turned toward *Mamm*.

Bethany smiled at Micah, and he responded with a shy grin that made her pulse flutter to life.

"This is *mei fraa*, Darlene," *Dat* continued. "And these are our *kinner*, Bethany and Anthony."

"You remember Magdalena," Richard said. "You already know Micah and *mei dat*." He pointed to the young woman. "And this is *mei dochder*, Laverne. And her husband, Al, and their *dochder*, Krissy."

"So nice to meet you." *Mamm* shook their hands.

"How have you been?" *Dat* asked Richard.

"*Gut, gut.* The farm keeps me busy," Richard said. "I hear you build gazebos."

"*Ya*, that's right," *Dat* said.

Anthony shook hands with Micah's family and then excused himself to go meet his friends over by the pasture fence. The fathers were soon discussing their businesses and laughing as they reminisced about their time together years ago.

Laverne stuck her hand out to Bethany. "We've heard so much about you."

"Really?" Bethany turned to Micah, who gave her another sheepish smile. If he had told his family about her, could he possibly care for her as more than a friend? The idea made her stomach dip.

"It's so nice to put a face with the name," Magdalena said as she shook Bethany's hand. Then she turned to *Mamm*. "And it's great to meet you too. Since our husbands grew up together, I would imagine they got into a lot of mischief together."

Mamm laughed. "That's what I've heard."

While Bethany's and Micah's parents continued talking, Bethany leaned down to Krissy. "I heard you're four, Krissy. Is that right?"

Krissy held up four fingers. "*Ya*."

Bethany laughed and glanced over at Micah, who smiled adoringly at his niece. She turned back to Krissy. "I'm so glad I got to meet you."

"How are you?" Micah suddenly asked.

"I'm okay." Bethany hugged her arms to her chest. "It sure feels like January today."

"It does." His brown eyes seemed to gleam as he looked at her. "I could sure use a cup of your *kaffi* to warm me up right now."

Bethany laughed and looked over at Laverne, who gave her a curious expression. She turned back to Micah, grateful for this moment to talk to him. Their conversation had been brief yesterday at the Coffee Corner.

Enos suddenly faced Micah, and Bethany noticed that he looked pale. "I need to sit down. I'm going on into the barn."

"You okay, *Daadi?*" Micah's expression clouded with worry.

"*Ya*, I just feel a little dizzy." Enos started toward the barn door.

"Are you all right, *Dat?*" Richard asked.

Micah pointed toward the barn. "I'll go with him, *Dat*. You get caught up with Harvey." Then he turned to Bethany. "Hopefully I'll talk to you soon."

"*Ya*." Bethany watched him walk away as worry surged through her. She looked at Laverne. "Micah mentioned that Enos has been tired lately. Do you know if Micah has taken him to the doctor?"

Laverne shook her head. "No, I don't. He hasn't said anything to me."

"I hope he's okay," Bethany said.

"I do too. He didn't look well when they came over for Krissy's birthday. I'm going to talk to Micah about convincing him to see a doctor. I think he looks worse now." Laverne glanced over at the barn and then back at Bethany. "I hear you have a booth at the marketplace called the Coffee Corner."

"And I heard that you sell the best *kaffi* in the county," Al, her husband, added as he picked up Krissy.

"*Danki*," Bethany said. "That's very kind."

"We should go into the kitchen with the other women and chat," *Mamm* said to Magdalena. "Before we freeze out here."

Laverne agreed and took Krissy from her husband's hands.

Bethany followed her mother, Magdalena, and Laverne into the kitchen. While her mother continued to talk to Magdalena, Bethany walked over to her cousins.

"Who is that?" Salina asked as she nodded at where *Mamm* stood.

"That's Micah's mother and *schweschder*."

"Really?" Leanna said, looking behind her. Then she frowned. "Uh-oh."

Christiana groaned as she held Kaylin against her shoulder and rubbed her back.

"What?" Bethany spun, and nausea bloomed in her stomach as she took in the scene—Sara Ann had Laverne cornered as she spoke animatedly, waving her arms about. "Why is she still attending our service?"

"Do you really want me to answer that question?" Leanna asked with a sigh.

Bethany looked at her oldest cousin. Leanna twisted her lips.

Bethany shook her head. "We all know Simply Sara Ann. She isn't going to give anyone a chance to compete with her, including me."

"From what you've told us about him, I think he's *schmaert* and knows which *maedel* is genuine," Christiana said. "Don't give up faith."

"Exactly." Salina rubbed Bethany's shoulder. "Just keep being your sweet self."

Bethany nodded, hoping her true self would be enough.

Micah sat with his father, brother-in-law, *daadi,* and Harvey while they ate lunch after the service. He looked on as Harvey and *Dat* tossed stories back and forth. He still marveled that his father was friends with Harvey when they were such polar opposites.

Still, he tried to keep his grandfather's explanation about his father's temper and his impatience in the back of his mind, hoping someday his father would apologize. Perhaps Micah would apologize, too, and then his father would insist they start over with their relationship.

He had started praying nightly for his father, begging God to give them a fresh start as father and son. He dreamed of having the close relationship with his family that Bethany seemed to have with hers. If only he had the kind of close friendships with his cousins that Bethany enjoyed.

When Micah's gaze moved to his grandfather, the familiar worry that had lingered over the past weeks rushed forward again. He'd been trying to convince *Daadi* to see a doctor, but he refused, saying he was just a tired old man. Still, Micah worried it was something more.

"Remember that time we went camping, and you were assigned the task of starting the fire?" Harvey asked through chuckles, wiping his eyes as he laughed.

"And I set my shoe on fire?" *Dat* responded, also laughing.

The two men guffawed so loudly that a few men at the opposite end shot them curious stares. Micah shook his head. He couldn't remember a time when he'd heard his father laugh so hard. He glanced over at Al and then *Daadi*, who were also grinning.

Micah looked toward the barn entrance, eager to catch a glimpse of Bethany. When he didn't see her, he turned his gaze back to his plate filled with pretzels, lunch meat, and bread. He'd hoped to have a few minutes to talk to her since their visits at the Coffee Corner had been so brief in recent weeks that they had left him craving more.

Lately he'd seen her in a different light. She seemed more beautiful and intriguing than ever before. During the service today, he'd kept stealing glances over to where she sat with her cousin Phoebe. She looked radiant in a light-blue dress that made her sky-blue eyes seem bluer. More than once she'd caught him studying her, and she had graced him with a shy smile as her cheeks blushed pink. He felt his heart warming for her, and his pulse jumped.

"Micah?"

"*Ya?*" Micah glanced over to where Al watched him.

"You okay?"

"*Ya.*" Micah glanced toward the barn exit, where he spotted young women carrying in more food. Now was the best chance for him to sneak away and try to steal a few minutes alone with Bethany. He climbed off the bench. "Excuse me. I'll be right back."

Al lifted an eyebrow as he watched him go.

Micah zigzagged past the women, excusing himself until he reached the barn door. When he stepped out into the cold, he shivered as he scanned the women walking from the house to the barn holding trays of food, hoping to see Bethany. Not seeing her, he slipped in the back door of the house and looked around. He smiled when he found Bethany in the kitchen, talking to Leanna as they filled carafes with coffee.

He leaned on the doorway and watched her for a moment, taking in her gorgeous profile, her small nose, pink lips, long neck. His pulse quickened, and he racked his brain for words to say.

"Micah?"

He glanced over his shoulder and felt his smile flatten as Sara Ann started toward him, walking from the family room toward the kitchen. He swallowed back his disappointment. "Hello."

"I thought that was you." She was talking a little too loud. Was she trying to draw a crowd?

"I looked for you earlier. I had a very nice conversation with your *mamm* and your *schweschder*. They are just lovely! It's so nice they came to church with you and Enos today. I told Laverne I made the quilt you bought for Krissy for her birthday."

Her smile became haughty, and his stomach twisted. "Laverne and your *mamm* were very impressed. They said it's the best quilting they've seen in a long time. I told them to come by the marketplace so they can see my booth."

"*Ya*, maybe they'll do that sometime." He started to turn back toward the doorway, hoping she'd take the hint and walk away.

"I told them you and Enos go there every Saturday to get coffee from Bethany's booth."

"Uh-huh," he mumbled without looking at her.

He saw movement out of his peripheral vision, and when he turned Sara Ann was beside him, looking up at him, her eyes reminding him of a puppy dog. He pressed his lips together. How was he going to get her to leave without appearing rude?

"I was thinking, Micah, that maybe they could come some Saturday, and we could all go out to lunch or something."

Micah studied her expression. What was she after? Was she waiting for him to ask her out? That would never happen.

"What do you think?" she asked, her eyes expectant. "Maybe we could take your family to Zimmerman's Family Restaurant some Saturday afternoon. Wouldn't that be fun?"

He paused, then looked over his shoulder. Bethany and Leanna were gone from the kitchen. He turned back toward Sara Ann's sugary-sweet smile.

Her brow crinkled, and her smile faltered. "Micah? Are you all right?"

He worked to move past her and head for the side door. "I'm sorry, but no. Excuse me."

"Is that a yes on lunch?" she called after him.

He snorted. Was she serious?

Ignoring her, her wrenched open the side door and marched toward the barn. Surely he could still manage a moment to talk to Bethany.

But when he reached the barn, he found her moving down one of the tables, filling cups and nodding warm greetings to the congregants. Micah remained at the doorway as irritation and disappointment warred inside of him. Why had he allowed Sara Ann to ruin his opportunity to talk to Bethany? He should have just walked into the kitchen and asked Bethany if she had a minute to talk. But he had hesitated, enjoying a moment to just watch her.

Now his chance was ruined. Since the men and women ate lunch in shifts after the service, he needed to return to his table and finish his lunch before the men left so the women could eat.

His shoulders hunched as he walked over to the table and climbed back into his seat. He looked over his shoulder one more time and spotted Bethany talking to Lamar as she filled his cup.

"So, Micah," Harvey said. "How have you been?"

"Fine." Micah nodded. "*Daadi* and I have been building some gliders and rockers."

"That sounds great," Harvey said. "Are they your biggest seller?"

"*Ya*," *Daadi* said.

Micah snuck in one last glance at Bethany before turning back to Harvey and *Daadi*. If he didn't have a chance to talk to her today, he would have to be patient and wait for next Saturday to talk to her again.

But could he wait that long when his heart craved more?

Chapter 16

⟊

Micah rushed around the kitchen as the delicious aromas of frying eggs and sizzling bacon filled the room. He set two plates and a pile of utensils on the table before turning toward the hallway that led to his grandfather's bedroom.

"*Daadi!*" he called. "Breakfast is almost ready!"

Then he turned back to the stove and flipped the eggs. He glanced out the kitchen window and looked up at the dark clouds clogging the sky. He'd awoken cold in his bedroom located at the top of the stairs. It was a dreary morning in late January, and the newspaper had reported a chance of snow. But the bad weather wouldn't bring down his sunny mood. It was Friday, the end of the week. That meant tomorrow he'd be able to go to the marketplace and see Bethany.

Thoughts of her had teased his mind throughout the week. He'd only had a moment to say good-bye to her before leaving church on Sunday when *Daadi* had said he was tired and wanted to nap. If only Sara Ann hadn't foiled his plan to talk to her when he went into the house.

Throughout the week, Micah had thought about visiting Bethany at night or even at the market, but each time he considered going, something had come up—a phone call from one of their suppliers or a request from his grandfather to do a task around the house.

Still, nothing would stop him from seeing Bethany tomorrow. He couldn't wait to talk with her again. He'd found himself no longer worried about losing Bethany the way he'd lost Dawn. Instead, he couldn't stop wondering if Bethany would consider dating him. Maybe tomorrow he'd find the nerve to ask her how she felt about him. Maybe he'd ask her if he could come visit her one night soon at her house.

The thought sent excitement thrumming through his veins.

He turned toward the doorway that led to *Daadi's* room. Where was his grandfather? He looked up at the clock and found it was seven thirty. His grandfather was normally up and dressed by six forty-five. Had he chosen a more leisurely start to his day today?

"*Daadi*! Are you up or are you sleeping in?" He smiled as he awaited a grouchy response.

But Micah heard nothing. No response. No sound of his grandfather shuffling around in his room. Only the sound of the sizzling bacon.

Micah slipped the bacon and eggs from skillet to a platter and started down the hallway. "*Daadi*! Come on out here and enjoy this *schee* day that the Lord has made."

He went to the bathroom and tapped on the door. It creaked open slowly, revealing that the room was empty.

"*Daadi?*" Micah continued to the large, first-floor bedroom *Daadi* had once shared with *Mammi*. "Hello? Are you getting dressed?" He peeked into the bedroom and spotted a lump under the pile of quilts on the bed.

Micah tapped the doorframe. "*Daadi?* Are you getting up today?"

He waited for his grandfather to move, but he didn't.

"*Daadi?*"

Nothing. Not a snore nor a sigh.

Panic began to rise in Micah's chest as he crossed the room to his grandfather's bed. "*Daadi?*"

He found his grandfather lying on his back. His skin was pale, and his eyes were partly open. The hair rose on the back of Micah's neck, and tears filled his eyes as he took in his serene expression.

No. Surely *Daadi* was fine. He just needed some extra rest today, and he'd wake up soon.

"*Daadi?*" Micah croaked as tears stung his eyes. "Are you all right?"

He touched the old man's cheek and found his skin cold, like marble. Micah gasped as he pushed the pile of quilts off of his grandfather and touched his arm. Like his face, it was cold and stiff. He shook his arm, praying for a response.

"*Daadi.* Please wake up. Please." Micah dropped to his knees as tears started to fall. "No, no, no, no! God, please don't take him! Not now. I need him. Please, God. Please!"

Swallowing back his tears, Micah jumped to his feet. He had to find help. Maybe the doctors in the emergency room could wake him.

He rushed out of the bedroom, through the kitchen, and out the back door. The cold leached through his socks as he sprinted toward the workshop to use the phone, and he shivered.

Something wet hit his face and mixed with the hot tears there. Looking up, he spotted white, puffy snowflakes drifting down from the gray clouds.

Micah ran into workshop and dialed 911. After telling the dispatcher to send help immediately, he dialed his sister's farm.

"Pick up, pick up, pick up," he seethed into the phone. When the voice mail answered, Micah wanted to scream. He waited for the beep and said, "It's me. There's something wrong with *Daadi*."

When his voice faltered, he cleared his throat. "I called the rescue squad, and they're on their way. I'll call you back and let you know where they take him. I'll be in touch soon. Pray for him." His voice broke, knowing in his heart that no prayers could help. His *daadi* was already gone.

He hung up the phone and dashed back through the snow, which had turned from flurries to a steady fall, seeping through his tan shirt and soaking his hair as he ran back into the house. He glanced toward the pasture as he went and spotted a line of bare, gnarly trees covered in snow that reached up toward the sky. The macabre scene sent a shiver deep into his bones.

Inside, he rushed to his grandfather's room, hoping *Daadi* had miraculously woken up to say he was hungry and ready for some bacon and eggs.

"*Daadi*." Micah dropped to his knees next to the bed again and took his grandfather's cold hand in his. "Please wake up. You're all I have. Please, *Daadi*. I need you. Wake up. Wake up!"

Dropping his head to the quilts, Micah let his tears flow, his sobs echoing eerily throughout the large, cold room.

When sirens sounded in the distance, Micah jumped up and ran to the front door. Wrenching it open, he watched an ambulance and fire truck park in the rock driveway. A young man and woman who looked to be in their late twenties jumped out of the ambulance and headed up toward the front door, the man holding a bag that Micah assumed was full of medical supplies.

"Are you Micah?" the woman asked him.

"*Ya*. Please help my grandfather," Micah pleaded with them, holding the front door open.

Four men dressed in uniforms jumped off of the fire engine and hurried toward the house.

"Where is he?" the male EMT asked, loping up the porch steps.

"In here." Micah led them down the hallway toward *Daadi's* room. "He's cold, and he hasn't moved." He stood back as the two EMTs went inside.

The four firefighters came down the hall and nodded at him as they, too, walked into the bedroom. Micah leaned back against the wall, waiting to hear his grandfather's voice, but all he heard were the murmurings of the emergency medical technicians. He held his breath and stared up the ceiling as tears poured down his cheeks.

Please, God. Please save him. Please wake him up.

Finally, the female EMT stepped out into the hallway. The tears in her eyes and the sad expression on her face gave him the news he feared the most.

"Micah, I'm so sorry," she whispered. "He's already gone."

Covering his face with his hands, Micah sobbed as grief pulled him under, sucking the air from his lungs and drowning him.

Bethany hummed as she set up her coffeepots and dropped donuts into the oil to fry. Once they were golden brown, she covered the donuts with strawberry glaze and then prepared another dozen donuts for the fryer.

She was glazing another round in chocolate when she heard a loud meow. Turning, she smiled down at Daisy and Lily as they blinked up at her. "*Gude mariye.* How are you two this fine Saturday morning?"

When the cats meowed in unison, she smiled and beckoned them to follow her over to their bowls, which she filled. She gave them fresh water before washing her hands and returning to her donuts.

"*Gude mariye,*" Leanna sang as she leaned over the counter.

"Hello, there." Bethany handed her a cup of caramel-flavored coffee.

Leanna added creamer and sweetener and took a sip. "Oooh. It's fantastic."

Bethany felt her smile brighten. "*Danki.*"

Leanna took another long drink. "What did you think of that snow we got overnight?"

"It was so *schee* this morning. The trees were sparkling in *mei dat*'s pasture." Bethany turned to glazing a dozen donuts in vanilla.

"I thought it was nice too. I hope it doesn't keep the shoppers away."

"*Ya,* I know." Bethany's heart gave a little kick as she thought of Micah. "I just hope it doesn't keep Micah and Enos away."

"*Ya.*" Leanna smiled. "Have you heard from him at all this week?"

"No." Bethany sighed as she finished glazing. She turned toward her cousin. "I keep thinking about how I saw him talking to Sara Ann at church. It still makes me wonder if he likes her, but he did make a point of saying good-bye to me before he and Enos left the service. I'm choosing to hold on to the hope that maybe our friendship can turn into something more. I have to be patient and let him come to me."

"I agree. Sometimes a relationship develops over time."

"Right." Bethany fingered the edge of the counter. "Maybe one of these Saturdays my booth will be quiet, and Micah and I will have extra time to talk."

Leanna chuckled. "Your booth is the most popular in the market, so I seriously doubt that. What if you suggested he come to see you at your *haus?*"

Bethany looked at her cousin. "I guess I could do that."

Leanna nodded. "Invite him and Enos for supper again. Didn't you say you got to sit alone with him and talk when they came last time?"

"*Ya.*" Bethany nodded. "But I got a strange feeling when he was there. He was really quiet with my family."

"Hmm." Leanna tapped her chin. "Maybe you could ask him to meet you for lunch one day. You could go to Will's restaurant."

"*Ya.*" Bethany's chest buzzed with excitement. "That's a *gut* idea."

"I'm full of *gut* ideas." Leanna winked, then stood and brushed her hands against her apron. "Well, I need to get my booth ready. Have a *gut* morning."

"You too." Bethany waved at her cousin.

She concentrated on glazing donuts until she heard the marketplace doors open and the murmur of customers entering. She thought she heard voices moving toward her booth, and her anticipation soared as she imagined Micah and Enos making their way to her for their usual Saturday-morning coffee and donut. She turned, but when two young Amish couples stepped into the booth instead, Bethany's heart sank. She quickly recovered, pasting a smile onto her lips and lifting her chin.

"*Gude mariye*," she said as they lined up in front of her counter. "Welcome to the Coffee Corner. This morning's coffee specials are caramel, white-chocolate, and peach-cobbler. I also have a dark-roast and a decaf."

As her customers gave their orders, Bethany rushed around filling them. More people entered her booth, and she searched the crowd for Micah and Enos. Her heart sank a little lower each time she realized they weren't there. By the time lunch rolled around, Bethany was feeling sick with worry about them. Questions poked at her like pins into a pin cushion as she pulled a stool up to a high-top table with Leanna and began eating her turkey sandwich.

"I hope Micah and Enos are okay," Leanna said as she took her liverwurst sandwich out of her lunch bag. "It's strange that they didn't show up."

"I know. I'm trying not to think the worst. Were they in an accident?" Then Bethany gasped. "Enos didn't look well the last time I saw him. Maybe Enos started feeling bad?"

"Oh, I hope not."

"Or did Micah decide he didn't want to see me anymore?"

Leanna rolled her eyes. "I highly doubt that."

"Maybe he met someone new!"

"Bethany, you have to be kidding."

"I'm not. I've told you the men in our youth group always preferred Salina and Christiana over me. When they talked to me, I used to think they liked me. Then I'd find out they were only using me to learn more about our cousins. I was never the first choice, so why should now be any different?"

Leanna's face clouded with a dark scowl. "You need to stop that. You don't fade into the woodwork when Salina or Christiana are around. You're just as *schee* and sweet as they are. You don't give yourself enough credit."

Two teenaged girls dressed in black parkas, jeans, boots, and matching purple knitted hats stepped into the booth. Bethany hopped down from the stool and rushed to the counter. While she served them peach-cobbler coffee and cinnamon donuts, she noticed Sara Ann walk into the booth and make her way over to Leanna. Bethany's shoulders tightened with irritation as she watched Sara Anna speak animatedly to Leanna, waving her arms. To her surprise, Leanna cupped her hands to her mouth, and her eyes widened.

Leanna turned toward Bethany, and a look of horror passed over her face. The expression caused Bethany's stomach to dip. Something was wrong.

"Thank you for coming by the booth today," Bethany told the girls as she gave them their change and a receipt. Once the girls were gone, Bethany rushed over to Leanna and Sara Ann. "What's going on?"

"Bethany!" Sara Ann grabbed her arm as she approached. "Did you hear the news?"

"What news?" Bethany divided a look between Leanna and Sara Ann. "What did I miss?"

Leanna patted the stool beside her. "Bethany. Sit."

"Why?" Bethany's chest constricted. She looked at Sara Ann. "Tell me, Sara Ann."

Sara Ann took a dramatic breath. "Enos passed away yesterday."

"What?" Bethany's voice was too loud, and she noticed customers at the other tables turn and look at her. She felt as if the wind had been knocked out of her, leaving her with a body made of lead. Off-balance, she grabbed the back of the stool beside her. "What do you mean? What happened?"

"*Mei bruder* is a volunteer firefighter, and he heard the call come through to go to Enos Zook's home yesterday morning. He heard from another firefighter that an Amish man had been found dead in his bed yesterday morning. Apparently he had a massive heart attack overnight, and Micah found him."

A small noise escaped Bethany's throat as tears leaked from her eyes. "Oh, no, no, no . . ."

"I'm so sorry." Leanna took Bethany's hand in hers. "That's why Micah didn't come by today."

"It can't be true." Bethany stared at Leanna as she wiped her eyes.

Sara Ann nodded with such vigor that the ties from her prayer covering bounced off her shoulders. "It is true. The funeral is Monday."

Bethany stood. "I need a minute." She turned to Leanna. "Would you please watch my booth?"

"Sure." Leanna gave her a warm expression. "Take your time."

Bethany hurried out of her booth and past knots of customers and the Candle Shop and Used Book Stand as she rushed to the far corner of the marketplace and into the ladies' restroom. She practically ran to the last stall and locked herself inside. Then she leaned back against the wall, covered her face with her hands, and let her tears break free as sobs tore from her throat.

The remembered echo of Micah's voice telling her that Enos was his best friend rang in her ears. Her heart cracked open as she imagined the depth of Micah's grief and pain.

Please, God, bring Micah comfort today. Please let me be a ray of light to him. Let me be the friend he needs right now. And help me be strong.

With a shuddering breath, Bethany picked herself up and headed back to her booth, praying she could face the remainder of the day.

Chapter 17

Micah stood in the family room Monday morning and felt as if he couldn't breathe. The room was packed with people walking in to speak to him and his family as they waited by the coffin.

This all felt like a dream—a surreal, horrific nightmare. *Daadi* was gone. For days now Micah had been alone in his grandfather's house. His greatest fear had come true. He kept hoping he'd wake up from this heartache and hear *Daadi* complaining that his bacon was too burned or his fried eggs were overdone. But no. Instead, Micah had awoken this morning alone again in a big, cold house and had to force himself out of bed to prepare for a funeral.

His mother and sister had come over to help him clean yesterday. Today Micah had worked hard to keep his tears at bay while getting himself ready. Now that he stood with his family by the coffin, he felt numb.

"I'm so sorry, Micah. Your *daadi* was a *wunderbaar* man," Will Zimmerman said as he made his way through the line with Salina in tow.

"Danki." Micah felt as if he was in a daze as he continued to thank members of the community.

Salina shook his hand next. "I'm so sorry."

"Danki." Micah was certain he spotted tears in her eyes, and he looked away. He couldn't allow himself to get caught up in his overwhelming grief again. Instead, he glanced toward the doorway and found a long line of community members on their way to share their condolences. The room felt too small and too hot, even though it was early February.

Micah greeted a few more church members and then turned toward his brother-in-law beside him. "I need a break. I'll be back."

"Okay." Al gave him a quick nod before turning back to another community member.

Keeping his head down and avoiding eye contact, Micah slipped past the line and out the back door. He welcomed the frigid morning air that settled into his bones as he started across the yard. The small mounds of snow lining the walkway had turned brown and sad after the snowfall Saturday.

Picking up speed, he once again kept his head down, avoiding the sad eyes of the community members filing up toward the house. He hurried to the large workshop, unlocked the door, and slipped inside the cold cinder block building. Once there, he released the breath he hadn't realized he'd been holding and enjoyed the comforting smell of wood and stain.

Flipping on the overhead propane lights, he surveyed the large work area and spotted the glider *Daadi* had been working on before he started feeling bad last week. His eyes filled with tears as guilt squeezed his lungs, eating him alive.

Why hadn't he insisted *Daadi* go to the doctor? If he had, would that have prevented the massive heart attack? If so, then

Daadi would still be here, working with him, not lying unmoving in a coffin as people walked by, staring at his empty shell.

"Why, God? Why did you take him?" Micah's lips trembled as he walked over to the workbench and picked up a piece of the glider.

Grabbing a piece of sandpaper, he rasped it over the wood. The repetitive motion gave him a tiny bit of relief from the ache in his chest. He kept going, smoothing the paper back and forth over the wood.

"Please, God." His voice came out in a strangled whisper. "Please stop this loneliness and grief from smothering me. Please, God. Help me."

Then he squeezed his eyes shut and worked to keep his tears at bay.

Bethany carried a large casserole dish as she hurried up the back steps at Micah and Enos's house. Her parents and Anthony followed her as she walked through the mudroom and into the kitchen, where she nodded at familiar faces and then set the chicken alfredo casserole beside a mountain of other serving dishes.

She made her way to the family room, where she found the long line of community members sharing their condolences with Enos's family. She stood up on her tiptoes, scanning the family members for Micah. Her stomach dropped when she didn't see him.

"What are you doing?" Anthony hissed in her ear.

She spun to face him behind her. "Do you see Micah up there

with his family?" she asked since he was several inches taller than she was.

Anthony's lips flattened as he gazed toward the family and the coffin. "No, I don't."

"Where is he?"

"How should I know?" Anthony shrugged. "Maybe the restroom?"

Worry twisted up her insides as she made her way down the line toward the family. When she reached Micah's mother, she held out her hand. "I'm so sorry for your loss."

"*Danki*," Magdalena said.

Bethany repeated the words when she shook Richard's hand and then turned to Laverne. "I'm so sorry for your loss."

"*Danki*," Laverne said, her dark eyes sparkling with tears.

"Where is Micah?"

Laverne looked past her husband beside her. "He's not there?" She tapped Al's arm. "Where did Micah go?"

"He told me he was going to step away for a few minutes, but it's been a while," Al said.

"Where do you think he went?" Bethany asked.

Laverne paused for a minute, then nodded toward the doorway. "Try the workshop. It's the large cinder block building past the big barn."

"Oh." Bethany nodded, but doubt pummeled her. Was it her place to look for him? "Would you like me to check on him?"

Laverne took Bethany's hand in hers. "*Ya*, please. He's been a mess. I think he needs someone to talk to."

"Okay." She shook Al's hand and then glanced back at Anthony. "Do you think it would be too forward of me to assume Micah wants to talk to me?"

"Go," he said.

Bethany started for the back door but stopped when she felt a hand grab her arm and gently spin her around.

"Bethany," Leanna said as she stood with Salina, Will, Christiana, and Jeff in the corner of the room. "Are you okay?"

"*Ya.*" She nodded, but her voice sounded raspy. "I was looking for Micah. His brother-in-law said he stepped away a while ago, so his *schweschder* told me to check the workshop. She said he's been having a hard time, and I'm so worried about him. Do you think it's okay if I go out there to see him alone?"

"Definitely. Go to him," Salina said. Leanna and Christiana nodded in agreement.

Bethany took a deep breath. "Pray I say the words that will comfort him."

Leanna touched Bethany's shoulder. "Sometimes when someone is grieving, the best thing you can say is nothing. Instead, just be there for him and listen when he needs you to."

Bethany nodded and hurried past the crowd of mourners and out the back door. She hugged her shawl closer to her body as she rushed through the bitter cold toward the cinder block building. When she reached the door, she clutched the cold handle and closed her eyes. "Lord, let me be a ray of light to Micah in a time of darkness," she whispered. Then she wrenched open the door and stepped into the workshop, breathing in the familiar scents, just like her father's shop. The hum of the propane lights filled her ears as she glanced around.

When she heard a scraping sound, she looked over to the far corner. Micah sat hunched over a worktable, sanding a piece of wood.

She closed the door with a soft *click* and started toward him.

Her heart thudded against her rib cage as her eyes stung with tears. She hugged her arms tightly against her chest as she reached him and held her breath, waiting for him to look up at her.

When he didn't, she hopped up onto a stool beside him. She watched him, taking in his eyes as they kept their fierce attention focused on his work, his hand moving back and forth, sanding the long piece of wood.

He suddenly looked up at her, his eyes wide as his mouth formed an O.

She shifted her weight on the stool.

"Bethany." His voice was ragged, as if he'd been crying all night. "I didn't hear you come in. How long have you been sitting here?"

"I-I just got here."

"Oh." He looked back down at the piece of wood and began sanding again.

She watched him for a few moments, then hopped off the stool. "I'm sorry to intrude. I'll go."

"No." He reached out and took her hand in his. "Please, don't go."

She froze in place, enjoying the feeling of his warm skin against hers.

"Sit with me." His thin voice pleaded with her, and the grief in his eyes nearly ripped her in half.

"Okay." She sat on the stool again and fiddled with a loose string on her shawl. "I'm so sorry," she whispered.

"*Danki.*"

He stared down at the piece of wood as silence stretched between them for several moments. She held her breath, waiting for him to speak. Leanna's words echoed in her mind: "*Sometimes when someone is grieving, the best thing you can say is nothing. Instead, just be there for him and listen when he needs you to.*"

She sent up a silent prayer. *Lord, use me to comfort him as you see fit.*

"This is the last project he worked on," Micah's voice rasped softly. "He started it two weeks ago, but he stopped working on it last week when he said he didn't feel well. I should have made him go to the doctor. I pleaded with him, but he was so stubborn. Still, I should have insisted. I should have made the appointment, called our driver, and forced him to go. But I didn't." He sniffed and wiped at his eyes. "If I had, maybe he would still be here."

"It's not your fault." She reached for his arm and then stopped, pulling her hand back.

He gripped the edge of the workbench. "Friday morning I was making breakfast. It was his favorite—eggs and bacon. He liked his bacon extra crispy but not burned."

She bit her lower lip.

"He normally gets up before seven. I thought it was strange that it was later than that and he still wasn't up. I called him a few times, and he didn't come. And when I checked on him . . ." His voice trailed off, and he traced the piece of wood with his thumb. "I went in, and he was already gone. His body was cold like stone. And he was so still and peaceful. I called nine one one, but it was too late."

A strangled sound escaped his throat, and he sucked in a breath.

"If you need to cry, just cry." Bethany leaned closer to him. "It's okay."

He wiped at his eyes and looked over at her. His face was blotchy with tears as it twisted up with grief and guilt. "I just can't believe he's gone. I keep expecting him to come out and tell me it's time to get to work. But he's gone. The *haus* is too quiet."

"I'm so sorry, Micah," she whispered again as tears trailed down her face. "I know you two were close."

"He was all I had."

"That's not true." She reached over and touched his arm this time, resting her hand on his hard bicep. "You have your family, and you have your *freinden*." *You have me!*

He shook his head. "You don't understand."

"What do you mean?"

He took a heaving breath, and his body shuddered as if he were reaching down into his toes for the right words. "I didn't only come here to work with *Daadi* because I wanted to become a carpenter."

When he hesitated, she pulled back her hand and nodded slowly. "Why else did you come?"

"I've never been close to *mei dat*. We've always had problems."

"What do you mean?"

"We don't get along. He has always criticized me for everything. I've never done anything right in his eyes, and we argue constantly. I've never felt like I fit into my family."

She blinked, confused by his words. "I'm sorry to hear that."

"I had always planned to move off *mei dat*'s farm."

"Are you saying you came to Bird-in-Hand to get away from your *dat*?"

"Not exactly. I had to leave White Horse to escape him, and the painful memories."

She tried to comprehend his words. "The painful memories of how he treated you?"

"No." He licked his lips and looked down at the workbench

again, fiddling with a piece of loose wood there. "I was engaged once."

Bethany swallowed as her shoulders tightened.

"Her name was Dawn, and I knew her practically my whole life. We grew up together. We started dating when we were about eighteen after we were baptized. We were going to get married. I had proposed to her, and we were planning the wedding. We were going to build a *haus* on her *dat*'s farm. Eventually I was going to take over the farm for her *dat*. We wanted a family. We were going to grow old together."

"What happened?" Her voice was so soft, it was barely audible over the propane lights.

"She wasn't feeling well, so she went to the doctor." He looked up at her and wiped at tears that trickled down his cheeks. "She was diagnosed with leukemia, and six months later she died. That's when I lost everything I'd ever hoped for. I was devastated. I wasn't sure how I would make it through another day without her." He wiped away more tears and sniffed. "She was everything to me."

"Micah, I had no idea." Bethany's throat swelled, making her voice sound thin. "What a horrible thing to endure."

He looked down and rested his elbow on the workbench and his cheek on the palm of his hand. "Once Dawn was gone, I needed to get away. I didn't want to face her family and the memories at every church service. And *mei dat* wasn't supportive when she passed away."

"What do you mean?"

His expression hardened. "He told me to get over it and find someone else."

"That's—that's terrible."

"I needed a new start, and *mei daadi* was always supportive of me. When I was little, we used to build things together. Those are my best memories . . ." He paused. "*Daadi*'s assistant had moved away, and I saw that as an opportunity to stay with my grandparents and start a new life here. I had a new job and a new opportunity to heal and move on. In the beginning I thought I would never get past the hurt or the heartache, but I slowly rebuilt my life. When *mei mammi* died, I was where I needed to be to help *mei daadi* through it. We did everything together. He was my source of strength.

"But now's he gone, and I don't know what to do." He looked down at the workbench again. "I've lost everything again. I don't understand it. I can't figure out why God chose to take him. I knew he would have to go eventually. But . . . I wasn't ready yet."

"We're not supposed to question God's will," she said.

"I know." He looked over at her, and his eyes were full, gleaming with fresh tears once again. "But it hurts so much." He covered his face with his hands.

"Oh, Micah." She reached for him, held his arms. "I'm so sorry. I know how much Enos meant to you."

He pulled his hands away and wiped his eyes with his sleeves before he looked over at her. "You must think I'm a mess."

"No, I don't think you're a mess at all. I feel your grief." She shook her head and sniffed as water filled her eyes. "I just don't know how to help you."

He rested his hands on top of hers. "*Danki* for being here."

"You're not alone, Micah. You have so many people who care about you." Her mouth dried as warmth prickled her skin where their hands touched. His touch made her feel momentarily light-headed.

He opened his mouth to respond, but the door to the shop opened, and he pressed his lips together. Bethany pulled her hands away and smoothed out her shawl as heat crept up her neck.

"Micah?" Al stepped into the workshop and looked around, his gaze finally landing Micah and Bethany. "The service is about to start."

"Thanks, Al. I'm on my way," Micah said.

Al nodded and disappeared through the door.

Clearing his throat, Micah stood and turned toward Bethany. "We should get back inside."

"*Ya.*" She started toward the door. Micah followed her, turning off the lights as they stepped out into the cold.

As they walked up toward the house together, Bethany looked over at him. "If you need someone to talk to, I'm always here. Just let me know."

"*Danki.*" He nodded.

She took in the sadness in his dark eyes and once again asked God to help her be the friend he needed during this difficult time.

Chapter 18

Micah tried to concentrate during the funeral, but his thoughts continued to spin with sadness and grief. He'd lost *Daadi*, and he was alone. The reality crashed around him, drowning out the bishop's holy words. Although he was surrounded by dozens of members of his community, he felt as if he were sitting by himself in the large barn.

The hollow loneliness sat beside him in his buggy as he processed to the cemetery for the burial. He stood beside Al, but he once again felt as if he were standing alone, watching his grandfather disappear from his life forever.

Lord, how will I go on now that I'm alone? What will I do to make it through another day? You've already taken Dawn and Mammi from me. Why do you need Daadi too?

When the graveside service was over, Micah made his way back to his house and was surprised to find a few of the women from the community working in the kitchen. He nodded at them and then walked into the family room. He glanced around, hoping to see Bethany one last time before she and her family left. But the family room was empty. Then he recalled that she had said good-bye to him before he and his family left for the gravesite. What had she said?

The words came back to him. She'd touched his hand and whispered, *"If you need someone to talk to, I'm always here. Just let me know."*

He closed his eyes, and her beautiful face filled his mind. She had listened to him talk and blubber in the workshop, her blue eyes full of sympathy that seemed to understand the depth of his grief. She was the friend he needed.

If only she were here now. But why would she want to spend the day listening to Micah go on and on about how forlorn he was? Of course she had gone home with her family. She most likely had chores she had to complete. She had more important things to do than sit with him and keep him company.

He sank down into his favorite, worn armchair and let his head drop into his hands.

"Micah?"

He looked up, and disappointment wrapped around his chest as Sara Ann walked toward him, her expression twisted with sadness that seemed more forced than sincere.

She sat down in a chair beside him and faced him. "I was hoping to speak to you before I left. I wanted to share my deepest condolences."

"Danki." His jaw clenched. He was tired of hearing the same words repeated to him, tired of repeating back the expected response. He wanted someone to say something more meaningful, more heartfelt, more real.

"If you need anything, please let me know." Sara Ann reached out and touched his hands.

Micah pulled away. "*Danki.*"

She sat up straighter. "Micah, I want you to know that I care deeply for you, and I would like to get to know you better. I'm here for you anytime you need me."

He studied her. From the moment he'd met her, he'd sensed Sara Ann had an end game. She seemed to be searching for something superficial—something less genuine than what Bethany had to offer. As he took in her expectant expression, something inside of him broke apart, and his patience fizzled. He felt his lips twist as his brow furrowed.

"What do you want from me, Sara Ann?" His voice seemed to vibrate with his irritation.

Her mouth opened and closed. She reminded him of a fish he had once caught while fishing with his *daadi*. From the looks of her, he assumed she wasn't often caught speechless.

"I'm—I'm not sure what you mean," she stammered.

"From the first time I met you, I've had the distinct impression that you wanted something from me. So I need you to be completely honest. What do you think I can give you?"

She blinked and then shrugged as she laughed. It sounded a little nervous. "I just thought maybe we could get to know each other better. You know, we could spend some time together and become better *freinden.*"

"Why?" he pressed. "So you could date me?"

She gave another forced laugh. "Sure. Why not? After all, we're both single, and we're not getting any younger."

"I'm sorry, Sara Ann." He stood. "I'm not the man for you." He started toward the stairs, then stopped and spun, taking in her shocked expression. "*Danki* for coming by today to pay your respects. I'm going to rest."

Micah walked upstairs, his heavy footfalls echoing in the stairwell. Then he slipped into his room, changed from his church clothes into everyday trousers and an old shirt, and flopped onto the bed. He stared up at the white ceiling and waited for sleep to find him. But he couldn't stop his mind from spinning.

He rubbed his eyes, trying to stop the cyclone of emotions that tortured him. When he heard footsteps, he stood and moved to the doorway.

Laverne had reached the top of the stairs. "Micah. I was looking for you. We're warming up one of the casseroles. Do you want some?"

"No." He shook his head. "I can't eat." He tapped his doorframe. "I'm going to try to take a nap."

She paused, and he held his breath, waiting for a lecture.

"You shouldn't be up here all by yourself. You should be with your family. We'll all work through our grief together."

He loosed a sarcastic snort. "You make it sound so easy. *Dat* can't stand the sight of me, and *Daadi* was the only one who truly supported me. I've lost the one person who cared."

"That's not true." Tears sparkled in her eyes. "I care about you. So do *Mamm*, Al, and Krissy. And *Dat* cares about you too. He just doesn't know how to express it."

"Laverne, stop making excuses for him. I moved in with *Daadi* to get away from *Dat*." Micah squeezed his eyes shut, trying to ward off the headache pulsing between his ears. "Don't you remember what he said when Dawn died? He told me to get over it and find someone else. I don't think I can stomach advice like that from him right now. I'd rather be alone."

"Please give him a chance. Maybe this will change him. Maybe *Dat* will realize what he's lost and appreciate his family more.

You can't give up on him. You and I lost our *daadi*, but he lost his *daed*."

"Why do you always take his side?" Micah's voice vibrated with resentment. "You and *Mamm* have *never* defended me against him. Instead, you both beg me to take the high road—as if his hateful words don't hurt me. Then you stand by silently while he rips me apart. *Daadi* was the only one who ever made me feel like I was worthy of any love and respect from my family."

He ran his hand down his face while he took a deep breath. "So, no, I'm not going to give *Dat* another chance. Why should I? He needs to acknowledge how badly he's treated me my entire life and apologize."

Laverne stared at him for moment, then nodded. "Well, you can wait for that day to come. In the meantime, you're only hurting yourself by staying up here alone. Maybe you can come downstairs and spend time with *Mamm* and me. You have us."

"No, I don't have you or *Mamm*. Not if *Dat* is here. Besides, you don't understand how I feel." Micah pointed at her. "You have your family. I have nothing but a big empty *haus*. I have no one."

She wagged a finger back at him. "That's your choice, Micah. *Daadi* said you have two *maed* who are interested in you. You could be dating. You could settle down and have a family, too, but you have chosen not to. You chose to completely give up after you lost Dawn." She held up her hands. "I know losing Dawn broke your heart, but it's been more than two years now. You have to choose to move on."

"That's not fair." He nearly spat the words at her. "I had a future planned with Dawn, but she was taken from me. If she had lived, we could have easily started a family by now."

"God had a reason for taking her, Micah. You need to accept

that and keep living. Your life is a gift." She reached for him, but he stepped back from her. "Look, I don't want to fight with you. I know you're in pain, but we all are. Come downstairs and be with your family. We all need each other now."

He shook his head. "No. I want to be alone."

Her lips twisted. "Fine. Suit yourself." Then she pointed at him again. "But you're only hurting yourself."

He turned and walked back into his room, where he threw himself back onto his bed. Turning to face the wall, he hugged his arms to his waist.

"Please, Lord," he whispered. "Heal my heart."

Bethany sat with Phoebe during church the following Sunday. She looked over at the unmarried men's section, and her heart sank when she didn't see Micah there.

Phoebe leaned over. *"Was iss letz?"* she whispered.

"I don't see Micah."

"Maybe he went to see his family today?"

Bethany nodded, but a thread of doubt wiggled through her. He hadn't visited her at the booth yesterday, which caused her to wonder if their Saturday visits had been his grandfather's suggestion and not something Micah himself had looked forward to each week.

But missing church seemed much more serious than missing his Saturday coffee at the market. It sent a renewed sense of concern through her.

She spent the service praying for Micah and his family, begging God to send them peace and healing. She couldn't stop recalling what Micah had said about his father's treatment of him. She couldn't imagine having a parent who berated her. When she imagined Richard criticizing Micah, it baffled her, and it caused her heart to break for him even more. She wished to talk to Micah and help him work through both his grief for Enos and his grief for what his father had put him through, even if she didn't quite know how.

The service ended, and she hurried to the kitchen and sidled up to her mother.

"*Mamm*," she said. "May I speak to you alone?"

"*Ya*, of course." *Mamm* followed her into the Eshes' family room, where they could find a quiet corner to talk. "*Was iss letz?*"

"Micah isn't at church today. I'm worried about him."

Mamm's expression turned sad. "I know. We all are, but not everyone grieves the same way."

"I know, but I want to help him. Maybe we should go by to see him on our way home."

"I don't think so." *Mamm* shook her head. "He could be visiting his family."

"That's what Phoebe said, but I doubt it. He shared with me that he's not close to his *daed*."

"He's not?" *Mamm* looked confused.

Bethany shook her head.

"I still think you need to keep your distance for now. Why don't you just give him some space? Let him grieve in private for a while."

"Okay." Bethany nibbled her lip. She couldn't shake the feeling that Micah needed her, but she also couldn't disobey her mother.

As Bethany followed her mother back into the kitchen, she

tried to imagine Micah visiting his parents and sharing sweet memories of Enos while they laughed and cried together. But if what Micah said about his family was true, Bethany knew he was suffering alone.

Micah sat at his kitchen table and sipped a cup of coffee. The house was silent and empty, as if the walls themselves mourned. The only sound was the ticking of the clock on the kitchen wall.

Over and over he found himself looking down the hallway toward *Daadi's* room, expecting him to come out and ask for a cup of coffee or a plate of eggs and bacon. He missed their morning conversations where they'd discuss their plan for the day, talking about projects and trips out for supplies. He even longed to argue with *Daadi* about advertising more with local stores.

But there would be no more breakfast discussions or afternoon disagreements with *Daadi*. He was truly gone.

Micah imagined his church district setting up for the noon meal while he sat by himself at his house. He had considered going to church, but he couldn't bring himself to pull on his suit and ready the horse and buggy. He didn't feel a connection to God or his community today. Without his grandfather, he didn't feel a connection to anything at all.

He took another drink of his coffee and grimaced. This bargain-brand coffee was not even close to Bethany's delicious flavored coffees he had enjoyed each Saturday for the past year.

He had thought about going to see her yesterday for his routine of coffee, delicious donuts, and a warm conversation with her. But after he had taken care of his horses, he couldn't find the strength to hitch up the buggy and make the trek to the market. It wouldn't be same without *Daadi* at his side, making conversation during the trip to town.

He finished his bland coffee, then set the mug in the sink and stared out the window. He tried to imagine a horse and buggy coming up the rock driveway toward his house. Maybe it could be Bethany and her family on their way to check on him, bring him a meal, offer their condolences again. But the driveway was as empty as his spirit.

He sighed as he considered the past week. He had tried to stay busy finishing up the glider *Daadi* had started before he died and then worked on a patio order. But the reality had hit him—he didn't have enough spring orders to keep him busy and sustain him. It was time for him to face the truth.

This coming week he had to tackle his grandfather's files and determine his financial situation. There had to be reasons why his grandfather would never allow him to help with the accounting books. *Daadi* was keeping secrets from Micah, and Micah knew it.

Micah dropped into a nearby kitchen chair, rubbed his hands down his face, and slumped back. The business was in trouble, and he had no time to waste. He needed a plan.

Chapter 19

The following Saturday morning, Micah turned toward the percolator sitting on the counter in his kitchen, and an image of sweet Bethany's smile filled his mind. He had spent all week by himself with his somber thoughts, whispering to himself and longing for another soul to answer to him and offer him some hope.

He was sick of being alone. He was also tired of listening to the sounds of the creaking floors below his feet and the bang of his hammer in the workshop.

He needed some human interaction.

Go to the marketplace. See Bethany. Enjoy her smile.

Yes, that was just what he needed.

Pushing himself away from the counter, he marched back upstairs to his bedroom. He would dress, shave, and brush his teeth. Then he would head to the marketplace for a decent cup of coffee, a delicious donut, and a conversation with the woman who could always make him smile.

His heart couldn't wait.

"I miss the smell of Christiana's Bake Shop," Leanna said as she sat across from Bethany at one of the high-top tables in the Coffee Corner.

"I do too. A jewelry booth just isn't as appealing, you know?" Bethany picked up her cup of butterscotch coffee and took a sip. "I miss seeing her too."

"And Salina." Leanna frowned. "But at least Salina will be back in the spring."

"*Ya.*" Bethany glanced toward the booth entrance as Micah crossed her mind once again. Thoughts and worries for him had tugged at her since the funeral. She prayed for him constantly, begging God to send him peace and strength.

"Hopefully he'll come to see you today."

Bethany turned toward her cousin. "Who?"

Leanna lifted one eyebrow as she picked up her chocolate-glazed donut. "Come on, Bethany. I know you're thinking of Micah. I'm worried about him too. I'm praying he shows up today. It's a shame you don't have a helper in your booth so that you two could talk." Her eyes widened as if an idea had just slapped her. "Would you like me to shut my booth down? I could help customers while you talk to Micah."

"That's really sweet, but it's not necessary. If he comes by, I'll make do with the time we have together."

Leanna sipped the coffee. "I love this butterscotch flavor."

"*Danki.*" Bethany studied her own cup. "It's *gut*. Not my favorite, but I wanted to try something new." She hopped down from the stool. "While you finish that *kaffi*, I need to make sure I'm all set up before the customers come." She started toward the counter.

"Bethany, is something else bothering you?"

Bethany spun to face Leanna, who watched her with concern in her eyes. "No, I'm just worried about Micah, and I feel so helpless. I want to reach out to him, but my parents told me to give him space. I can't disobey them, but I feel like I'm not doing enough. Aren't we supposed to minister to each other? Shouldn't that be more important than appearing too forward?"

Leanna nodded. "You're right. We should take better care of each other, especially when someone is grieving. But you can't go against your parents."

Bethany lifted her chin. "I'm going to reach out to him if he doesn't come by today. I can't spend my days wondering how he is. I'm praying for him, but I want to see him, look into his eyes, and remind him that he has a *freind* in me."

"That's a *gut* plan." Leanna slipped off the stool and tossed her napkin into a nearby trash can. "I'll see you at lunchtime. Sell a lot of *kaffi* and donuts."

Bethany smiled at her cousin. "And you sell a lot of jams and jellies."

Lifting her cup, Leanna said, "I plan to try."

Bethany straightened her counter and her stack of cups. Then she sat up on her stool and stared at the clock. Soon, she heard the doors to the market open and the sound of customers talking while they walked to booths.

She looked toward her booth entrance just as Micah walked in, and her pulse immediately fluttered. Jumping up, she rushed around the counter, meeting him as he approached her. She suppressed the urge to throw her arms around him and hug him.

His brown eyes were dull and outlined with purple circles. Also, his face looked thinner, as if he hadn't eaten much for days. The sadness in his expression sent a shard of ice through her heart.

"How are you?" she asked.

"I'm making it." He shrugged. "And you?"

"I'm just glad to see you. I missed you last Saturday here at the market and then Sunday at church. I wanted to come see you, but *mei mamm* felt I should give you space in case you were with your family."

He looked down at the toes of his boots and then back up at her. "I couldn't bring myself to leave the *haus* last weekend. I felt like I needed to be alone. But when I stay home, I'm lonely. I know it doesn't make sense, but I'm a mess. I feel like I'm hanging on by a thread."

"Maybe coming to church would help you feel better. Your community cares about you, Micah." *I care about you.*

He rubbed the back of his neck. "Even so, I don't *feel* connected to the community right now. People don't understand what I've been through."

"We may not know exactly how you feel, but we've all experienced some kind of loss. And we're all praying for you."

"I guess I'm a little lost." He huffed out a nervous laugh. Then he sniffed. "Anyway . . . What have I missed here at the Coffee Corner?"

"Just my worrying about you." She hoped her words weren't too honest, too forward.

Something unreadable flickered in his expression. "I appreciate that."

A group of teenaged girls walked into the booth giggling, and Bethany felt her lips flatten. Her time alone with Micah had come to an end.

"I guess I'd better get *mei kaffi* and donuts." He seemed as disappointed as she felt as he pointed toward the counter. "What are your flavors today?"

She slipped behind the counter and gestured to the chalkboard on the wall. "I have butterscotch, apple-strudel, banana cream–pie, regular, and decaf."

"Oh." He rubbed his chin as he looked at the board. Then he looked at her. "What do you recommend?"

She leaned forward and lowered her voice. "Honestly, I think the banana cream-pie is the best."

His lips tipped up in a weak smile. "I'll have that." He pulled his wallet out of his pocket. "And two chocolate-glazed donuts, please."

"Coming right up." She poured his coffee and found a small box for his donuts before she handed him a handful of sweetener packets and a pitcher of cream. As she took his money and gave him his change, a line began to form behind him. If only she could have ten minutes when her booth wasn't busy!

"*Danki.*" He sipped the coffee and nodded. "So much better than the bland stuff I brew at home."

"I'm glad you came back for the *kaffi.*" She wished she could ask him if he'd missed her too. Was it only the coffee that drew him to her booth?

He glanced behind him at the line of customers and then back to her. "I'd better let you get back to work."

"Have a *gut* day, Micah," she told him.

"I hope you do too." He gazed at her a moment longer before he headed out of the booth, taking a piece of her heart with him.

Bethany watched him go and then turned to the group of teenagers. "Welcome to the Coffee Corner. How may I help you?"

She hoped her smile was bright enough to cover the disappointment she felt at having said good-bye to Micah.

Bethany spent the rest of the morning filling orders. During the midmorning lull, she wiped down the high-top tables while she prepared for the late-afternoon rush. When she saw movement in the corner of her eye, she looked up as Simply Sara Ann sauntered into the booth.

"Hi, Bethany," she trilled as she walked over to her. "How's business today?"

"The usual." Bethany shrugged. "I've sold quite a bit, but winter is never as busy as the spring and summer when tourist season is in full swing. How about you?"

"I've sold three quilts today, so it's been a pretty *gut* day."

"That's great." Bethany leaned against a table and studied Sara Ann while wondering why she was being so friendly. Was she finally turning over a new leaf? "Would you like a cup of *kaffi*?"

Sara Ann held up a few bills. "*Ya*. Please."

"What sounds *gut* to you?" Bethany slipped behind the counter and pointed to the blackboard.

"I'll take the apple-strudel."

"Coming right up." Bethany poured the coffee and handed it to her.

"*Danki*." Simply Sara Ann gave her the money. After adding creamer and sweetener, she took a sip.

"Do you like it?"

"*Ya*." Sara Ann wrapped her hands around the cup as a strange smile overtook her face. "Did I see Micah walk out of here earlier?"

Bethany nodded. "*Ya*, he came for a cup of *kaffi* and a donut."

"Interesting." Sara Ann tilted her head. "My cousin said he didn't go to church last week."

Bethany blinked, suddenly realizing Simply Sara Ann hadn't been at her district's church service either. Did that mean she knew Micah wasn't going to attend? Or was she giving up on pursuing him? The latter made Bethany's spirit lift.

"That's right. He wasn't at church." Bethany held her breath, waiting for Sara Ann to respond.

Sara Ann leaned forward and smirked as if she had a tasty secret. "Laverne told me something interesting when I saw her at that last church service I attended."

Bethany stilled. "What did she say?"

"She told me that Micah and Enos had supper at your *haus* one night in December."

"That's true. I invited them to come for chili."

"Enos said Micah thought your family was too loud for him. He said he was overwhelmed, and he felt like he needed some peace and quiet when he left the house. What a funny thing for him to say!" Then she tittered loudly, making a big show of it before turning toward the booth exit. She looked over her shoulder and lifted the cup of coffee. "Anyway, *danki* for the *kaffi*. Have a *gut* afternoon."

Sara Ann sashayed out of the booth while Bethany stared after her, her mouth hanging open.

So Bethany had been right all along. When Micah had been quiet that night he'd come for supper, she couldn't shake the feeling that he had seemed a little off. He had been uncomfortable with her family, and the knowledge of that stung her like the hot coffee had blistered her skin.

She bit at her lip as she tried to swallow the truth—Micah

could never love her. She'd been pinning her hopes on a man who could never see himself as a part of her family.

Leanna appeared at the entrance of Bethany's booth. "I saw Simply Sara Ann just walk out of your booth. Since it's quiet I thought I'd come to see what she wanted." She pointed in the direction in which Sara Ann had gone. Then her expression filled with worry. "Bethany. Are you all right?" She walked over to the counter and leaned her elbows on it.

Bethany shook her head as she climbed up onto a stool. "Simply Sara Ann just bought a cup of *kaffi* from me. I thought she was being too nice, and she was." She shared what Laverne had told Sara Ann about the dinner Enos and Micah had shared at her house. "It turns out I was right when I thought Micah didn't feel comfortable at *mei haus*."

Leanna looked unconvinced. "How do you know what she said is true?"

"Why would she make it up?"

"Because she obviously likes Micah. She probably knows he cares about you, so she *wants* to hurt you."

"But it *is* true that Micah and Enos ate at *mei haus*. She didn't make that up. If Laverne told her about the supper, then she told her something."

Leanna shook her head. "I don't believe it."

"He came to see me today."

"And? How was he?"

Bethany shook her head. "He looked like he hadn't slept or eaten in days. He doesn't think anyone will understand how he feels if he comes to church. I tried to convince him that we all care about him."

"That's *gut*." Leanna touched her hand. "He came to see you, but he didn't go to church. That means he feels a connection to you. See, Bethany? He does care about you."

Bethany shook her head. "No, he just missed the *kaffi*. He said *mei kaffi* was much better than his bland *kaffi* at home."

Leanna clucked her tongue. "You don't honestly believe that."

"I do." Bethany sighed. "Besides, if he doesn't feel comfortable around my family, he'd never see a future for us."

"Not necessarily. I think he does care about you, but he's just overcome by grief right now. If you continue to be an emotional support to him, then maybe he will want a future with you after he finds his strength again. It's hard to think about love when you're in pain, Bethany."

Bethany nodded to satisfy her cousin, but the doubt Simply Sara Ann had planted in her mind started to grow like a noxious weed.

Micah would never love her. He would never want a future with her.

Yet she still wished to be his friend and help him through this difficult time.

Chapter 20

Micah walked into the Bird-in-Hand Marketplace the following Saturday morning and was greeted by the warmth of the heating system, along with the sweet smells of chocolate, candy, and coffee.

He imagined Bethany standing behind the counter, preparing her coffee and donuts for the day. For the past week he had pored over his grandfather's accounting books to see just how badly the business was failing. He was still researching the problems, but so far the numbers looked dire. Amid the loneliness of that task, thoughts of Bethany had served as bright spots in his otherwise dark days.

Avoiding Sara Ann's Quilt Shop, he walked quickly past the lunch meat counter, used-book booth, candy booth, candle shop, and the Jam and Jelly Nook before he came to the Coffee Corner. He felt his spirit lift when he spotted Bethany, standing in front of her chalkboard while writing the flavors of the day. She wore a purple dress and black apron, along with her usual prayer covering.

Micah walked slowly up behind her and looked back over his shoulder, grateful to find no other customers had walked in yet. There hadn't been a line at the door, so he hoped the plunging temperatures and threat of snow would hold off the crowd today.

Bethany turned, and her beautiful face lit up with a wide smile when she saw him. "Micah. Hi. I was hoping you'd come by today. How was your week?"

He shrugged, not wanting to admit he was truly coming apart at the seams. "How are you?"

"I'm *gut*." She pointed to the blackboard behind her. "I thought I'd test some new flavors."

"Blueberry, French-toast, and coconut. Hmm." He tilted his head. "I don't know what to pick."

"I also made peppermint mocha just in case you came by." She pointed to a small pot on the burner in the corner and gave him a shy smile.

For the first time since he'd lost *Daadi*, he felt warmth swirl in his chest. Bethany had been the only thought that had made him feel better all week, and now, knowing she'd made his favorite coffee flavor just for him, he felt his heart come alive. Someone had actually thought of him and wanted to do something nice—just for him.

Since before *Daadi*'s death, Micah had been wondering if he ought to put his heart on the line for the possibility of a future with Bethany. But so much had changed since then. How could Micah envision a future when he was an absolute wreck both emotionally and financially? He couldn't provide for a wife if he was going to lose his business. And he couldn't truly love Bethany when his heart was in shambles. Bethany deserved someone who would love her completely and could provide for her and their future children.

Still, he needed her friendship.

"Micah?" Her brow pinched. "Are you all right?" She pointed to the board. "You don't have to choose the peppermint mocha today if you'd prefer one of the other flavors." She gave him a little smile. "You won't hurt my feelings."

"No, I want the peppermint mocha, please."

She raised an eyebrow. "You sure? You can pick something else. The French-toast is actually pretty *gut*." She cringed. "I didn't mean to sound prideful."

"I know you're not prideful." He pointed to the little pot on the burner. "I definitely want the peppermint mocha. And also a strawberry-glazed donut. Please."

He pulled out his wallet and counted out the bills while she worked to fill his order. When she handed him the coffee cup, he held out the money.

"I can't take that."

"Why?"

She shook her head. "I'm just really glad to see your smile today. That's payment enough for me."

"No." He placed the money on the counter in front of her. "I can't take this for free. You're here to make a profit, and I have a feeling it's going to be quiet today since we're supposed to get some snow." He added creamer and sweetener to his cup.

She looked at the money and then at him. "No."

He sighed as he felt a smile turn up the corners of his mouth. "You're really stubborn, Bethany Gingerich."

She laughed and tapped her chin. "Funny. I've heard that before."

He pointed to a table. "Would you sit with me for a moment?"

She looked at the booth entrance, checking for customers, and grinned at him. "I'd love to."

She poured herself a cup of coffee and added creamer and sweetener before they moved to the closest high-top table and sat beside each other.

"Tell me about your week," she said.

He sipped the coffee and blew out a puff of air. "I'm trying to make heads or tails of *mei daadi's* accounting books. And so far it looks like the business's finances are a mess."

"*Ach.* No." Bethany shook her head, and her prayer covering's ribbons fanned her face. "I'm sorry to hear that."

"*Ya*, well. Unfortunately, it's the truth. He never let me help with the financial side of things, and now I think I know why. He's been hiding the business's decline from me the whole time."

"That's a lot to deal with on top of losing him. Let me know if there's a way I can help you."

"*Danki.*" He clutched his cup. "I miss him so much. I keep expecting him to walk into the kitchen and say it's time to get to work. And when I'm in the shop I expect him to tell me I'm not sanding right." He shook his head. "I don't mean that he was criticizing me all the time. He liked to tease me."

"He did seem like he enjoyed joking around." Bethany smiled.

He laughed as a memory floated up from somewhere in his mind. "One time when I was a kid, I was staining a chair, and he told me I was using the wrong side of the paint brush. He said one side of the bristles was the top and the other was the bottom. And I believed him."

Bethany chuckled. "That's too much."

"Another time we went fishing when I was about twelve, and

he told me we had to switch sides of the boat halfway through the day to make sure we caught the same amount of fish from each side of the pond."

She giggled. "How funny!"

He smiled, enjoying the sound of her merriment. "He really liked you."

"I really liked him too." She beamed.

I like you, too, Bethany. I like you a lot. He took a sip of coffee, then bit into the donut.

She studied him. "Are you coming to church tomorrow?"

"I don't know." *Probably not.*

"Do you still feel disconnected from the church?"

"I do."

Bethany's eyes met his as she listened, waiting for him to continue.

Micah looked down at his donut. "It's hard to say out loud. I guess I don't understand why God would take Dawn and then *Daadi* from me, and I'm angry." His voice wobbled. "I wanted what *mei schweschder* has—a spouse, a family, a home. I thought I'd have those things with Dawn, but I didn't get the chance to. Then I moved here, thinking I would start a new life, and now that has been taken from me as well. I've lost *Mammi* and *Daadi*, and now I might lose my business. It's difficult to imagine facing everyone when I'm so broken and full of questions."

He looked at her and found her staring at him with an intensity that sent a shock wave thundering through him. "What do you want to say?"

"You're young, Micah. You're not even thirty. You can still have a *fraa*, a family, a home, and a business. If this business is failing, then you can build another one. It's too soon to give up, and your church district will never give up on you. God will never give up on you. He loves you."

The words formed a new knot in his stomach. He took a drink of coffee.

"Please come to church tomorrow. Everyone wants to know how you are."

He picked up his donut and took a bite, enjoying the sweetness as he avoided the passion in her eyes.

"Will you, Micah?"

He swallowed and wiped his mouth with a paper napkin. "I'll try to come."

Her expression softened. "That's all anyone can ask for."

But in his heart, he knew he wouldn't try very hard.

Bethany sat down in Salina's parents' barn to eat lunch with her cousins after church the next day. Micah hadn't come to church again, and disappointment had followed her like a dark cloud all morning.

She couldn't stop thinking about what he'd shared yesterday at the Coffee Corner—that he'd missed his chance to have a family since his fiancée had died. When he'd said those words, it took all of her strength not to blurt out that she wanted those things, too, and that she could imagine herself having them with him.

The truth was she longed to tell him that she loved him. Because she did. She couldn't deny it. She didn't want to deny it. Instead, she wanted to beg Micah to let her show him he could be happy again if he just gave her a chance.

But she hadn't said that. Instead, she'd concentrated on encouraging him to come to church, and she'd hoped he would. When she realized he wasn't there, she'd spent the service praying for him, begging God to show him that he could be happy again if he just came back to his community.

As she sat with her cousins, she told them about Micah's visit to the Coffee Corner, leaving out how she'd almost confessed her feelings to him.

"Let me get this straight," Salina began as she sat across from Bethany. "Micah came to see you yesterday, and you begged him to come to church today."

"But he didn't come," Christiana filled in the rest. Since Jeff was feeding Kaylin, Christiana was able to sit with her cousins and enjoy her lunch.

"I want to help him, but I don't know how." Bethany was almost certain they could hear the desperation in her voice. "He looks so sad and lonely. I worry about him. He's alone all week in that *haus*. He has to miss some human interaction."

Leanna shrugged. "So go visit him."

"But he's *alone*," Bethany repeated. "People would say it's inappropriate for me to be there alone with him."

"Take your *mamm* or Anthony," Christiana said before popping a pretzel into her mouth. "I'm sure Anthony would go with you. I've seen him chatting with Micah before. They get along. And Anthony is just as friendly and social as you are."

Bethany nodded slowly as excitement filled her. "That's a *gut* idea."

Salina swallowed a bite of her sandwich. "Make him a meal and take it to him. I'm sure he'll appreciate that. You mentioned that he looked skinny. Maybe he didn't like the food the community members left for him the day of the funeral. You could bring him something he might prefer to eat."

"I love this idea." Now Bethany just had to convince her family to allow her to visit him.

Later that evening she sat on the sofa in the family room reading a book while her parents sat in their favorite recliners. She'd watched the clock all afternoon, waiting for Anthony to arrive home from his youth-group gathering.

When he stepped into the family room, she set her book on the coffee table and squared her shoulders.

"I wanted to discuss something with all of you," she announced, her body shaking with anticipation.

"Oh? What is it?" *Dat* asked, setting down his own book and peering over his reading glasses.

"I've been very concerned about Micah. He hasn't been to church since Enos passed away, but he has come to see me at the Coffee Corner. He shared with me that he doesn't feel a connection to the community, which is why he hasn't come to church. I was hoping maybe Anthony and I could go visit him and take him a meal." She looked at her brother. "We could stop over there one afternoon this week. Maybe Tuesday?"

"It's fine with me." Anthony shrugged.

Bethany looked at her mother. "I could make him a beef stew, along with a few rolls and some brownies."

"I think that's a great idea." *Mamm* looked at *Dat.* "Don't you, Harvey?"

Dat nodded. "*Ya.* That's a nice gesture. I have a feeling that's just what he needs."

Bethany hoped her father was right and she could convince Micah to come back to the church.

Tuesday afternoon Micah sat at the desk at the back of the workshop and dropped the accounting ledger onto the desktop with a loud *thwap*! He'd been studying it all day, along with the pile of unpaid bills he'd found in the bottom drawer. Things were much worse than he thought. Not only did he owe suppliers for wood and tools, but Enos had also used the farm as collateral to take out a loan to get caught up on overdue tax bills. To make matters worse, Enos had defaulted on those loan payments, and the bank had recently sent a letter threatening to foreclose on the farm.

"Why did you let everything go, *Daadi*?" he growled under his breath. "Why didn't you tell me that we were in trouble? I could have helped!"

He slammed his hand down on the desk. While pain radiated up his wrist, he stood and glanced around the shop at the row of gliders that sat lonely and still, waiting for someone to buy them and sit on them on cheerful porches on a sunny day. He looked over at the Adirondack chairs, porch swings, and picnic tables that also needed homes and families to enjoy them.

As he'd studied his grandfather's accounts, the truth had become clearer to Micah: if he couldn't pay his suppliers and he couldn't find someone to buy the furniture he had on hand, he would need to sell off the business, piece by piece. And if he didn't make enough money on the furniture and the tools, he might need to sell everything—including the house and the land that had been in his family for generations. *Daadi* had passed on with unpaid debts, and the reality threatened everything Micah had to his name.

He suddenly recalled the day *Daadi* had told him that he

planned to leave everything to Micah. He had started to say that he wished he could have left him more. Did he know about the debts then? Or perhaps he hadn't realized the extent of the debts. Maybe *Daadi* hadn't really believed the bank planned to take the farm.

Anguish set in. Where would he go if he sold everything? Would he have to move back in with his parents at the age of twenty-seven? That would mean dealing with his father's daily abuse—as well as saying good-bye to Bethany forever.

But he had no hold on Bethany. Most likely she would find a man who could love her and care for her, and she'd forget all about her friendship with Micah.

The idea sent envy coiling in his belly like a venomous snake.

Shoving the thought away, he walked over to the door, flipped off the propane lights, and headed outside. He'd had enough stress for the day. It was time to go inside and find something to eat before he showered. Then he would spend the evening in a newly predictable way—lying in bed and waiting for his thoughts to dissolve so that sleep could overtake him.

When he stepped out into the afternoon sunlight, he found a horse and buggy sitting at the top of his driveway. He glanced up at the back porch and was stunned to see Bethany and Anthony standing by his back door. Bethany held two portable serving dishes, along with a basket. She grinned as Anthony waved.

"There you are!" Anthony called. "We've been knocking for a couple of minutes now."

"Sorry. I've been in the shop all day." He picked up speed as he hurried to the door.

Bethany's smile was bright as he loped up the back steps. "It's *gut* to see you."

"You too." Micah opened the door and motioned for them to come in. "I'm sorry you were standing out in the cold."

"It's okay." Bethany's smile didn't fade. "I was about to send Anthony to the shop to check to see if you were there." She set the serving dishes and the basket on the counter. "I brought you beef stew, rolls, and brownies."

"Wow." Micah rubbed his hands together. "That sounds amazing. You really didn't have to."

"We wanted to," Anthony said. "We've all been concerned about you."

Bethany nodded. "That's right. I told you everyone misses you at church."

"*Danki.*" Micah pushed his hand through his hair, not sure what to say.

"Have you been working today?" Bethany asked.

Micah looked past her to avoid the concern in her blue eyes. "I've just been going through the financials for the business, trying to figure some things out."

Now Anthony looked concerned. "Is your business okay?"

"It will be." And that wasn't a lie. If he found some buyers, it would be okay. At least the bills might be paid.

"That's *gut.*" Bethany glanced around the house. "Do you need help with anything? Do you need me to do some laundry or mending?"

"No, though that's a generous offer."

"Okay." Bethany looked around. "Well, I guess we should get going, then. I need to help *mei mamm* with some chores."

She hesitated, and he wondered if she wanted him to ask her to stay for supper. Would she stay if he asked? Would it be awkward for her and Anthony to eat with him?

Though happy to see Bethany's cheerful face, Micah wasn't in the mood to chat. He had too much on his mind to struggle through small talk. If he asked them to stay, he imagined the supper would be full of uncomfortable pauses and silence.

Anthony reached out and shook his hand. "Please call us if you need anything. We mean it. You're a *gut freind*, and we care about you."

"I appreciate it." Micah turned to Bethany, and she held out her hand. When she shook it, he felt a jolt of heat sizzle up his arm. He wanted to hold on forever and never let go. "*Danki* for the food."

"*Gern gschehne.*" Her smile faded, and her expression became serious, intense. "I hope to see you soon. Call me—even if it's just to talk."

He nodded.

Micah walked them to the door and stood on the porch as they climbed into their buggy and disappeared down the driveway.

And the familiar crushing loneliness set in once again.

Chapter 21

Bethany knocked on the door of Leanna's parents' large white farmhouse the following afternoon. She held a tray with two cups of macadamia-nut coffee, and a tote bag full of fudge brownies hung off of her arm.

While she waited for someone to come to the door, Bethany glanced around at the three rows of red barns, the small *daadihaus* where her grandparents lived, and the large pasture dotted with cows. She breathed in the familiar scent of animals and the moist air as she shivered in the late-February cold.

The door opened, and Leanna smiled at her.

"Hi, Bethany! Oh! Let me help you!" She took hold of the tray and motioned for Bethany to come in.

"Where is everyone?" Bethany asked as they walked into the large kitchen.

"*Mei mamm* and *Mammi* went to the grocery store. Chester went for supplies with *mei dat.* So I'm the only one home." Leanna pointed toward the doorway. "I was just mending a few pairs of Chester's trousers. He's always ripping them when he works in the barn."

Bethany pulled out the container of brownies. "I made your favorite—chocolate-fudge."

"*Danki*." Leanna took two plates and a knife from the cabinets, then sat down at the table and sipped her coffee. "Oh, and macadamia nut–flavored *kaffi*." She looked over at Bethany. "I was surprised when you called yesterday and asked if you could come to visit. What's the occasion?"

Bethany bit her lip as she sat down across from Leanna. She sighed and looked down at the table as she thought about her visit with Micah.

"Anthony and I went to see Micah yesterday. We took your advice and brought him a meal. I'm just so worried about him. I wanted to get your advice on how I can best help him."

Leanna opened the container of brownies and cut two before setting them on the plates and pushing one over to Bethany. "You want to ask me about when I lost Marlin."

"*Ya*. Is that too personal?" Bethany held her breath, hoping her cousin would be honest with her and also not find her curiosity offensive.

"Of course not. I always feel comfortable talking to you, Salina, and Christiana." Leanna sipped more coffee. "In the beginning I felt like I was stuck in a fog, just going through the motions. Chester was only nine, and I was more worried about taking care of him than myself. That wasn't the best way to handle things, because when the grief would hit me, I would crash hard. But it was the only way I knew to survive. I just kept praying, begging God to hold me up so I could take care of Chester."

Bethany nodded and swallowed as her throat became thick. Memories of Marlin's funeral hit her like waves—Leanna as pale as a sheet as she held on to Chester during the church service and the graveside ceremony. Bethany recalled wanting desperately to take away her cousin's pain.

"Grief is different for everyone, and I'm not sure my grief would feel the same as Micah's."

"It might be. He's actually experienced something similar to what you have."

Leanna's brown eyebrows lifted. "What do you mean?"

Bethany pressed her lips together as she considered sharing the secret Micah had told her.

"What is it, Bethany? He's not a widower because he doesn't have a beard." Then Leanna snapped her fingers. "Did he lose a girlfriend before he moved here?"

Bethany groaned as she sat back in the chair. "I've wanted to tell you, but it's not my secret to share."

Leanna leaned forward. "I won't tell anyone, but you don't have to tell me if you feel you should keep it to yourself."

"Do you remember when I went out to the workshop looking for Micah the day of Enos's funeral?"

"*Ya.*"

"Well, I found him sitting alone while he sanded a piece of wood that he said was part of the last project Enos had started."

Leanna shook her head as tears glistened in her eyes. "That's heartbreaking."

"*Ya,* it was." Then Bethany shared what Micah told her about Dawn. "He said he was all alone because he lost his fiancée, and then he moved here and he lost his grandparents."

Leanna shook her head. "He's engulfed in his grief. What about his family?"

Bethany hesitated, not wanting to completely betray his confidence since she'd already shared too much. "He's not close to his family."

"*Ach*, this is so *bedauerlich*."

"I know, and I want to help him but don't know how. He looks so sad and lonely. I keep telling him that his community cares for him, but he looks at me like he doesn't believe me." Bethany traced the lip of her coffee cup with her thumb. "It hurts because I'm in love with him, and I know he could never love me back."

"Whoa." Leanna reached out and touched her hand. "You're in love with him?"

Bethany stared down at her coffee. "*Ya*. My feelings for him are so intense that it hurts sometimes. I can't stop thinking about him and worrying about him, but I also can't stop thinking about what Simply Sara Ann said. If he thought about me the same way, he never would have said my family is too much for him. So I just keep on concentrating on being his *freind*. Maybe I could even be a comfort to him until he falls in love and marries someone else." The words tasted bitter in her mouth, but she had to face the truth.

"Bethany, I think you're wrong." Leanna held up her hand to stop Bethany from disagreeing. "Just think about this. He says he doesn't feel a connection to the community or God, but he still comes to see you every Saturday for a cup of *kaffi* and conversation. Didn't you tell me that he sat at a table with you and talked for a while last Saturday?"

"*Ya*, but that's just because he trusts me. I'm nonthreatening. Like I've been told, nearly a hundred times, I'm cute and perky. None of the men in our community see me as an equal or someone they'd want to date or marry."

"Stop that." Leanna shook a finger at her. "You have to stop putting yourself down like this. You have so much to offer, and Micah would be blessed to call you his girlfriend—or more. I think you're doing everything right with him. After Marlin died, my family helped me. My parents insisted I move in with them since I couldn't afford to keep renting the *haus* Marlin and I had in Gordonville. I became closer to you, Salina, and Christiana than I ever had been. I found my way to peace with the help of prayer and my family. You're being a *gut freind* to him, and I believe that when he finds his way through this storm, he'll realize you've been there all along." Leanna held her coffee cup toward Bethany. "He'll see you're the one he wants by his side always."

Bethany tried not to snort. "You think he's going to fall in love with me after he realizes he can count on me?" She shook her head. "I doubt it."

"Why?"

"What if Dawn was the love of his life? What if he never loves anyone the way he loved her?"

Leanna sighed and sipped her coffee.

"What?" Bethany leaned forward, desperate to hear what her cousin was contemplating. "Do you believe you can find love again?"

"For me?"

"*Ya.*"

Leanna twisted her lips. "I believe in love and that God has plans for everyone." She paused. "But for me, I don't think I could ever find a man I could love as much as I loved Marlin."

"And that's probably how he feels about Dawn." Bethany's voice was almost a whisper.

Leanna frowned. "You don't know that for sure."

"But when he told me about Dawn, he spoke as if he'd found

the love of his life in her. Now that she's gone, he's probably given up on love and the idea of spending the rest of his life with someone special."

"*Ya*, he might have, but God may have another plan for him. And don't forget God can change hearts."

Bethany nodded, hoping Leanna was right. But deep in her bones, she was filled with doubt.

Micah walked around the workshop Friday morning as the gravity of his situation pulled down on his shoulders. He'd made some calls to possible buyers, including the one Harvey and Anthony had mentioned the night he and *Daadi* had joined them for supper. Now he had to wait for return calls, praying he could unload some of the furniture he had on hand ready to go to stores.

He flopped down into the desk chair and dropped his head into his hands. If the buyers weren't interested in the furniture, he would have to consider selling the business and letting his supplies, furniture, and tools go to try to pay off the debt *Daadi* had left him. But that still didn't resolve the issue of losing the farm. While *Daadi* had insisted he had money in savings, a trip to the bank had confirmed that while Micah was listed on the account, there wasn't enough money to cover what they owed.

Added to that, one of the suppliers had repeatedly left messages asking Enos or Micah to call him, and now Micah knew why—he wanted money for the wood Enos had ordered from him but then never paid for.

Now Micah had a choice to make—was he going to try to crawl out of this debt or sell everything and start over somewhere else. If the latter, where? He couldn't consider moving back home. He didn't want to be a farmer. Plus, living and working with his father would be worse than living on the street. He couldn't spend the rest of his life arguing and being berated for not being the son his father had prayed for.

He considered asking Laverne if he could stay with her family until he was back on his feet. But would that situation be much better? His relationship with her had been strained for years. Plus, he didn't want to return to his old church district and all of the heartbreaking memories of the life he could have had with Dawn.

Maybe he could go out to Ohio and look up his cousins on his mother's side. Perhaps they would welcome him into their family, and he would find a relationship like Bethany had with her cousins. Would his mother's family even want to help him?

Leaning back in the chair, Micah stared up at the propane lights buzzing above him. He had hoped to start a new life here, but it seemed that new life would be cut short.

"Why didn't you tell me the truth, *Daadi?*"

Micah swiped a pen off the desk and hurled it across the room, where it bounced off a can of stain and disappeared behind a tool bench.

He looked around the shop at the piles of wood, unfinished furniture, and also the finished gliders, tables, chairs, and benches. Would he be able to sell all of this? Would one of the suppliers consider buying the unused wood back?

His thoughts turned toward the thousands of hours he'd spent in this workshop building furniture and bonding with his grandfather. The times they had worked side by side. The times they'd laughed at his grandfather's silly jokes. The times they had shared precious memories of *Mammi* while wiping their tears. How could he walk away from those memories and sell them off as if they meant nothing?

He rubbed at his eyes with the heels of his hands as his thoughts turned to Bethany and her beautiful smile. His visits with her on Saturdays continued to be the only happy moments in his long week—the only nourishment for his soul. What would it be like to have a woman like her in his life? Would she offer him daily words of encouragement? Would she hold his hand and tell him everything with the business would be okay?

But how could Bethany ever love him? He was a loser with a failing business who was also an emotional wreck. Why would she want to get involved with him and his problems?

He felt as if he were sinking in his sadness, loneliness, and grief. He couldn't sleep. He couldn't eat. He walked around in a daze all day, hopeless about the future and racking his brain for a path forward that didn't involve confronting the demons of his past.

He closed his eyes to talk to God and then stopped. He'd felt so disconnected from God lately that he couldn't even bring himself to pray.

Micah pushed himself off the chair and stood. He hoped one of the buyers would call him back and take his furniture to sell. Perhaps at least one would agree to allow him to advertise on their website, and if he made enough money, he might be able to refinance the loan on which *Daadi* had defaulted. If not, then he would have to look for a buyer to take over the entire business and move on with his life.

But how could he live with himself if he sold everything his grandfather had built?

Chapter 22

❧

Bethany swallowed a gasp as Micah walked into the booth the following morning. The purple circles under his eyes were darker than she'd remembered from Tuesday, and his face also looked thinner and more gaunt. She forced herself to smile as he approached the counter, and she was grateful there weren't any customers waiting behind him.

She recalled what Leanna had told her about how she survived her own grief after Marlin passed away. She would do her best to be Micah's strength. She would try to minister to him and offer her encouragement.

"*Gude mariye,*" she called out. "How are you today?"

"I'm okay." His expression was sober and unreadable as he leaned on the counter and looked up at her specials.

"I have peppermint mocha for you." She pointed to the small pot on the burner.

"That sounds *gut. Danki* for making my favorite."

"Would you also like a cinnamon donut? Or chocolate-glazed?" She worked to keep her tone light and happy despite the worry for him that continued to course through her.

"Sure. Either would be fine."

"It's cold out there this morning. I don't know about you, but I'm ready for spring." She quickly poured the coffee and gathered up one of each flavor of donut and pointed to one of the empty tables nearby. "How about we sit and get caught up?"

"Sure." He set his money on the counter and took the cup of coffee and two donuts from her.

Bethany poured herself a cup of one of her new flavored coffees, then grabbed a handful of creamers and packets of sweetener before she walked over to the table and hopped up on a stool beside Micah. She added creamer and sweetener to her cup.

He did the same and then stared down at his cup. More concern filled her. She decided to do what she did best—talk and fill the space between them until he spoke to her.

"I thought I'd try a new flavor today," she began, keeping her voice as perky as possible. "I've been doing some research, and I found this Brazilian nut–crunch *kaffi*. Doesn't that sound interesting?" She pushed her cup toward him. "Smell it."

He leaned down and took a whiff. "It smells *gut*."

"Do you want some?" She pointed toward the counter. "I'll pour you a cup."

He shook his head. "No, thanks." He took a sip of his peppermint mocha.

"How was your week?"

He set his cup down and pushed his hand through his hair, leaving it standing up at odd angles, making his face look younger and giving him an innocent aura. "I've had a lot on my mind." His voice was quiet and seemed to vibrate with anguish.

Her heart was sick for him, but she was careful to keep her expression sunny. "Do you want to talk about it?"

He hesitated, then shook his head. "No."

She masked her disappointment and searched for something else to lighten the mood, just talking as subjects came into her mind.

"My week has been busy," she began. "On Wednesday afternoon I went to see Leanna and check on her. Then I stopped by to see Christiana. Her *boppli* is getting so big. It's difficult to believe Kaylin is almost two months old now. She said she's starting to get Kaylin on a schedule, but she's still not getting much sleep."

Micah took a bite of his donut and looked at her, nodding as she spoke. She was surprised to see his shoulders actually relax slightly. Was her constant prattling helping him?

"And then, like I was saying, I did some research on *kaffi* flavors. When I went to the store where I buy my grounds and flavorings, I looked for something new." She pointed to the blackboard. "I also picked up black-satin and chocolate cherry–kiss. Do you think those sound *gut?*"

He nodded.

An awkward silence fell between them, and she tried not to panic. Bethany was not used to silence. She wanted him to open up, but she didn't want to push him away by pressuring him to speak. She knew he had to be the one to tell her what burdened his heart, and forcing it out of him and becoming aggressive like Simply Sara Ann would *not* do the trick.

"*Danki* for the beef stew, rolls, and the brownies. They were *appeditlich*," he finally said. "I meant to bring you your containers, but I forgot."

"Oh, it's okay. You can keep them. *Mei mamm* and I have plenty."

He took another bite of his donut.

"Is there anything else I can do for you?"

He looked up at her as he swallowed, and she felt this strange sensation that he wanted to tell her something. She could feel his sadness coming off of him in waves. Would he ever trust her enough to tell her his deepest secrets? After all, he'd told her about Dawn and his volatile relationship with his father. Perhaps that meant he did trust her. But could he ever trust her with everything that bothered him?

"No, but I appreciate you asking." He took another bite, chewed, and swallowed. "I have to run some errands today."

"Oh? Where do you have to go?" *Please tell me. Please talk to me. Please let me help you!*

"I have to see one of the suppliers we get our wood from." He fingered his coffee cup.

"Do you need more wood?"

"No." He kept his eyes down. "I have too much."

"Too much?"

He nodded.

"Does that mean you don't have enough orders to fill?"

He sipped more coffee, then set the cup on the table. "How are your parents doing?"

She blinked, stunned by the sudden subject change. "They're fine." She talked on about her father and brother working long hours trying to get ready for the busy season. She discussed her mother working in the house.

Soon she spotted customers coming into the booth, and her heart sank.

"I guess it's time for you to get back to your own work." His tone told her that he might be as disappointed as she was to end their time together.

"*Ya.*" She looked into his sad eyes, sorry their time had been cut short again. "I hope you have a *gut* day, Micah."

"You too." His expression remained dark and bleak.

Oh, how she missed his smile!

He pushed back the stool and stood. "Take care, Bethany."

"You too." As she watched him walk away, she sent a fervent prayer up to God.

Please, God, please show Micah the depth of your love and heal his broken heart. Please let him know I care and want to help him. Please lead him back to our community and to you.

Then she squared her shoulders and walked over to the counter, where an Amish couple who looked to be in their thirties waited for her. "*Gude mariye,* and welcome to the Coffee Corner."

❧

Micah sat in his buggy outside of Parkers' Home Improvement. He looked down at his empty coffee cup as he recalled his conversation with Bethany. Listening to her talk and seeing her smile filled him with a warmth he hadn't felt in a long time. She was an angel, the only ray of hope he had since *Daadi* had passed away. He had longed to stay in her booth all day today, just listening to her talk on about her family.

If only things could have been different between them. If only he wasn't broke and didn't have to leave Bird-in-Hand. If only he wasn't an emotional wreck.

But he had to go inside and talk to the owner of Parkers' Home Improvement about buying him out. The other buyers had called him back. A few of them had already made deals with other furniture builders for their spring and summer stock. Others said they would talk to him later in the spring, which would be too late for Micah. That meant Micah had no other choice. He was going to have to try to sell the business his grandfather had owned for close to fifty years. He just didn't know if he had the emotional strength to do it.

Closing his eyes, he allowed an image of Bethany's gorgeous face to fill his mind. When she'd asked him what was wrong, he'd wanted to confess everything. He'd considered telling her the truth about the mess his grandfather had left him and about how he was thinking of moving to Ohio and leaving Bird-in-Hand behind.

But he couldn't form the words. He was too embarrassed to admit that his life was in shambles when she had everything—a family who loved her, cousins who were her best friends, a thriving business, and a close relationship with God. When *Daadi* had died, he'd left Micah with nothing but an empty house, a failing business, unpaid bills, and a feeling of complete alienation from his community and God.

But Micah also couldn't bring himself to tell her the truth and run the risk of smearing his grandfather's name. He loved his grandfather too much to tarnish his legacy, no matter how bad the finances were.

And now Micah had to somehow pick up the pieces and try to rebuild his life.

Micah climbed out of the buggy and walked to the front door of Parkers' Home Improvement. He stepped into the large store and glanced around at the display of patio furniture and the aisles that contained everything from nails and screws to lumber, batteries, and cleaners.

He breathed in a mix of wood, rubber, and cleaning chemicals as he walked over to the front desk where a young man stood. He recognized him as the owner's son, Taylor.

"May I help you?"

"Hi. I'm Micah Zook. I was wondering if I could talk to your father."

"Oh, of course." Taylor picked up a phone and pushed a few buttons. "Hey, Dad. Micah Zook is here to see you." He nodded and then, after hanging up the phone, looked at Micah. "He'll be right out."

"Thanks." While he waited, Micah walked over to a rack of key chains and turned the display around so that the key chains swayed, making a *tink, tink* sound as they zoomed past him.

"Micah. So good to see you."

He turned, faced Brandon Parker, and shook his work-roughened hand. "You too," Micah said. "Is there a place where we can talk?"

"Absolutely." Brandon pointed toward a row of doors at the front of the large store. "Why don't we go to my office?

"Perfect."

"I'm ready for spring. How about you?" Brandon made small talk about the weather as they walked.

"*Ya*, I sure am."

Micah tried to gather his thoughts as they walked into the large office, decorated with a long cherry desk; matching shelves filled with photos of Brandon smiling with his wife, Taylor, and two daughters; and a few filing cabinets, a sofa, and two chairs. Micah took a seat on one of the chairs situated in front of the desk.

Brandon sat in the chair behind the desk. "I was sorry to hear about your grandfather."

"Thanks."

"So, what can I do for you?"

Micah sat back in the chair and cleared his throat. "I've been going through the books for the business, and I've found that my grandfather didn't tell me how steeped in debt we are."

Brandon nodded slowly.

Micah continued. "I realized that he hadn't paid you for the last supplies we received just before he passed away. I've gotten your messages, and I'm sorry I didn't call you back. I've been trying to figure out what to do first."

"I heard that your grandfather had passed away, so I wanted to give you some more time to grieve before I bothered you with business issues. Besides, I've known your family my whole life. My father owned this store before I took it over, and he worked with your grandfather for years. So if you need more time, I understand. We can definitely work something out."

"Thanks, but I don't need more time." Micah sat up taller. "I think I need to sell off everything and move on. I wanted to see if you would be interested in buying me out."

Brandon blinked and tilted his head. "Wait a minute." He held his hands up. "You want me to buy your business?"

"I know we owe you for the lumber." Micah gestured toward the front of the store. "You sell patio furniture here, so I hoped you could offer me something for the furniture and accept a return on the wood, minus any interest I owe. Then you can buy the rest and sell it here for a profit."

Brandon studied him. "Are you sure about this, Micah?"

"I am, and frankly, I don't see another solution. I'm also going to talk to a Realtor about selling the property. My plan is to start over somewhere else."

Brandon shook his head. "I hate to hear that you're going to sell the business. Your grandfather ran it for such a long time."

Micah nodded. His windpipe felt pinched shut.

"Well, let me see when I can come out there and look at everything. I'll be in touch, and we can work out the details."

"Great." As Micah shook his hand, he felt his heart breaking.

"Did you see Micah yesterday?" Salina asked Bethany as she sat with *Mammi* and their cousins in *Mammi's* small kitchen Sunday afternoon. Since it was an off Sunday without a service, they'd all gathered at Leanna's father's farm to visit for the afternoon.

"He came to see me at the Coffee Corner yesterday." Bethany grasped her cup of coffee. "He had dark circles under his eyes, and he looked as if he hadn't slept in a week. His face was so thin. I wanted to drag him over to your restaurant for a big meal."

"*Ach*, that's so *bedauerlich*," *Mammi* said.

"Poor Micah." Christiana cradled Kaylin in her arms as she fed her a bottle. "What did you say to him?"

"I mostly babbled about things. I tried to get him to talk to me, but he said he didn't want to talk about whatever was bothering him. He said he had to run some errands and he had a lot on his mind. But that was all he would tell me."

Leanna picked up an oatmeal cookie from the large plate in the center of the table. "I told Bethany she did the right thing by just being there for him and offering support. That's what helped me when I lost Marlin."

"That's the best you can do," *Mammi* said. "It says a lot that he comes to see you, but he hasn't been to church since Enos passed away."

Bethany shook her head. "He just likes the *kaffi*."

Salina snorted. "You can't be serious, Bethany. He could get *kaffi* anywhere!"

Christiana shook her head. "I think we all know it's more than the *kaffi*."

"That's what *I* keep telling her," Leanna sang, "but she won't listen!"

Bethany told them what Sara Ann had said—that Laverne had shared about how Micah didn't feel comfortable with her family. "Why would he want to be more than *freinden* if my family is too 'overwhelming' for him?"

Mammi reached over and rubbed her shoulder. "If that's even true, it's not stopping him from coming to see you. You offer him a solace he doesn't find anywhere else if he comes to see you every Saturday. In fact, you might be his only *freind*."

"That's what I told her," Leanna said. "But she doesn't believe me."

"Well, I'm older than you and wiser, so she'll believe me," *Mammi* said with a grin. Then she turned to Bethany. "You are most likely a balm to his troubled soul. Just keep trying to encourage him."

Bethany nodded. "I pray for him constantly, asking God to give him peace and comfort and lead him back to the community."

"That's all you can do. You are reminding him of the light amid the darkness," *Mammi* said.

"Thank you, *Mammi*," Bethany said. And she hoped her willingness was enough to help him.

Micah stood on the porch later that evening and stared out into the eerie dark. Then he stepped back into the house and stood in the center of the kitchen and glanced around. The deathly quiet felt like it would swallow him whole.

How he missed his grandfather. He missed his company, his laugh, his stories, and even his grumpy moods. He had been his best friend, his buddy, his business partner, his confidant. He was the one who had taught him everything he knew about being a carpenter. If only Micah could hear his voice one more time.

He needed some relief from the numbness and the isolation that set in every week and stayed until Saturday. He sank into a chair and covered his face with his hands. If only he could escape from himself. He'd rather feel anything else than the way he felt today. Even numbness would be an improvement to his condition.

Suddenly a memory drifted across Micah's mind. He had been sixteen, and he'd had one of the worst fights ever with his father. After storming out of the house, he'd met a group of his friends from youth group in a secluded section of woods behind his friend Ervan's farm. Ervan had stolen a few bottles of alcohol from his other brother, who ran with a wild crowd. He'd opened the bottles and passed them around while they sat in the circle. Micah had taken a long drink of whiskey, and after his throat stopped burning, a numbness had settled over him, making him forget how much his father's abuse had shattered him that day.

Micah needed to find the numbness again.

Tomorrow he would go to town and find some relief. Then he would face selling off his grandfather's legacy and try to find the strength to rebuild his life once again in a strange community.

Chapter 23

Bethany stood on the porch the following morning and hung a pair of her father's trousers on the clothesline. Then she pushed the line out toward the barn.

She had spent the morning doing the laundry, and now she was almost done hanging out the clean clothes. Although today was the first day of March and it was still bitterly cold, the laundry would dry by the end of the day. She glanced down at the basket and picked up another pair of his trousers, finding there were only two more pairs left.

"Bethany!" Anthony called as he headed out from the workshop. "I need to run to Parkers' for some supplies. Do you want to swing by the grocery store?"

"*Ya.* Let me just finish hanging out the clothes," she called back.

"I'll hitch up the horse and buggy." He started toward the barn.

Bethany hung up the last pairs of trousers, then walked into the house and set the basket in the laundry room. She found her mother in the kitchen, filling a bucket with water while the mop stood leaning against the counter.

"Anthony has to run to town for supplies, and he offered to take me to the grocery store." Bethany crossed to the counter where the list they'd made earlier sat.

"Oh, *gut*," *Mamm* said. "Take some money out of my purse. I'm going to mop the bathrooms."

"Okay. I'll be back soon." Bethany waved good-bye and hurried out to meet her brother in the driveway.

As she and Anthony rode toward town, Micah crossed her mind. She'd spent the morning praying for him while she washed and hung the clothes. She imagined Micah waking up in that big house alone, eating a silent breakfast, and walking out to his workshop with no company but his own thoughts. Her heart broke at the images that filled her mind.

Bethany couldn't imagine living without her loud family. As much as they drove her crazy at times, she still enjoyed eating breakfast while they all competed to tell their stories and laughed at something that had happened the day before. Their presence always brightened her spirits.

Anthony guided the horse into the parking lot at the grocery store. After they purchased everything on the list, they loaded up the buggy and headed to Parkers' Home Improvement. Anthony bought a few gallons of stain and some bolts before they loaded up the buggy again. Bethany peered out the passenger window as they headed back toward home.

At a red light Anthony halted the horse and tapped Bethany on the shoulder. "Hey. Isn't that Micah?"

"Where?" Bethany leaned over him and looked out toward the strip mall. She gasped when she saw a man who resembled

Micah walking out of a liquor store holding a box. She looked at her brother. "Surely not. I mean . . ." She squinted her eyes for a better look. "Do you *really* think that's him, Anthony?"

Her brother nodded. "I'm afraid I do."

Bethany's body shook as anger and worry boiled in her chest. "We need to stop him."

"How?" Anthony asked.

"I don't know, but this can't be good. We can't let him drink his life away." She pointed toward the store. "Let's go see if he'll talk to us."

A car tooted a horn behind them.

"Oof, I have to keep moving. The light is green," Anthony said, flicking the reins.

"Then let's follow him to his house."

"Bethany, I think we should mind our own business. Micah is a grown man. He's older than both of us."

"But what if he's throwing his life away?" She turned toward her brother and folded her hands as panic gripped her. "Please, let's go to his *haus*. We have to help him."

Anthony frowned and then sighed. "Fine. I need to find a place to turn around."

"*Danki*, Anthony."

As they made their way to Micah's house, Bethany wrung her hands and prayed for the right words to convince Micah not to lose himself in alcohol.

Anthony guided the horse up the long, rock driveway toward the farmhouse. When they reached the top of the driveway, Bethany spotted Micah standing at the back of his buggy. He stared over at them with a confused expression twisting up his handsome face.

Bethany jumped out of the buggy and marched toward him. "What are you doing?"

Micah blinked and divided a look between her and Anthony. "I'm not sure what you're talking about."

"We saw you." Her voice shook as she neared him. "You were walking out of the liquor store. What did you buy?"

Storm clouds gathered across his face, grim and foreboding. "That's none of your business."

"It *is* my business because I care about you." Her eyes stung with furious tears as she stopped in front of him. "Why would you buy alcohol?"

His jaw tightened as he stared at her. Then, without another word, he turned and stalked toward the workshop.

She started after him, her body shuddering with nerves. "Do you think the alcohol will solve your problems, Micah? Do you think drinking will make you feel better? It won't. Alcohol just makes everything worse."

When he kept walking, she racked her brain for something to say.

"Bethany," Anthony called, his voice holding a hint of warning. "Bethany. Stop. Back off."

Her desperation flared. "Micah, please listen to me. Alcohol won't bring your *daadi* back."

Micah stopped and spun, his face a twisted mask of fury. "I know that, Bethany!"

She winced and took a step back.

"You think I don't know that?" He took a step toward her and pointed at the house. "I know it every time I walk through that big *haus* by myself." Then he pointed toward the shop. "And then when I walk through the workshop alone. You have no idea what it feels like to be completely alone. How dare you stand there and judge me when you have no idea what my life is like!"

"Micah." She held her hand up as her body continued to tremble. "I'm sorry. I didn't mean to hurt you."

He gave a derisive snort. "Really? So then why come over here if not to lecture me about all the mistakes I've made? Right now you sound just like *mei daed*."

She blanched as if he'd struck her. She was speechless for a moment as her mouth worked, and no words escaped her lips. "I'm—I'm sorry. I didn't mean to sound that way at all. I just want you to know you don't need alcohol to help you feel better. You need God." She pointed to the gray sky above them. "And you need your community." She pointed to herself and to Anthony as he walked over to them. "We'll help you. Just tell us how."

Micah shook his head as a sneer overtook his face. "You have no idea how I feel."

"You keep saying that, and you're right. I don't know how you feel, and I'll never know unless you tell me."

Micah ran his tongue over his teeth as he stared at her. Bethany hugged her arms over her black sweater as she waited for him to speak. *Please open up to me, Micah. Please!*

"You'll never understand." He spun on his heel and started toward the shop again.

"Micah," Anthony called to him. "Don't leave. Bethany and I care about you. We're worried about you, and we want to help."

Micah faced them again. "You can't help me. You might as well give up."

"Why can't we help you?" Bethany asked, desperate for him to stop and talk to her. "Tell me."

"Because there's no way to fix it, and you can't possibly relate to me." He pointed a finger at her. "You have your loving family. You have your cousins, your *bruder*, your parents, and your business. What do I have? Absolutely nothing. My business is failing. I'm all alone here . . ." His voice broke, and the sound was like a knife to her chest. "I have nothing at all."

"That's not true." She wiped her face as a few tears escaped her eyes. "Your community loves you." *I love you.* "We all want to help you. You just have to tell us how. That's why we're here now."

He shook his head, and his lip trembled. "You can't. Please, just go." Waving her off, he walked over toward the shop again.

"Micah," Anthony called. "Stop. Don't push us away. It's obvious you're hurting and you could use some *freinden* right now. I feel like we could have done more to help you after you lost Enos, and I'm sorry. But we're here now, and we're ready to help you. So don't push us away. Talk to us. Let us help."

Micah wrenched open the door to the shop and faced them. "Just go."

Then he walked into the shop, and the door slammed behind him.

Bethany looked at her brother. "I don't know what else to do," she whispered as helplessness clawed at her chest.

Anthony shook his head. "We tried. We have to go."

"But he needs us."

"We can't help someone who doesn't want our help." Anthony pointed toward the waiting horse and buggy. "Come on, Bethany."

"Anthony, we can't leave him like this." Her voice quavered as tears blurred her vision.

"We need to go home." He started toward the horse and buggy.

Bethany stood facing the shop, waiting for the door to open

and for Micah to come walking out to talk to her. When he didn't appear, she headed toward the shop.

"Bethany, stop!" Anthony called from the buggy. "He's asked us more than once to leave him alone. He'll reach out to you if he changes his mind."

But would he?

"Come on, Bethany," Anthony yelled. "We need to get home."

Bethany heaved a deep sigh and turned back toward the buggy. As she climbed in beside her brother, she closed her eyes and sent up an urgent prayer to God.

Please, Lord. Please help Micah see that the community wants to help him. Let us help him and bring him back to you.

Then she hugged her arms to her chest as her tears began to trickle down her face.

Micah pushed open the workshop door and peered out as Anthony's horse and buggy headed down his driveway. A cold fury squeezed his chest as he stalked out to his own buggy and unloaded the box from the back.

His thoughts spun with anger and regret as he replayed everything he'd just said. He had never expected Bethany to show up at his house today. He had hoped to make a quick run out to the liquor store in peace. All he wanted was a moment's relief—but he couldn't have counted on Bethany to appear out of nowhere and lecture him about how he should find his relief in the community and God.

He gritted his teeth. How could she judge him when she'd never experienced the alienation he had?

With his free arm he closed the back of the buggy and started toward the shop. Bethany said she cared about him, but then why did she lecture him? Couldn't she see that her judgmental words wouldn't help him?

He walked into the shop and set the box on the desk, glancing around at the unfinished projects, supplies, and finished furniture. He would find out Friday if Brandon wanted to buy it all. Could he hold on for four more days?

His thoughts moved back to Bethany and the fierceness in her eyes as she harangued him. Then he recalled how she'd blanched and stepped away from him when he'd yelled at her. He'd sounded just like his father when he barked at her.

Guilt twined in his gut. He'd hurt her. Did she deserve that after she'd been his friend throughout this entire fiasco? He'd managed to push away the one person who seemed to care about him. And the one person for whom he cared.

He was just like his father! He'd made her feel as badly as he felt when his father browbeat him.

Micah groaned and pulled out a bottle of whiskey. He didn't deserve a woman as wonderful as Bethany. He didn't deserve to be a member of her community either.

Twisting open the bottle, he held it up to his mouth and took a long swig. He nearly choked on the sting of the drink, then wiped his mouth with the back of his hand and dropped hard into the desk chair. Closing his eyes, he sucked in a breath. Then he took another long drink. He needed relief. And only alcohol could do it.

He just hoped it was enough.

Bethany managed to hold back her tears as she sat at the kitchen table with her mother and brother. She had arrived home and immediately begun telling her mother what had happened as she and Anthony carried in the groceries.

"I can't believe you followed him to his *haus*," Mamm said.

Bethany twisted a napkin in her hands. "But I'm so worried about him, Mamm. He's headed down a destructive path."

Mamm shook her head. "I don't know what to say. You should tell your *onkel* Lamar and Neil. They'll go visit him and talk to him about his transgressions."

"But then he'll get in trouble," Anthony said. "He'll be shunned."

"Maybe that's what he needs to bring him back to the faith," *Mamm* said.

Bethany shook her head. "No, I think that would drive him further away. I wanted to express that we care about him. I also wanted to tell him I love him, but I couldn't bring myself to say it."

"What did you say?" Anthony asked.

Bethany shrugged as if the words didn't make her heart lurch. "I care about him. I love him. I just don't know how to make him believe my intentions are good. No matter what I say, it doesn't come out right."

Mamm reached over and placed her hands on Bethany's. "You just have to pray for him. God will lead him down the right path."

"But what if he doesn't?" Her voice was a hoarse whisper.

"Keep praying for him," Anthony said. "We'll all pray for him."

"*Ya.*" Bethany sniffed.

Please, God. Please help Micah.

Chapter 24

Micah stood in the driveway with Brandon on Friday afternoon. He shoved his hands into his trouser pockets as Brandon glanced around the property once more. He had toured the workshop while they discussed the contents—the tools, finished projects, unfinished projects, and supplies. Micah had made sure his bottles of whiskey were tucked away.

Then they'd talked about the house, two barns, row of storage sheds, and the pasture. And to Micah's shock, Brandon wanted to buy all of it—the house, the workshop, barns, and the land.

Everything.

Brandon was ready to buy Micah's grandfather's entire legacy.

Micah held his breath as Brandon looked around once more, and suddenly doubt hit him. Was he making a mistake? What would *Daadi* say if he knew Micah was selling everything?

Micah missed his grandfather more than anything, but *Daadi* had left behind a mess. Wasn't this what *Daadi* deserved?

No, he hadn't really deserved it. After all, *Daadi* had started to express his regret over the debt. Perhaps he believed this spring they would climb out of the hole and find a way to pay back the bank for the defaulted loan, as well as pay back the suppliers they owed.

"Are you happy with the price?" Brandon asked.

"*Ya*, I definitely think it's fair."

It was more than fair. In fact, it was more than Micah had ever dreamed of receiving for everything. The money would enable Micah to pay off his grandfather's debts, including the loan with the bank, and then travel out to Ohio and find a home to rent. It would also buy him a little time while he searched for a job.

Micah looked toward the house. "What did you say you would do with the farm?"

Brandon pointed toward the house. "My wife has been bugging me to build her a bigger house for a while now. We like our neighborhood, but we don't have any land. We live in one of those cookie-cutter places where all of the houses look the same, and the house sits on a postage stamp-size lot." He rolled his eyes. "This place is gorgeous. There's so much room to grow. We might either add on to this house or knock it down and start over. I'll ask her what she wants. After all, she's the boss." He chuckled.

Knock it down and start over.

Micah swallowed. How would his grandparents feel if they knew someone was going to knock down the house where they had raised their family and grown old together?

"Well, I need to go to the bank and see a lawyer about getting the paperwork together." Brandon shook Micah's hand. His grin suddenly faded. "You look a little green. Are you okay? Are you sure this is what you want to do?"

Micah tried to force a smile, but it felt more like a grimace. "I'll be fine."

"Well, it's going to take me about a week or so to get it all worked out. Just let me know as soon as you can if you change your mind. This is a huge decision."

"I'm sure I won't, but thank you."

Brandon walked over to his black Chevrolet Tahoe sitting in the driveway waiting for him. He pulled open the driver-side door and looked over at Micah as the keys jiggled in his hands. "I'll let you know when it's all set, and we can talk about a closing date."

"Sounds good." Micah gave him a wave. "Talk to you soon."

Brandon climbed in the driver's seat, and the truck roared to life before backing down the driveway.

Micah made his way toward the shop. He glanced up at the dark sky as the smell of rain filled his nostrils. At the door to the building, he stopped and looked toward the house. He tried to imagine his grandparents sitting together on the porch, each moving back and forth in their favorite rockers, which *Daadi* had built for them as a wedding gift.

Their life together had begun and ended in this house, and their only child had been born in this house—a historical marker of their joys, their sadness, their love.

His heart twisted.

What would Bethany say if she knew what he was about to do?

Micah sucked in a breath. She had haunted his thoughts all week as he walked around the house and shop by himself. He couldn't get her hurt expression out of his mind.

Somehow he knew what Bethany would say. She would tell

him he was letting everyone down—his grandparents, his community, and even God. But what choice did he have in the face of such debt?

A drop of water hit his straw hat and another his shoulder. He looked up as rain began sprinkling down from the heavens. He breathed in the fresh, sweet scent and closed his eyes, allowing the early-March droplets to pour down on his face. It was cold but also refreshing.

Was this a sign from God? If so, what was God trying to say?

Micah wrenched open the shop door and walked over to the sofa in the corner. This was where he had spent last night, curled up with a blanket. The shop felt more like home than that big, empty house.

He sank down on the worn upholstery and glanced across at the box of liquor bottles he'd set on a low shelf behind some other supplies. He'd sipped on it all week, and he felt as if he needed more to dull the ever-present emotional pain.

Standing, he crossed to the box and picked out a new bottle of whiskey, which he opened and started drinking. He closed his eyes and waited for the pain to slip away and the numbness to overtake him.

Guilt and regret filled Bethany as she stood in the Corner Coffee booth and put a small pot of peppermint mocha on a burner. She'd spent all week worrying about Micah. Their heated discussion had spiraled through her mind over and over, and each time she recalled what she'd said to him, she felt worse. A chasm opened in her chest every time she thought of him.

If only she could apologize.

She'd prayed for him numerous times every day, each time asking God to help him. And she'd also asked God to send him to the Coffee Corner so that they could work things out and she could apologize—even though she assumed he'd never want to talk to her again after what she'd said to him. After all, he'd accused her of sounding like his father! She cringed at the memory as guilt whipped through her.

Bethany had her coffee and donuts ready when the doors opened and customers began making their way around the marketplace. Disappointment filled her when Micah wasn't her first customer. Her disappointment turned to sadness when an hour passed and she still didn't see him.

Salina walked in an hour later when Bethany had a lull in her line.

"Hi, Salina," Bethany said.

"*Gude mariye.*" Salina leaned on the counter and pointed to her list of today's flavors. "May I please try the caramel-nut-fudge *kaffi* and a strawberry-glazed donut?"

"Sure." Bethany filled the coffee order and handed her the cup and donut. "What are you up to this morning?"

"I told Will I would help out at the restaurant, but I decided to drop by to see you and Leanna first." She sipped the coffee. "Oh, wow. This is fabulous." She looked at Bethany. "You seem preoccupied. *Was iss letz?*"

Bethany felt her lips twist into a deep frown.

"Is it something to do with Micah?"

Bethany nodded. "*Ya.* It's gotten worse."

"Tell me."

Bethany summarized what had happened on Monday when

she and Anthony saw Micah buying liquor. She shared about their argument and how terribly it had gone. "I've been worried about him all week and feeling guilty for how I handled the situation."

Salina shook her head. "That's so *bedauerlich* that he felt he had to turn to alcohol for relief." She sat a moment, frowning in thought, and Bethany's eyes widened as she suddenly recalled what her mother had said about telling the bishop and the deacon. Would Salina share his transgressions?

Salina's eyebrows careened toward her hairline. "Why are you looking at me like that?"

"You won't tell your *dat* and *bruder,* will you? I think shunning him for his sins would push him even further away from God, as well as the community."

"Oh, no, no, no. I would never do that to him. It's not my place." She glanced at the clock on the wall and back at Bethany. "You know, I told Will I wanted to spend some time with you since we don't see each other much lately. Why don't you pack up Micah's favorite donuts and *kaffi* and take them to him? It could it be a care package and also a way to apologize for the argument. If you give him an olive branch like that, he might open up to you." She gestured around the booth. "I'll run the booth for you until you get back."

"Are you sure? It gets crazy here now that it's March and spring is coming."

"Go on." Salina moved behind the counter. "You go check on Micah and work things out. He needs you."

"*Danki.* I'll do it." Bethany nodded as excitement moved through her. "I'll put together a box of donuts and two cups of peppermint mocha. Then I'll ask Kent if I can use his phone in the office to call Anthony and ask him to come get me and take me to Micah's."

"Now you're talking," Salina said.

Bethany quickly explained which coffee makers held which flavor and showed her the price sheet.

"I got this. You go take care of Micah." Salina looked toward the booth entrance as a middle-aged couple walked in. "Good morning. Welcome to the Coffee Corner. What can I get for you?"

Soon Bethany was riding in her brother's buggy. Her hands shook as Micah's large farmhouse came into view. Anthony guided the horse up to the back porch and Bethany hopped out, carrying the two cups of coffee while Anthony held the box of donuts.

Bethany rushed up the back steps and banged on the door. She glanced around the farm as she waited, spotting the empty pasture, along with the two barns, the row of storage sheds, and the workshop. Everything felt too still and almost eerie, despite the brilliant and cloudless blue sky and the bright sun shining above them.

After a few moments, she knocked again. She peered in through the storm door, trying to see through the back door, and knocked again.

"Micah!" she shouted. "Micah! It's Bethany and Anthony. Please let us in. Micah!"

Tenting her eyes, she looked in through the side window that faced the kitchen. She found the room empty. The counter and table were clear, no signs of movement or breakfast dishes.

She looked at her brother. "Where do you think he is? Maybe he's in the shop?"

Anthony shrugged. "Possibly. Or maybe he went to town?"

"But he didn't stop in to the market." She knocked again. "Micah? Are you in there?"

"Is the door unlocked?" Anthony asked.

She pulled on the storm door, and it opened. But when she tried the main door, it didn't budge. "No."

Anthony jammed his thumb toward the front of the house. "I'll go try the front door. You keep knocking here. Then we can check the barn and the shop." He set the box of donuts on the railing and jogged toward the front of the house.

While her brother was gone, Bethany continued to knock on the door and peer through the windows.

After a few minutes, Anthony ran back to the porch. "He wasn't there." He pointed toward the barn. "I'll go see if his horse and buggy are in the barn."

"Okay." Bethany knocked again. "Micah? Micah, if you're in there, we just want to talk. I want to apologize to you. Please let me in. Please."

"Bethany!" Anthony called from outside the barn. "His horse and buggy are here."

Panic began to rise in her chest. "What if he's hurt and needs help? He's all alone in there!"

"Calm down, Bethany." Anthony spoke in measured tones. "I'm sure there's a reasonable explanation. I'm going to try the shop. He's been in there when we've come to visit before."

Foreboding filled her as Anthony pulled on the door to the workshop and it opened. She walked to the end of the porch and picked up the box of donuts before she started down the porch steps. She quickened her pace as she headed toward the shop.

After a few moments, Anthony reappeared at the door, a deep frown lining his face. "I found him."

"Micah!" Bethany hurried toward the shop. "Is he okay?"

Anthony pressed his lips together and didn't respond.

Bethany rushed into the shop. She let out a gasp when she spotted Micah lying motionless on the sofa in the corner of the shop. She dropped the box of donuts onto the desk and set the coffee down beside it before running over to him.

"Micah!" she yelled. "Micah!" She dropped to her knees beside him and shook him. "Micah! Wake up!"

When he didn't move, tears began to stream down her face as she felt his arms and his hands. They were warm, but he wasn't responding.

"Something's wrong." She looked over at Anthony as tears continued to rush down her face. "Call nine one one!"

Chapter 25

"He's sick, Anthony!" Bethany yelled at her brother. "He needs help!"

Anthony shook his head.

"Why aren't you calling nine one one?" she demanded, pointing to the desk. "The phone is right there."

"He's not sick, Bethany. Well, he is, but he doesn't need a doctor. He needs to sober up."

"What do you mean?" She stared at her younger brother as her frustration flared. "I don't understand."

Anthony pointed to the floor beside her. "Look."

Bethany looked down and found three empty bottles. She looked back at her brother.

"He's drunk, Bethany. He drank until he passed out."

She stared down at the bottles again. "How did you know?"

"Remember when I used to go camping with my youth group when I was on my *rumspringa*? You know, before I was baptized." Anthony paused. "Let's just say some of *mei freinden* liked their vodka." He held up a finger. "And if you tell *Mamm* and *Dat*, I'll never speak to you again."

Just as Bethany opened her mouth to respond, a moan escaped Micah that sounded more like a guttural groan from somewhere deep in his chest.

"Micah?" She leaned down and took his hand in hers. "Micah?"

"Shhhhh," Micah hissed. "Stop yelling."

"I'm not—" she began.

Anthony interrupted her as he took her arm and pulled her back. "Give him some space."

Bethany stood and wrung her hands as she waited for Micah to wake up. Worry and confusion rushed through her as her heart continued to pound against her rib cage.

Micah groaned again, and his eyes blinked open. He tented his hand over his eyes as if the propane lights were as bright as the afternoon summer sun.

"*Gude mariye, mei freind*," Anthony said with exaggerated brightness. "It looks like you had a wild night."

Micah moaned and sat up, his dark hair standing up at odd angles, making him look much younger than twenty-seven. He rested his elbows on his thighs and cradled his head in his hands.

"What are you doing here?" Micah's words were muffled by his hands.

"We came to check on you," Bethany said. "I was concerned when you didn't come to the Coffee Corner this morning."

Micah looked up at her, his eyes dull, bloodshot, and rimmed with dark circles. "You left your booth to check on me?"

"*Ya*. Salina is running it for me." Bethany rushed over to the desk and retrieved the coffee and donuts. "I brought you breakfast."

"Uh, Bethany. I wouldn't give him that," Anthony warned.

She handed Micah the cup of coffee. He smelled it and gagged, covering his mouth.

"He's hung over, Bethany." Anthony took the cup from her and set it on the floor. "He needs water and aspirin."

"Oh." Bethany pointed toward the house. "If you give me a key, I can run to the *haus* and get you some."

"No, thanks. I'll get it." He rubbed his eyes. "Just go. I can take care of myself."

Bethany shook her head. "It doesn't look like you can. Let me help you, okay?"

Micah held up his hand. "Please don't start. I'm not in the mood for another one of your lectures."

"Why are you doing this to yourself?" Sadness overcame her.

"Bethany . . ." Anthony warned again.

"Why would you drink until you passed out?" Bethany ignored her brother and continued. "I really don't understand."

"Of course you don't." Micah's voice was suddenly flinty and sharp, his expression fierce.

"So then help me understand, Micah. Tell me what I can do to help you. I'm here because I care about you."

His lips curled with bitterness as he stared down at the coffee cup at his feet. "I sold the business and the farm. I'm moving to Ohio."

"What?" Bethany felt as if the ground had dropped out from under her feet. She sank down on a nearby stool. "You sold everything and you're moving? You're leaving?"

"Why Ohio?" Anthony asked.

"Most of *mei mamm*'s side of the family is there. Since starting a new life here hasn't worked out so well, I thought I might try again in my cousins' church district."

Bethany shook her head, trying to comprehend his words. "Why would you do that?" A cold feeling started in the pit of her stomach and began to spread to other parts of her body.

"Because I can't afford to stay here." Micah looked up at her, and his anger seemed to melt away, leaving anguish in its wake. "*Mei daadi* didn't tell me that we were drowning in unpaid bills. I only found out when I started investigating the books. Not only do we owe suppliers, but *mei daadi* had also taken out a loan to pay overdue tax bills. He used the farm as collateral and then defaulted on the loan. I've tried selling my furniture stock to different buyers, but I was turned down. There's no way I can climb out of the debt. So I met with Brandon Parker to discuss options."

"The owner of Parkers' Home Improvement?" Anthony asked.

"*Ya.*" Micah nodded. "He's the supplier I owe the most. Well, the business does. He wants to buy everything—the business, tools, supplies, finished projects, the *haus*, everything. That will allow me to pay the bank as well as the suppliers."

His voice wobbled, and his next words came out in a choked whisper. "I'll walk away with just enough money to head out to Ohio, find a place to rent, and search for a job. I haven't seen *mei mamm*'s side of the family for years. So if my cousins aren't *froh* to see me, then I have no idea what I'll do. I have nowhere else to go."

"You're just going to leave?" Bethany shook her head as her lungs constricted.

"I have no choice."

"You have plenty of choices," Bethany said.

"Like what, Bethany? What choices do I have?" His voice challenged her, but the pain in his eyes was so raw that she had to look away for a moment.

"Keep trying and don't give up," Bethany said, her voice pleading with him.

"I'm sorry to hear this, Micah," Anthony said as he sank down on a paint can. "We'll hate to see you go. I feel like we were just really getting to know you."

Micah nodded and pushed a hand through his thick hair.

"Is this what your *daadi* would want?" Bethany asked as her throat thickened.

"I don't know what he would want. He never told me how bad things were, and he's not here to explain why he kept the truth from me." His eyebrows made a V. "Do you think this is what I want, Bethany?"

"What *do* you want?" she asked.

Micah didn't respond. Instead, he blew out a puff of air and stood. He walked to the back of the shop and opened a small refrigerator. After pulling out a bottle of water, he took a long drink.

Bethany cleared her throat as the lump of emotion began to swell there.

Anthony stood and motioned for Bethany to get up. "We should go."

"No." Bethany looked over at Micah. "I want to know what your family thinks of this."

Micah hung his head. "I haven't told them yet. They haven't contacted me since the funeral. I don't think they really care how I am. If they did, they would have checked on me."

"Well, I think your *schweschder* would be sad to hear you want to leave. I know I am." She started toward the door. "Let's go, Anthony."

She looked over at Micah, and he studied her, his expression twisted with what looked like despondency. When she felt a wave of tears building in her eyes, she spun and rushed out to her brother's waiting buggy. As she climbed into the vehicle, she dissolved into tears, gasping for breath as sobs bubbled up in her throat. She covered her face with her hands as she cried.

Her heart broke as she imagined Micah packing up his belongings and moving to Ohio. She'd no longer see him at the market or at church. He'd be erased from her life, taking her heart and her dreams with him.

Why, God? Why? Have you heard any of my prayers?

After a few moments, she felt a hand on her shoulder.

"Breathe, Bethany," Anthony mumbled. "It's going to be all right. Just take a deep breath and let it go."

She felt the horse pull the buggy forward. Taking a handful of tissues from the pocket of her apron, she wiped her eyes and nose.

Anthony kept his eyes focused on the road ahead as she sniffed. "Do you want me to take you home?" he finally asked.

"No. I have to go back to the market."

He looked over at her. "You're not in any shape to run the booth today. You can close it down, and I'll take you home."

"*Danki*, but no. I'll be fine."

"You sure?"

She nodded. "*Ya*, but thanks."

She stared out at the passing traffic as the buggy moved down Old Philadelphia Pike toward the marketplace. When they reached the parking lot, Anthony looked over at her again.

"What's going on with Micah's family? The last time we saw him, he said you sounded like his *daed*. This time he said his family hasn't spoken to him since the funeral. That was a month ago. I guess they're not close at all?"

She shook her head. "He told me he and his *daed* don't get

along. It sounds like his relationship is strained with his *mamm* and *schweschder* too."

"That's *bedauerlich*. He really doesn't have anyone."

"He has me, but he's too blind to see it."

A silence fell between them, and Bethany took deep breaths to stop her tears and settle her emotions.

"If it's any consolation," Anthony began, "I think he does care about you, but he's too lost right now to tell up from down. We'll keep praying he finds his way back to the community."

Bethany nodded. "Thanks, but it's not going to work out."

"You never know what God has planned."

"Thanks for going with me." She pushed the door open and climbed out.

"Bethany."

"*Ya?*" She faced him.

"If you tell *Mamm* and *Dat* about my camping trips—"

"I won't." She placed her hand on her chest. "Your secret is safe with me."

"*Danki.*" Anthony looked relieved, and she tried not to laugh despite her disappointment in Micah. "It's *gut* to see you smile. See you later."

"See ya." She pushed the door closed and hurried up the front steps, past the planters that would be full of colorful, cheery flowers once warmer weather came back to Lancaster County. She moved down the aisle, past the lunch meat counter, and waved at Menno, the Amish man who ran the booth, as he handed an elderly *English* man a package of meat. Then she walked by the candy booth and breathed in the sweet smell of the chocolate as Laurie, the woman who owned the booth, handed a package of chocolate-covered pretzels to a middle-aged Amish man.

Bethany weaved past a group of customers standing by the used-book booth and arrived at the Coffee Corner. She breathed a sigh of relief when she found the booth was relatively quiet. Salina wiped down a table while three young women who looked to be in their early twenties sat and talked at a table in the corner.

When Salina looked up, she smiled at Bethany. "How did it go?"

Bethany frowned and shook her head as she pointed to the counter, indicating they needed to speak in private.

Salina followed her behind the counter. "What happened?" she whispered.

"He was drunk and passed out in the workshop," Bethany answered just as quietly as they both stood with their backs to the tables and chairs.

Salina gasped, and Bethany shushed her.

Bethany shared what he said about selling everything and moving to Ohio. "I feel like my heart has been stomped on." She shook her head and touched the hem of her apron. "I don't want him to go."

"*Ach*, Bethany, I am so sorry."

"You should have seen the floor, Salina," Bethany said. "It was littered with empty bottles of alcohol. What would Enos say if he knew Micah was drinking until he passed out? He would be mortified."

"Hello there."

Bethany spun and found Simply Sara Ann watching them, a devious smile turning up her lips. *Oh no! Had she heard everything they'd just said about Micah?*

"Hi, Sara Ann." Bethany gulped. "How are you?"

"I'm just fine." Sara Ann divided a look between them. "A

few of my customers told me your caramel-nut fudge *kaffi* was spectacular."

"Oh. *Danki.*" Bethany looked at Salina, who somehow managed to stay cool. "Would you please pour her a cup?"

"Of course." Salina grabbed a cup and filled it while Bethany took Sara Ann's money.

"Have you spoken to Micah lately?"

"No." Bethany shook her head and tried to seem casual. "Have you?"

"Oh, no." Sara Ann waved her off. "I haven't seen him or spoken to him since the funeral."

"Huh," Bethany said as Salina handed Sara Ann her cup of coffee.

Simply Sara Ann added a splash of milk and sipped. "Yum! It is fantastic." She grinned. "Well, when you see Micah, please give him my love." Then she turned on her heel and flounced out of the booth.

Bethany moaned and cupped her hand to her forehead. "Do you think she heard us?"

"Surely not." Salina shook her head.

"But she was standing right there when I talked about the empty bottles and asked you what you thought Enos would say."

"Don't worry about it." Salina rubbed her shoulder. "Even if she did hear, I'm sure she wouldn't tell anyone."

"Please, Salina! She'll tell everyone at her next quilting bee. You remember how she was the one who told you Will had broken up with Caroline. She had heard it through the gossips at one of her bees." Bethany groaned and looked down at the counter. "This is a disaster."

"Just have faith. Keep praying for him. He's not gone from the district yet. And if he does leave, that doesn't mean he'll stay gone forever. If he reaches out to you, you could write letters." Salina's smile was hopeful. "He might get settled in Ohio and then realize he wants to have a relationship with you. He could come back for you or he might ask you to come to Ohio. We'd all miss you if you left, but we could visit you. And you and Micah could still come here to visit your parents, Anthony, and the rest of us. We'd all keep in touch."

"You're way ahead of yourself, Salina. I don't think he wants me to go to Ohio with him. I don't think he wants me to go anywhere with him." Bethany shook her head. "He doesn't want to date me. And he probably hates me now since he keeps saying I'll never understand how he feels."

"How could anyone hate you, sweet Bethany?" Salina touched her arm. "You're most likely the only one who has gone to check on him. You've been a loyal *freind*. He'll realize that."

"I hope so."

But deep in her heart, Bethany knew she'd lost Micah forever.

Chapter 26

Bethany walked with her parents to the buggy after church on Sunday. She'd been disappointed that Micah hadn't come to church again this Sunday, but she wasn't surprised.

Throughout the service she prayed for Micah again, begging God to heal his heart and make him feel strong enough and worthy enough to give up the alcohol. She also selfishly prayed that he would consider staying in Bird-in-Hand and giving his business another try.

When the service ended, she helped the women set up for the noon meal, and she tried to chat with her cousins when they ate. She dodged questions Leanna and Christiana asked about Micah because she didn't want to recount her heartache or risk anyone from the congregation hearing about his sin of drinking.

After lunch was over, she hurried to follow her parents to their buggy and avoided any other conversations. She just wanted to rest at home and nurse her wounded heart.

"Bethany!"

She turned and found Salina's brother, Neil, who was also the deacon of their congregation, walking toward her. She swallowed a groan as her cousin caught up to her.

At thirty-two, Neil reminded Bethany of her *onkel* Lamar, his father. He had the same long nose, the same dark hair, the same light-blue eyes, the same bushy eyebrows, the same long beard, and also the same stoic focus on the good of the community.

Bethany worked to keep a sunny smile on her face despite his stern expression. "Hi, Neil. What did you need?"

"I was wondering if I could ask you something."

"Okay." She fingered the edge of her white apron.

He touched his beard and glanced around. Then he lowered his voice. "I heard you were *freinden* with Micah Zook."

Bethany swallowed as her throat filled with a messy knot of worry. "I speak to him from time to time."

"There's a rumor that he has been doing a lot of drinking."

Bethany stilled and everything inside of her froze.

"*Mei dat* and I have been concerned that he's been missing church, and then we heard he was drinking. We're worried about him."

"Are you going to shun him?" Her voice shook.

"I can't discuss that with you." Neil studied her. "Do you know anything about the drinking?"

"If you shun him, he'll leave for sure. Please don't shun him."

"What do you mean he'll leave for sure? Is he considering leaving the community?"

Bethany looked behind him at her parents as they stood by their buggy talking to Leanna's parents, completely oblivious to her conversation with Neil.

"Bethany?" Neil asked. "If you know something, you should tell me. We're concerned for his welfare."

"Did Sara Ann King tell you he was drinking?"

"I can't reveal who told me, but I need to know the truth."

Bethany sighed. "He told me he was going to sell everything to an *Englisher* and move to Ohio."

"And the drinking?"

She couldn't lie to her deacon. "*Ya*, it's truth. He's been drinking. Anthony and I found him after he had had too much alcohol." She pressed her lips together, fighting back her rioting emotions. "I tried to convince him to stay. He needs to know his church district cares about him."

Neil gave her a curt nod. "I'll keep that in mind when I go to visit him."

"Please don't shun him."

"I have to do what's right for the church and what's right for God."

"I understand."

"*Danki*, Bethany," Neil said.

She nodded and turned, almost walking right into her brother. "How long have you been standing there?"

"Long enough." Anthony gestured in the direction Neil had walked. "What was that about?"

"Micah." Bethany worried her lip as an idea that might keep Micah from leaving Bird-in-Hand formed in her head. "Would you do me a favor and not go out with your youth group today?"

"Why?"

"I have an idea I want to propose to *Dat*, and I need your help convincing him."

Anthony eyed her with suspicion. "Is this about Micah?"

"*Ya.* If you let me ride home with you, I'll spell it out."

Anthony released a sigh. "Fine, but this better be one really *gut* idea!"

"*Danki.*" Hope took root in her heart as she walked with him to his horse and buggy.

❧

Later that afternoon Bethany sat in the family room with her parents and Anthony. "*Dat,* I want to tell you something."

"What is it, Bethany?"

"Neil stopped me when we were walking to your buggy and asked me about Micah."

"What did he ask you?" *Mamm* asked.

Bethany shared how she and Anthony had gone to visit him and found him passed out from drinking too much, and her parents gasped.

"I had told Salina about it, and I think Sara Ann King overhead our conversation. I have a feeling she told *Onkel* Lamar or Neil about it. Or maybe she gossiped to someone who told them."

"Why would she do that?" *Mamm* asked.

"She's a terrible gossip," Bethany said. "My cousins and I have seen plenty of evidence of it at the market."

"Why didn't you tell us that you found Micah passed out?" *Dat* asked.

Bethany shrugged. "I don't know. I guess I was afraid to tell you. He also said he's going to move to Ohio to reconnect with his *mamm's* side of the family." She shared how he'd said he was in the process of selling everything and wanted to start over with the help of his cousins. "It's breaking my heart to see him go. I want to help him."

"I know you do, *mei liewe*, but he's an adult. He'll make his own decisions."

"That's true, but I have a solution." She glanced over at Anthony, and he nodded, encouraging her to go on. "Anthony once told me that Micah had asked your advice on his business. He said his *daadi* left him drowning in debt. The other day I was praying while I was cleaning the tables in the Coffee Corner, and I realized that your business is similar to his."

She paused and took a deep breath. "What if you combined your businesses? You said the man who owns the shed distribution place wants to buy gazebos from you because they are Amish made. What if that man sold your gazebos along with Micah's custom patio furniture? You would be a one-stop shop for Amish-made gazebos and patio furniture."

Dat's face lit up as he glanced at *Mamm* and then back at Bethany. "What an intriguing idea."

Bethany held up her hands. "I understand his business is in debt, and that means you're taking a risk. However, if it works out, it could be a successful endeavor for both of you. Maybe you can find a way to help him apply for a loan to pay off the debt or something like that. Or you can pay it off and take it out of his profits. I'm not sure what it would mean, but I just feel like he's giving up his dreams when all he needs is someone to help him when he's down. He told me moving here was a new start, and he loved working with his *daadi*. When I look into his eyes, I see the depth of his pain and what he's giving up by selling Enos's life's work."

She paused and took a deep, shuddering breath. "We need to help him. God calls on us to help one another in our time of need. Micah needs us now." Her voice cracked.

Dat gave her an encouraging smile. "I will definitely consider it. Let me think about it, okay?"

She nodded. "*Danki, Dat.*"

Her father reached over and took her hand in his. "Bethany, you have a kind and giving heart, and I am proud to call you *mei dochder. Danki* for caring for people the way you do. Micah is blessed to have you as his *freind.*"

Bethany nodded, and for the first time in many days, she felt hopeful for Micah.

Micah started down the stairs Monday morning and yawned. He'd spent another restless night trying to sleep while Bethany's words echoed in his mind. "*Well, I think your* schweschder *would be sad to hear you want to leave. I know I am.*"

He could still hear her shaky voice and see the tears sprinkling down her pink cheeks. He'd broken her heart, and she'd broken his.

If only things were different . . .

His feet hit the downstairs floor, and the linoleum sent cold seeping through his socks and into his skin. When he heard a loud knock on the back door, he hurried through the mudroom and wrenched open the door. Pure dread flowed through his veins when he found Neil Petersheim, the deacon, standing on his back porch.

Micah knew before Neil said a word that he was in trouble

with the church. He'd known it was coming. But did it matter if he was planning to leave this church district anyway?

"Neil. What a surprise." Micah worked to keep his expression pleasant as he pushed the door open. "Come in."

"*Gude mariye.*" Neil gave him a stiff nod.

Micah had always found Neil to be serious and rigid, but he seemed like a good man. At least he was pleasant enough when they made small talk at church during lunch.

Moving to the sink, Micah filled the percolator with water and glanced over his shoulder at Neil. "Would you like a cup of *kaffi*?"

"Oh. Uh. Sure." Neil gave him another stiff nod.

"Please have a seat." Micah pointed to the kitchen chairs. Then he turned back to the stove and set the percolator on a burner before sitting down across from Neil. "So, what brings you all the way out here today?"

Of course Micah knew the response. Most likely Neil was going to discuss his absence from church and possibly his drinking if Bethany and Anthony had told Neil about his episode on Saturday.

Anger punched him in the gut. Why couldn't Bethany and Anthony stay out of his business? It had been his decision to drink. He was a grown man and could live his life the way he chose.

"There are many members of the congregation who are concerned about your behavior. You've missed quite a few church services, and I heard a report that you had been drinking alcohol."

Micah nodded. Despite his swirling irritation, he couldn't bring himself to lie. Nor could he find any point in lying. "It's all true."

Neil blinked, seeming surprised Micah told the truth. Did most folks try to lie their way out of a shunning? "We're all concerned about you. Also, we want you to make yourself right with the church and God."

"You're talking about a confession and shunning, right?"

Neil nodded. "That's right."

Micah set his hands on the table. "It's not necessary."

"What do you mean?"

"I'm selling this place and I'm considering moving out to Ohio. I have family there. I have a buyer for my land, and we're supposed to work out the details later this week. There's really no point in my confessing because hopefully I'll be out of here on my way to Ohio in a few weeks or so."

"Oh." Neil looked puzzled. "Are you leaving the Amish church completely?"

"No." Micah stood and walked over to the counter. He opened the cabinet and pulled out two mugs. Then he retrieved sugar and creamer. "I have cousins out in Ohio, and I haven't seen them in years. I'm not close to my family here, so I'm going to see if I can reconnect with *mei mamm*'s family out in Middlefield. I'll make a new life there. I can complete my confession and shunning there after I move and start over."

Neil remained silent, but he looked as if he was contemplating something. Watching him, something shifted in Micah. His frustration faded, replaced by a weary resignation.

"Look, I know what I've been doing—how I've been handling things—is wrong, both with avoiding church and with the drinking. I've been . . . It's not an excuse, but I've been having a tough time dealing with losing my grandfather and then finding out my business was steeped in debt."

Neil's face registered surprise, along with a quiet compassion. His expression gave Micah the courage to keep going. As he prepared their mugs of coffee, Micah shared what he had found when he dug into the accounting books. "*Mei daadi* left me a mess, and I've been trying to figure out where to go from here."

Micah brought the two mugs of coffee to the table and set one in front of Neil.

"I can imagine this has been difficult for you, but we're supposed to live our lives in accordance with the *Ordnung*. That means attending church and avoiding alcohol. And your community cares about you. You can always come to us when you have problems. We're called to take care of each other, and I wish you'd given us the opportunity to do that." Neil added sugar and creamer, then took a sip.

Micah did the same, and he found himself craving Bethany's *kaffi*. How he would miss her flavors when he moved away. He closed his eyes as his heart twisted.

"Is there something else you want to discuss?" Neil asked.

Micah nursed his coffee as he considered asking about Bethany. But what would he ask? How silly would he look asking about Neil's cousin?

"Did Bethany or Anthony tell you about the drinking?"

Neil shook his head. "No, they didn't tell me, but Bethany confirmed it when I questioned her."

"Who told you?"

"I don't feel I am at liberty to share that information with you."

Micah studied him. "You know, I feel I should point out that gossip is a sin as much as avoiding church and drinking alcohol are."

"That is true." Neil sighed.

"Perhaps the person who told you about my sin needs to be reminded that he or she isn't sinless either."

Neil nodded.

Micah took another sip of his bland coffee and tried to think of something to say to Neil. "How's your family?"

Neil made small talk about his daughters. After his cup was empty, he stood, and Micah walked him out to the porch.

"*Danki* for the *kaffi*," Neil said.

"*Gern gschehne*, but it's not nearly as *gut* as Bethany's."

A strange look came over Neil's face. "I think you should consider finding a way to remain in the community. I have a feeling there are some church members who would be very *froh* to see you stay." He shook Micah's hand. "Have a *gut* day."

As Micah watched Neil walk to his horse and buggy, he wondered what church members Neil had been referring to when he told Micah he should stay. Possibly Bethany? Why would Bethany even consider him when he'd not only lost his business and his home but was now facing a shunning if he stayed in the community?

He stepped toward his back door just as he heard a truck engine rumble up his driveway. Pivoting, he turned as a dark-blue Chevrolet Silverado stopped at the top of the driveway and *Dat* climbed out of the passenger seat.

"Oh no," Micah grumbled under his breath. "Now *Dat* is here to fuss at me? Maybe I should have stayed in bed."

Dat walked around the front end of the truck and came to the bottom of the porch steps. "*Gude mariye*, Micah."

"Hello, *Dat*." Micah felt his jaw clench and the muscles in his shoulders coil as he stared down at his father.

"It's been a while."

"*Ya*. In fact, it's been a month since the funeral." Micah folded his arms over his chest and lifted his chin. "What brings you out here today?"

"I had to make a supply run so I thought I'd stop by to see how you're doing."

Micah snorted.

Dat pointed to the back door. "May I come in for a few minutes?"

"Why not? *Kaffi* is already made." He swiveled toward the door and wrenched it open, holding it for his father before they both walked into the kitchen. He placed Neil's mug in the sink and retrieved a fresh one for *Dat* before filling it with coffee. He carried it to the table where *Dat* sat.

"Did *Mamm* send you out to check on me?" Micah asked as *Dat* added creamer and sugar to the mug.

Dat nodded, and Micah pursed his lips.

"Who was leaving when I pulled up?" *Dat* asked.

"Neil Petersheim. He's the deacon in my district."

Dat's eyes widened. "The deacon? Why did he have to visit you?"

Micah leaned back in his chair. "Because I'm about to be shunned."

"Why?"

"Oh, let's see." Micah began counting off the offenses on his fingers. "Bethany and Anthony Gingerich found me passed out after a night of binge-drinking. And I've also missed quite a few church services since *Daadi* died."

Dat's eyes narrowed as his brow puckered. "Why would you behave like that, Micah? You're a grown man now, not a teenager."

"Please, *Dat*. Why are you surprised? I've always been a

failure to you." Micah nearly spat the words at his father as fury exploded through him. "You should expect me to mess up! That's what you've always said to me."

Dat's mouth worked, but no words came out. Then he blinked. "What would your *daadi* say if he knew you were going to be shunned?"

"What would he say?" Micah gave a humorless laugh. "I think he'd understand. After all, he left me a failing business, plus a farm that's in foreclosure."

"What are you talking about?"

Micah explained the debt and his plan to sell everything to Brandon Parker. His father listened, his sneer melting away as his mouth dropped open.

"I had no idea things were bad."

"Neither did I." Micah pushed back his chair, stood, and paced back and forth by the table before stopping in front of his father. "He's left me no choice."

Dat shook his head. "Why didn't you come to me when you found out how bad the debt was?"

"Why would I do that? And give you the satisfaction of telling me that you always knew I'd mess up *Daadi's* business?" He gestured widely. "You were the one who told me I was 'freeloading' off *Daadi* instead of building my own *haus* 'like a man.'" He made air quotes with his fingers. "You are the last person I'd come to for help."

Micah's body trembled as his mouth dried. "You've made it clear that I'm the biggest disappointment of your life, so I would never, ever consider coming to you for help or anything else."

Something unreadable flickered across *Dat's* face before he pushed his chair back and stood. "I'm sorry you feel that way." He pointed to the mug. "*Danki* for the *kaffi*."

Confusion swirled in Micah's gut as *Dat* started across the kitchen. Where was the argument? The yelling? The biting insults?

The silence was deafening.

When *Dat* reached the back door, he turned the knob. Only then did he pause. With a sigh, he peered over his shoulder at Micah. "I've never felt that you were a failure or a disappointment. And I'll miss you when you go to Ohio." Then he disappeared out the door.

Micah stood stunned a moment before he scrubbed his hand across his face and tried to make sense of what had just happened. He had imagined it would be cathartic to tell his father how he truly felt about how he had treated Micah all these years. But relief wasn't what coursed through him. Instead, confusion, regret, and sadness swirled in his gut as he stood alone in the kitchen. His father wasn't disappointed in him? And would miss him? None of it made sense!

But one thing was clear—Micah had now reached rock bottom in his life. And the only way to repair it was to cut his losses and start fresh in a new community.

If that was the best solution, though, then why did the idea of leaving hurt him to his very core?

Chapter 27

Bethany sat with her cousins in Christiana's kitchen the following Wednesday afternoon. The delicious smells of sticky buns, coffee cake, and Bethany's favorite apple-pie coffee filled the room. Kaylin slept in a bassinet in the next room while they talked and ate.

Working hard to keep her emotions in check, Bethany shared what had happened when she and Anthony went to see Micah on Saturday. And then she told her cousins about her visit with Neil after the church service. Her cousins' eyes were wide, and shock covered their faces when she finished sharing her stories.

"Neil asked you about Micah after church on Sunday?" Salina held her hands up. "I promise you I didn't tell *mei dat* or *mei bruder* anything. I stay out of church business. It's not my place. And trust me, I hear about it enough when I have family dinners with them. When you told me about what happened on Saturday, I kept it to myself. I would never betray your trust like that."

"I never thought you did," Bethany insisted. "I'm certain it was Simply Sara Ann."

Christiana groaned as she took another sticky bun from the plate in the center of the table. "Why can't she mind her own business?"

"I don't think that's how it happened," Leanna said as she placed her mug on the table. "I imagine Simply Sara Ann told her cousin Fern, and then Fern did her the favor of sharing the information with Neil and *Onkel* Lamar."

Bethany rested her cheek on the palm of her hand. "I'm sure you're right. I'm just so worried about him. If he's shunned, he'll leave Bird-in-Hand for sure."

"There's still a chance he might stay." Leanna rubbed Bethany's shoulder.

"I'll be positively heartbroken if he leaves."

Salina's eyes widened again as she pointed at Bethany. "So you're in love with him?"

Bethany sat up straight and nodded gravely. "I am. At first I had a crush on him. And then, as I got to know him, it developed into so much more. Now I feel like I'm losing a piece of my heart every time I think about never sharing another Saturday-morning chat with him at my Coffee Corner."

"Keep praying for him," Christiana said. "Ask God to change his heart."

"I'll always pray for him, but honestly, maybe it's better if he leaves." Bethany felt her shoulders slump as she looked down at her half-empty coffee cup.

"Wait a minute," Christiana said. "Why would you say you're in love with him and then say it would be better if he left?"

Bethany looked up at her redheaded cousin. "I've told you before—because he could never love me the way I love him. Maybe if he leaves I can move on somehow."

"Are you still convinced he can't love you because your family likes to talk a lot at suppertime?" Christiana asked, looking incredulous.

Bethany nodded. "That, yes. But also because I lectured him the day I saw him buying the alcohol. I know I hurt him. I said terrible things to him. And he was so angry."

"You need to stop that, Bethany," Salina said. "He'll forgive you when he comes through this hard time."

"Of course he will," Leanna added.

"It's not just that," Bethany said as she curled her hands around her mug. "We're just too different. How could we possibly get along if I'm perky and talkative and he's quiet? We'll never mesh as a couple."

"I disagree completely." Salina shook her head. "Will and I are very different. He loves to joke around, and he's very outgoing. You know I tend to be shy and clam up if I don't know someone. I'm organized, and his office was a complete mess when we met."

Salina waved her hands in the air as she rolled her eyes. "And you should see the mess he makes when he's working on a new recipe. Sometimes I look at the kitchen and cringe, and then I walk out and let him do his thing. And you all know that our backgrounds are different too. He grew up Old Order Mennonite, and *mei dat* is an Amish bishop. But those differences keep our marriage interesting. I think it would be boring to be married to someone who is just like me."

"*Ya*, that's true," Christiana said. "Jeff and I are different too." She put a hand on her chest. "What matters is what's in your heart. As long as you have the same basic beliefs and you want the same things, your relationship can work."

Leanna nodded. "I think Micah has some problems he needs to work out. First and foremost, he needs to stop drinking. If he can figure out the problems with the business and make himself right with the church, I think you two can definitely have a bright future."

Bethany considered what they had to say and shrugged. "But maybe I need to let him go. That way I won't be left completely heartbroken if he doesn't work those things out."

"Or you can keep having faith and praying for him," Leanna said with a smile. "That way you'll be ready to celebrate with him when he does work it all out and comes back to you."

Salina and Christiana nodded.

Changing the subject, Christiana turned to Salina. "Have you purchased all of your seeds for your new garden?"

"I have." Salina rubbed her hands together. "I'm waiting for it to warm up a little more so I can start my planting. I can't wait to get my garden going and get back to the booth." She divided a look between Bethany and Leanna. "Have you two missed me at the marketplace?"

"Of course we have," Leanna said. "We miss both of you. It's not the same." She looked at Christiana. "I miss the smell of the Bake Shop so much. That jewelry booth is no replacement for your *kichlin* and pies." She looked at Bethany. "Weren't we just talking about that the other day, Bethany?"

Bethany nodded and tried to smile, but her thoughts were stuck on Micah. She was grateful for her cousins who tried to cheer her up, but waiting for God to sort out Micah's life was a lesson in patience she knew she needed to learn.

❧

When a knock sounded on the back door Thursday morning, Micah looked up from the box of documents he'd been sorting through on the kitchen table. He hurried out to the mudroom and was surprised to find Harvey and Anthony standing on the back porch.

"*Gude mariye,*" Micah said as he shook Harvey's hand. "What a surprise." Hot embarrassment crawled up his neck as he shook Anthony's hand. The last time he'd seen him, Micah had awoken on the shop sofa after a night of drinking. He brushed off the thought and smiled at him. "What brings you out here today?"

"We wanted to stop by and talk to you for a few minutes," Harvey said. "We've been missing you at church."

Micah shoved his hands into his trouser pockets and tried to prepare himself for another lecture. On one hand, he didn't want to hear about how he'd been sinning and hurting himself. But on the other, it was nice to have company after spending so many days alone. Talking to another human was a welcome relief from the hours he'd spent shuffling around the house and workshop by himself, thinking about his discussion with Neil and his confusing conversation with *Dat.*

"*Ya.* Come in." Micah led them into the kitchen and motioned toward the table. "Please excuse the mess. I was going through some paperwork." He pushed the piles together in the center of the table. "Would you like some *kaffi?*" he asked, motioning toward the percolator.

"That would be great," Anthony said as Harvey nodded. "*Danki.*"

Micah nodded. "Please have a seat while I get it ready." After retrieving three cups of coffee, along with the sugar bowl and pitcher of cream, he returned to the table and handed them each a cup.

"What would you like to discuss?" he asked as he sat down and took a sip of his drink.

"Anthony told me you're planning to sell your business and your property to an *Englisher*," Harvey said as he stirred cream and sugar into his mug. "Is that true?"

"*Ya*, it is," Micah said.

Anthony poured cream into his own coffee and stirred. "Have you closed the deal yet?"

Micah shook his head. "No, not yet. He's still working out the legal side of things. I heard from him yesterday, and we're supposed to do the paperwork sometime next week."

"Hmm." Harvey took a sip of coffee. "What if I made you a counteroffer?"

Micah blinked. "What do you mean?"

Harvey set his mug on the table. "When you came over for supper, I told you about the shed distributor who wanted to order my gazebos because his customers ask for Amish-made items. There's a market out there for carpenters like us, and we should take advantage of it. If we combined our businesses, we could be a one-stop shop for Amish-made gazebos and custom patio furniture. What do you think of that?"

Micah was speechless as he looked back and forth between Harvey and Anthony, looking for any sign of a joke. "Are you serious?"

Harvey laughed, a loud, boisterous sound. "Why wouldn't I be serious? Zook's Custom Outdoor Furniture has been around for years and has a great reputation. It would be a shame for you to sell everything off and close the doors for *gut*."

"*Mei dat* is right," Anthony chimed in. "If we combined, it would be beneficial for all of us. We could even sell gazebos and patio furniture as a package deal. There are so many great products we could advertise together."

"Wait a minute." Micah held his hand up. "You both know why I'm selling, right? My business is going under because *mei daadi* didn't tell me the debts were piling up. I have a mountain of unpaid bills."

Harvey nodded. "I know."

"I told him," Anthony said.

"I've tried to sell my stock to several different buyers, and they turned me down." He listed the buyers he'd called. "The bigger problem I have is I'm going to lose the farm too. *Mei daadi* had overdue tax bills, and he used the farm as collateral on a loan. Then he defaulted on the loan. I have no way of getting out of this debt, and that's why I'm selling everything," Micah said. "If you already know that, then why would you want to combine businesses if mine is in shambles?"

"We can work that out," Harvey said.

"How?" Micah asked.

"We'll find a way to pay back Enos's debts and make you solvent again. It may take a little time, but we'd hate for you to lose everything you have."

"And what about the farm?"

Harvey rubbed his beard. "We can discuss it. I can either give you the money to get you caught up on the loan payments. Or I can cosign for you to take out a new loan. We can discuss it in more detail after you show me all of the debts you have."

Micah studied Harvey as confusion swamped him. "Why would you want to bail me out?"

"Because I think this could be *gut* for all of us," Harvey said.

"We can both increase our sales," Anthony chimed in. "Many people are looking for Amish patio furniture and gazebos because of our craftsmanship. We can go to suppliers as one company and make deals to get on their websites and their catalogs. It will be profitable for us all." He paused and then added, "And it would mean you'll stay in Bird-in-Hand. We want you to stay."

Micah's thoughts spun. If he stayed in Bird-in-Hand, he'd have to face the congregation and confess his sins. Then he'd have to make it through the shunning.

On the other hand, he'd still be able to see Bethany. And if he combined his business with her family's, he'd be a part of her life, seeing her more often than only at church and the Coffee Corner.

But Bethany had seen him at his lowest. How could she ever look him in the eye again without recalling how he'd behaved and how he'd treated her? Staying in Bird-in-Hand would mean that he would have to see her often, which meant facing how he'd ruined their special friendship.

Still, remaining in Bird-in-Hand almost surely meant he would have the opportunity to save his grandfather's legacy. Was that what he wanted to do?

His confusion morphed and became a dark cloud hanging over him, making his thoughts reel like a furious tornado.

"I can tell you're trying to work something out in your head," Harvey said, his expression warm and kind. "What are you thinking?"

"I just don't know what to do. Your offer is a complete surprise, frankly." Micah shook his head, hoping to knock his jumbled thoughts into logical order. "Also, Neil came to see me about missing church and also about drinking." He pressed his lips together as he looked at Anthony. "I'm sorry for that, Anthony. I'm sure you think the worst of me, and you have every right to. Neil said I'll need to confess, and I'm sure I'll be put under the *Ban*."

"But everyone will forgive you," Anthony said. "We all have sinned and fall short of the glory of God, but we're all forgiven."

Micah pinched the bridge of his nose. "I need to think about all of this and consider all of the pros and cons of staying and leaving."

"That's fair." Harvey folded his hands. "But I do believe Enos would be *froh* to see us combine our businesses. I think he'd be proud to see you taking the lead and bringing the business into the future."

Micah's heart squeezed at the thought of his grandfather being proud of him. Would he truly be proud? Would he want to see Micah lead his business into the future?

Harvey finished the last of his coffee and stood. "We need to run some errands, so we'll let you get back to work." He held out his hand and shook Micah's. "I hope you'll consider going into business with us. We would be honored to help you continue Enos's legacy."

"*Danki* for the opportunity," Micah said. "I will let you know."

"*Gut*," Harvey said before heading toward the back door.

"It was great seeing you." Anthony shook Micah's hand.

"You too." Micah stood at the mudroom doorway and watched them go. He suddenly had the overwhelming need to know how Bethany was. As Anthony reached for the door, Micah hurried over to him. "Anthony. Wait."

Anthony faced him.

"How's Bethany?"

Anthony frowned, and Micah's chest felt heavy with worry.

"She misses you," Anthony said.

Micah nodded as his mouth dried.

"See you later," Anthony said before he disappeared through the door.

Micah stood in the doorway, his thoughts swirling as Anthony and Harvey strode to their horse and buggy. Anthony's words echoed through his mind. If Bethany missed him, did that mean she cared for him? Even after everything they'd been through in recent days?

As hope bloomed in his heart for the first time since *Daadi*'s death, Micah realized the truth: he had fallen in love with Bethany. Although he'd tried to guard his heart, Bethany had found a way in. She had become important to him despite the turmoil between them. And he cared for her deeply. He loved her. He craved a future with her, but he had nothing to offer her.

He moaned, covering his face with his hands.

He was so confused he feared he might go mad from all his raging thoughts. And for the first time in weeks, Micah felt the urge to pray.

"Lead me, Lord," he whispered. "Guide me on the right path."

Then he turned and walked over to the kitchen table to continue sorting through papers, knowing he had a very big decision to make.

Chapter 28

Bethany smiled when she spotted her father and brother walking into her booth later that afternoon. She stood up from the table she had been wiping and waved at them. "What a surprise to see you here!"

"We were in the neighborhood and thought we'd stop by." *Dat* pulled out his wallet from his pocket as he looked up at the specials on the blackboard. "I'd like a cup of your Black Forest cake *kaffi*."

"That sounds *gut*," Anthony said as he sat at one of the high-top tables. "I'll take one also."

"Put your money away, *Dat*." Bethany waved him off as she slipped behind the counter and poured two cups. Then she grabbed two chocolate-glazed donuts before meeting them at the table where her father and Anthony sat.

She handed them their coffee and donuts, along with a handful of creamers, sweeteners, and stirrers, and they thanked her. Then she rested her elbow on the table and her chin in her hand. "You two rarely come by to visit me. So tell me the truth. Why are you really here?"

"We went to see Micah," *Dat* began before taking a bite of his donut.

Her heart stuttered with excitement. "And . . ."

"And I asked him if he would consider going into business with me. I told him that Zook's Custom Outdoor Furniture has always had a great reputation and that I thought we could both increase our sales if we became a one-stop shop for gazebos and outdoor furniture."

"And what did he say?" She could barely contain the excitement in her voice.

"He said he would think about it," Anthony said.

"Oh." Bethany's hope deflated like a balloon. She'd prayed Micah would take the offer, and hearing he had to think about the idea sent disappointment roaring through her.

"Did he at least sound like he liked the idea?" she asked, hating the desperation in her voice.

"I think so," *Dat* said.

Anthony wiped his mouth on a paper napkin. "He seemed a little stunned by the offer. He also seemed confused by the notion that *Dat* wanted to help him out of his debt."

Bethany nodded slowly. "But he still has to think about it."

Dat sipped his coffee. "This *kaffi* is fantastic." He took another sip. "I think he's confused and overwhelmed, but I have faith he'll make the right decision."

Bethany sat up straight and forced herself to smile and change the subject. "So, what else are you two up to today?"

"Well, we had planned to see Micah and then run for supplies. But your *mamm* gave us a list for the grocery store," *Dat* began.

Bethany smiled and nodded as her father went on about their errands, but her thoughts were stuck on Micah and his less than enthusiastic response to her father's offer to help save his business. It was obvious Micah had made up his mind and had already planned to sell everything to the *Englisher* and leave the district. Her heart cracked at the thought.

"Are you okay, Bethany?" Anthony asked as he lifted the last piece of his donut.

"*Ya*, of course." She pointed to their coffee cups. "I'm trying new flavors. Do you both truly like the *kaffi*?"

Dat gave her a warm grin. "It's spectacular. I'm so very proud of your success, Bethany. You've done such a great job with your Coffee Corner."

"*Danki, Dat*." Bethany smiled, but she felt a pang of sadness. Would she ever have a husband who would say he was proud of her?

Dat stood and tossed his coffee cup and napkin in the trash. "Well, Anthony, we'd better get going to the grocery store before your *mamm* starts to worry that we ran off to Mexico without her."

Anthony chuckled. "You're right." He gulped down the last of his coffee and threw away his trash. "*Danki* for the *appeditlich* snack," he told Bethany.

"*Gern gschehne*." She stood.

"I'll pick you up at the regular time," he added.

"I'll be ready."

Dat started toward the booth exit, but Anthony lingered behind.

"Before we left Micah's shop, he called me back," Anthony said. "And he asked about you."

"He did?" A tremor rolled through her.

Her brother nodded.

"What did he say?"

"He wanted to know how you're doing."

"What did you tell him?"

"I told him you missed him, and he looked surprised." Anthony glanced over at *Dat*, who stood in the doorway of the booth. Then he turned back to her. "I have a feeling he's going to decide to stay. I think you need to keep praying for him. And don't give up hope just yet."

She swallowed. "Okay."

As her father and brother left the Coffee Corner, Bethany sent up another prayer:

Please, God, show Micah how much he means to our community and to me. And please help him decide to stay in Bird-in-Hand.

The old, worn linoleum floors creaked as Micah walked out of the kitchen and headed toward the hallway leading to his grandfather's bedroom later that evening. He carried a lantern and moved through the family room past the bathroom to the bedroom.

He stood in the doorway and tried not to recall the day he'd found *Daadi* in bed and already gone from this life.

Glancing around the room, he took in all of the things that reminded him of *Daadi*. The tall dresser that held his socks, undershorts, undershirts, and handkerchiefs. The small closet filled with his shoes, trousers, and shirts. The shelves clogged with his favorite books. The nightstand that held his reading glasses, a battery-operated clock, and a Bible.

Micah sank down onto the edge of *Daadi's* double bed, and it creaked under his weight. He looked around the room and tried to imagine packing everything up and storing it all when he moved out. *If* he moved out.

Confusion had been his constant companion ever since Harvey and Anthony had come to see him this morning. Micah had spent most of the day contemplating what to do. He'd prayed, made a list of pros and cons, and wandered around the workshop, trying to decide what the best choice would be.

If he stayed in the community, he could save his grandfather's business and continue to do what he loved.

Still, Micah wasn't completely at peace with allowing Harvey to bail him out of his debt. Also, he had to consider his relationship with Bethany. Could he stand living in the same community with Bethany if he'd lost her friendship forever? The thought of life without her company made him feel empty.

Micah rubbed his forehead as the dull throb of a headache started behind his eyes. All of these decisions were driving him crazy! If only he had someone to talk to.

He glanced around the room, and suddenly grief overwhelmed him. He hugged his arms to his chest as tears filled his eyes.

"Why did you have to go, *Daadi*?" he whispered as he scanned the room. "I'm lost without you. We were partners. I wasn't ready to run the business alone, and you didn't prepare me. Why didn't you tell me we were in trouble? I could have helped you figure out how to fix things. We could have done it together. But now you're gone, and I'm stuck here trying to pick up the pieces and make decisions that seem too difficult. I just hope I make you proud. And I hope you'll forgive me no matter what I decide to do."

He wiped his eyes as he looked down at his lap. He had to pick himself up and figure this out on his own. After all, he was almost thirty. He had to start acting like a grown man.

With a sigh, Micah pushed himself off of the bed and started for the door. He stopped when he spotted a piece of paper sticking out from under the nightstand. Crouching down, he picked it up and unfolded it. It was a letter written in beautiful, slanted script. The paper was faded and wrinkled, but he could still read the words. The letter was to his grandmother from her sister, his great-aunt Dottie.

Dear Bertha,

It was so wonderful to get your letter. I'm glad to know you and Enos are doing well. Marvin and I are feeling better. Those colds did linger, but we're grateful we're on the mend now.

I was so happy to hear Micah had decided to move in with you and Enos to help out with the business since Enos's helper moved to Indiana to get married. I know you had always hoped Richard would take over the business someday, and you were disappointed when he decided to become a dairy farmer instead. But I'm sure it warms your heart that Micah has come to help out.

Micah was always such a kind and bright boy. I know you and Enos are very proud of him. I'm sure he'll do a great job. I remember you told me how much Enos enjoyed teaching Micah how to build furniture when he would come to visit. Micah has always enjoyed working with tools and wood more than his father ever did. It's funny how the love of carpentry skipped a generation when Richard was born. But now Enos has the opportunity to take Micah under his wing and teach him everything he knows. I'm certain Enos will enjoy every moment he has in the workshop with Micah. Enos will feel young again!

And like you said, Enos had always hoped to keep the business in the family. Your heritage will live on long after you're gone since Micah is there to run things. You can rest easy knowing your business will be in the best hands when you and Enos are too old to handle things at the house. Micah will take great care of you both! And he will carry on Enos's dream.

I must run now and make supper for Marvin and me. Please send my love to Enos and Micah. And write to me soon.

All my love,
Dottie

Micah stared down at the letter, reading it over and over again until the words were burned into his mind. The answer was right in front of him, written in his great-aunt's beautiful script penmanship—he was *called* to take over the business. He was *called* to stay in Bird-in-Hand and ensure his grandparents' legacy would stay alive and well now that they were both gone.

Micah's vision blurred as he looked up toward the ceiling.

"I hear you, God, loud and clear," he whispered as tears streamed down his hot cheeks. "I see I need to keep the business, the *haus*, and the land. I must make myself right with the church. And I also have to ask Bethany for forgiveness. I love her, and I want her in my life. I want to beg her to give me a chance to show her I can be the man she deserves. With your help, I can learn how to take better care of myself and then take care of her. I can find a future with her once I fix myself. But I can't do it without your help. Please continued to show me the right path for me, and also please help Bethany forgive me. I can do all of this through you because you give me strength. *Danki* for showing me what I need to do."

Micah folded the letter and put it on the nightstand. Then he jumped up from the bed, grabbed the lantern, and hurried out into the kitchen. He retrieved a garbage bag from under the sink. Then pulling on a coat and boots, Micah carried the lantern and trash bag out to the workshop. He picked up all of the empty alcohol bottles and dropped them into the garbage bag. They clinked together loudly as they fell inside.

When he walked back outside, he tied up the trash bag and dropped it into a trash can, then looked up at the dark sky and took in the stars twinkling above him. He breathed in the cool, fresh air, enjoying the aroma of animals, earth, and new life.

For the first time since he'd lost his grandfather, he felt hope igniting in his chest, and he felt his heart begin to heal.

"Lord," he whispered, "I'm sorry I lost my way for so long. I'm ready to come back to you. I want to redirect my life to you and to what you have in store for me. Please continue to show me the path you have chosen for me. Help me live a life that is pleasing to you. I am your servant, and I am ready to listen for your voice."

Then Micah picked up his lantern and started toward the house.

Tomorrow he would thank Brandon Parker for his offer but renege on their deal as gracefully as possible. Then he would talk to Harvey about combining their businesses and would reveal the extent of his grandfather's debt.

But first he would go to see Bethany.

With God's help, he would win her friendship back and convince her they could possibly be more than friends after he made himself right with the church.

Chapter 29

Saturday morning Bethany smiled at a customer as she handed back her change. "Thank you for coming by the Coffee Corner today," she told the woman, who looked to be in her forties. "I hope you have a great day."

"You too," the woman said as she slipped her change into her pocket and walked away from the counter.

"Hi. How may I help you?" she asked the next person in line, who was a young man who looked to be about her age.

Bethany glanced behind him as he gave his order, and she sucked in a breath when she spotted Micah stepping into the booth.

For the first time since Enos had passed away, Micah looked rested and refreshed. Although he was still skinnier than he had been before Enos died, Micah's eyes were bright, and his skin looked pink instead of pale. He was clad in a dark-blue shirt, and he had an air of confidence and assurance about him.

Her mouth dried as she took in his handsome face. When his eyes met hers, he smiled, and a sizzle of heat danced up her spine. But as he took his place at the end of the line, a niggle of worry filled her. Had he come to say good-bye to her before he left for his new life in Ohio?

"Miss?" the customer asked. "Did you hear my order?"

"I'm sorry. No, I didn't." Bethany felt her cheeks heat as her hands began to shake. "Would you please repeat it?"

She quickly filled his order and took care of the four people waiting behind him. By the time Micah reached her she was shuddering with anticipation, waiting to hear what he had to say to her.

"Hi," she said, her voice sounding breathy.

"*Gude mariye.*" He leaned forward on the counter, and his bright smile made him look so attractive she felt off-balance. "*Wie geht's?*"

"I'm well. You?"

"I feel great today." He pointed up toward her blackboard. "Could I please have a cup of blueberry-cinnamon-crumble *kaffi* and a cinnamon-sugar donut." He pulled out his wallet from his coat pocket.

"Coming right up." She tried to calm her jumping nerves as she retrieved his order. Her mind spun with questions. What had he come to tell her?

She set the coffee and donut in front of him and gave him his change. He leaned over the cup and grinned. "Oh, this smells amazing."

"*Danki.*" She glanced behind him and frowned as a group of six young Amish folks who looked to be about her age walked into the booth. If only her booth could have been empty this morning!

He looked over his shoulder and his smile faded. "You're busy today."

"Well, the first day of spring is next week. Tourist season will be in full swing soon."

283

He tapped his finger on the counter. "I had hoped to talk to you alone."

"I can't leave the booth now, but . . ." Her heart drummed hard and fast.

He rubbed at a spot on his cheek. "What if I picked you up and gave you a ride home this evening? Would that work?"

She swallowed. "*Ya.*"

"What time should I be back?"

They discussed a time, and then he lifted his coffee cup. "I'll see you later. Have a *gut* day."

"You too." Trepidation pinched her chest as she watched him saunter over to get creamer, sweetener, and a stirrer from the condiment station and then leave her booth. Then, forcing her lips into a bright smile, she looked at her group of customers. "*Gude mariye.* Welcome to the Coffee Corner. How may I help you?"

Later that morning Bethany breathed a sigh of relief when her line of customers dissipated. She grabbed a wet rag and began to wipe down her counter. A buzz of conversations filled her booth as people sat at her high-top tables enjoying their coffee and donuts.

Her mind continued to twirl with worry about Micah as she tried to keep her hands busy, organizing her workspace, cleaning up the condiment station, and sweeping up crumbs from the sprinkled donuts she had sold.

When she glanced back toward the booth entrance, she spotted Leanna rushing toward her.

"Hey," Bethany greeted her cousin.

"Hi." Leanna seemed out of breath as she reached the counter. "I asked one of the ladies in the candle booth to watch mine for a minute. I thought I saw Micah walk in here earlier, and I've been anxious to ask you about it. Was that him?"

Everything inside of Bethany twisted and tightened as she nodded. "*Ya*, it was."

"And . . ." Leanna glanced back behind her again. "Tell me quickly."

"I'm really not sure what he wanted." Bethany shrugged. "He said he needed to talk to me, but I had a line. He's going to pick me up and give me a ride home."

Leanna gasped. "That's so exciting!"

Bethany felt her brow furrow. "No, it's not."

"What do you mean?"

"He looked fantastic—like he'd slept for the first time in a month and a tremendous weight had been lifted off his shoulders." She drew invisible circles on the worn wooden countertop as she spoke. "He probably wants to tell me he's sold everything and he's moving at the end of the month."

Leanna clucked her tongue. "Bethany, you have always been a *froh* ray of sunshine, finding the *gut* in people and the silver lining in every cloud. Why are you always so negative when it comes to Micah's intentions toward you?"

"Because I feel in my heart he wants to leave." Bethany heard the quiver in her voice as she looked at her cousin. "If he cared about me, he would have told me by now. He would have come to see me at *mei haus* so that we could talk there in private. Coming to my booth on a Saturday morning is convenient for him. He's not going out of his way to talk to me."

Leanna tapped the edge of the counter. "But he is. He's coming back when you close. He wants to give you a ride home so that you can talk in the buggy and then maybe talk on your porch."

She touched Bethany's hand. "Your prayers are probably being answered right now. You just don't know it yet."

Unconvinced, Bethany frowned. "I guess we'll see."

Leanna looked over her shoulder as a group of middle-aged ladies headed toward her booth. "I need to go. We'll talk more at lunchtime. In the meantime, stay positive," she said before heading to her booth.

"I'll try," Bethany whispered, but she was already bracing herself for a painful good-bye.

Micah arrived at the Bird-in-Hand marketplace thirty minutes early after showering and putting on his best navy-blue shirt, clean trousers, and suspenders. He hurried into the market and made his way past the other booths, being sure to avoid Sara Ann's Quilt Stand on his way to the Coffee Corner.

When he reached the entrance to Bethany's booth, he glanced behind him and found Leanna watching him while she held a dust cloth. She gave him a little wave and a smile that sent encouragement rushing through him. If Bethany's cousin supported him, did that mean Bethany might forgive him?

Micah nodded at her, and Leanna returned to dusting the shelves in her Jam and Jelly Nook. He looked back into the Coffee Corner where Bethany wiped down her high-top tables with a spray bottle and paper towels. He squared his shoulders and stepped inside.

"Hi, Bethany," he said.

She looked up, glanced over at the clock, then back at him. "You're early."

"I'm sorry." He gave her a shrug. "I was worried about the evening traffic."

"That's okay." She pointed to one of the stools. "You can have a seat. I should be ready in a few minutes."

"Put me to work." He grinned. "I've worked in this booth before, you know. There was this one time when the owner burned her hand, and I ran the counter for an *entire* hour."

To his surprise, she laughed, her pretty face lighting up like sunlight on a summer afternoon. "Is that so? Well, it sounds like someone should put you on the payroll permanently." She held out the paper towels and the spray bottle. "If you finish wiping down the tables, I can start washing the coffeepots."

"Perfect." Micah took the cleaner and roll of paper towels from her and set to work while she slipped behind the counter. After a moment, he glanced back and found her working with her back to him. The silence between them was almost deafening.

He turned toward her as he wiped another table. "How was your day?"

"Busy." She kept her back to him as she washed a coffeepot at the utility sink in the back of the booth.

"I would imagine you ran out of your blueberry-cinnamon crumble *kaffi*. It was *appeditlich*," he said, hoping to pull her into a conversation.

"I sold quite a bit of it. The customers seemed to like it."

"*Gut.* I guess that means you'll feature it again?"

"*Ya*, I will. I keep a list of my bestsellers, and I plan to have them on the menu again."

"Great." He waited for her to elaborate, but she continued scrubbing the pot with her back to him.

He frowned as he took in her stiff posture and clipped responses. Contrary to her earlier laughter, she now seemed either angry or anxious. Worry threaded through him. Perhaps he'd missed his chance to apologize to her. He silently prayed God would soften her heart toward him as he returned to wiping down the tables.

Soon the furniture and the coffeepots were clean, and Bethany had packed up the leftover donuts in a large box. Then she turned her attention to closing the register. Micah grabbed a broom and kept himself occupied with sweeping the floor. He stole frequent glances at her, taking in her adorable expression. With her brow wrinkled, her lips moved as she silently counted the bills. Did she have any idea how pretty she was?

Micah swept the crumbs and dirt into a pile and then into a dustpan before dropping the dirt into the trash can. "I'll tie up the trash bags. Where do they go?"

"Oh. *Danki.*"

She gave him instructions, and he emptied the trash cans both in the back of the booth and out front by the tables. He deposited the bags out by the loading dock located at the back of the marketplace before returning to the booth where she was stuffing money into a zippered bank bag.

Micah leaned on a nearby table and tried to imagine what it would be like to pick up Bethany at the booth at closing every Thursday, Friday, and Saturday. How he'd love to help her clean up while they discussed their day. With Bethany around, even mundane tasks seemed to be filled with delight.

Bethany looked around the booth. "Well, I think I'm ready to go."

"Great."

Micah's shoulders tightened as Bethany gathered up her purse, tote bag, and the box of leftover donuts. As they walked toward the exit, he prayed she would listen to him with an open heart as he begged for her forgiveness.

Chapter 30

Bethany's hands shook as she climbed into Micah's buggy. She'd spent the afternoon worrying about what he would tell her when he arrived to take her home, and now she had to face whatever it was he had to say.

While she stared out the side window, she held her tote bag on her lap and touched a loose thread on the handle as Micah guided the horse through the parking lot and then out onto Old Philadelphia Pike. She searched her mind for something to say to him, but she came up blank.

"I'm glad you had *gut* business today," he said, his voice breaking through the sound of passing traffic, the *clip-clopping* of horse hooves, and the whir of the buggy wheels.

"*Danki.* How was *your* day?" she asked, her voice sounding thin and reedy.

"*Gut.*" He glanced over at her, and she was almost certain she found a twinkle in his dark eyes. "I ran some errands, and then I continued cleaning up my workshop. I've been slowly tidying it up over time."

She took a deep breath. The small talk between them felt

awkward and forced. If only she could find a way to bridge the chasm between them filled with the unfinished business of their last encounters.

He shook his head as he turned his attention back toward the road ahead. "It's taken me a while to get it all in order. I'm embarrassed by what a mess it had become since *mei daadi* passed away. I had old food wrappers, empty water bottles, and even some napkins strewn about. And then the liquor bottles."

She was almost certain he had blushed when he mentioned the alcohol. She hoped that meant he'd stopped drinking.

"Not to mention the piles of tools everywhere," he continued. "*Mei daadi* would be so disappointed in me if he saw that mess. He used to lecture me about always putting my tools away in the proper drawer of the toolbox after we finished a project. He said you always prepared for your next project by cleaning up after the last one."

Bethany licked her lips as Micah talked on and on about tidying his workshop. Was he cleaning up in order to get ready to sell all of the contents? Or maybe he was preparing to pack up the tools before sending them on a journey in a moving truck to his new home in Ohio. The thought sent sadness curling in her chest. She hugged her arms against her middle.

When he guided the horse onto Gibbons Road, she couldn't take the small talk anymore. She had to hear him tell her the truth, even if it shattered her heart.

She turned toward him. "Micah, why did you really want to drive me today?"

"What do you mean?"

"You said you wanted to talk to me about something, and the anticipation has been eating at me all day long. Please just say what you came to say. I can handle it. I'm not as naïve and weak as everyone thinks I am."

Micah's forehead puckered as he looked over at her. "Who said you were naïve and weak?"

"It doesn't matter." She waved him off as more irritation filled her. "Just tell me what you wanted to say when you came into my booth this morning. I'm tired of making small talk and playing games. I'm ready to hear the truth, so just be honest with me."

Micah guided his horse up her driveway and halted it at the top. When he turned toward her, his pleasant expression had dissolved, and the somber looked on his eyes rocked her to the depth of her soul.

This was it. He was going to tell her he was leaving. This was their last good-bye. She swallowed against her building emotions. She felt as if she were crying on the inside as she tried to steel herself against the grief in her chest.

"Bethany," he began, "I don't know how to say this. I've been racking my brain for the right words all day long."

"Just say it." Her voice was a hoarse whisper.

He reached for her hands, and she started to pull them away but stopped, allowing him to touch her. The feel of his warm skin against hers sent a thrill rushing up her arms. She tried to fight off the pleasure, but she couldn't. Why did his touch have to feel so right when she had to force herself to let him go?

"Bethany," he began, his voice strained. "I'm so sorry. I can't tell you just how sorry I am for hurting you so many times. You've always been so nice to me, and you were the *freind* I needed when my life was a wreck. You stood by me when *mei daadi* died, and you tried to reach out to me when I was at my lowest. I rejected you, and I said terrible things to you. I've never deserved your friendship. I don't know how to make it up to you, but I want you to know that I appreciate you. You've become important to me."

Her body began to vibrate as she stared into his eyes. Was he trying to let her down easy?

"My heart was in shambles after *mei daadi* died, and things took a darker turn when I found all of the debt he left me," he continued. "I had moved here to make a new start, but I thought my future was ruined. My Saturday-morning chats with you in the Coffee Corner were my only bright light throughout all of the darkness surrounding me. I turned to alcohol as a way to relieve the pain, but it only made things worse. I was on a destructive path. You were the only one who checked on me when I disappeared from church. And when you did, I was terrible to you. I yelled at you, and I said awful things. I behaved like *mei daed*. In fact, I treated you the way he has always treated me, and I'm embarrassed and furious with myself for doing that to you. You're the last person who deserves to be treated that way."

He moved his thumbs over the back of her hands, and she shivered with delight at the feeling.

"I don't deserve to have you in my life, but I am so very grateful for you," he continued, his eyes glittering with unshed tears. "I've gotten rid of all of the alcohol, and I've begged God for his forgiveness, because I had turned my back on him too. The deacon came to see me, and now I have to confess and make myself right with the church. But I wanted to make sure I had your forgiveness first before I faced the deacon and the bishop."

"You've had my forgiveness all along."

They were both silent for a moment, and then what he'd said clicked into place in her mind.

"Wait a minute." She pulled one of her hands back and held it up. "You're going to confess?"

He nodded. "That's right."

"If you're going to confess, does that mean you're not going to sell everything and move away?"

"No, I'm not. I'm going to stay here and make myself right with the community and the church."

Something inside of her broke apart, and she blew out a deep, shaky sigh of relief.

"Your *dat* and *bruder* asked me to go into business with them, and I'm going to accept their offer. I've done a lot of praying and soul searching, and I realized I belong here."

He leaned against the door behind him as he angled his body toward her. "I thought I should go to my family in Ohio because I've coveted the relationship you have with your cousins. But I can't keep running away from my problems. I belong here." He pointed to the seat as if indicating the ground below the buggy. "I need to continue *mei daadi*'s legacy. So I turned down Brandon Parker's offer this morning. I went to see him after I spoke to you. He completely understands that I want to stay, and I told him I would work out a payment plan for what *mei daadi* owed him. I'm also going to pay back the other suppliers and work something out with the bank so I don't lose the farm. All of this will be with your *daed*'s help, of course."

"Oh, I'm *froh* to hear it." Her eyes filled with happy tears.

"But I wanted to talk to you before I take the offer to join my business with your *dat*'s. I couldn't stand to work with your *dat* if you weren't still *mei freind*. It would be torture to stay in the district, work for your family, and not be able to talk to you."

"Of course I'm still your *freind*, Micah. And I'm sorry for all of those horrible things I said to you the day I saw you buying the alcohol. I was just so worried about you." She sniffed. "I had hoped you would stay if *mei dat* asked you to combine businesses. That's part of the reason why I suggested it."

His eyes rounded. "That was your idea?"

She nodded.

"You still want me to stay?"

"Very much." She took a fortifying breath and wiped at her eyes. It was time to tell her truth. "I-I've had a crush on you since you first started coming to my booth. I know you could never like me as more than a *freind*, but that's okay. I've accepted it. I'll be fine as long as you're still *mei freind*."

He sat up straight and shook his head as he studied her. "I'm confused. Why would you think I would only want to be your *freind*?"

"I know you don't like me that way, and it's okay."

"Bethany, what are you talking about? Whatever gave you the idea that I couldn't ever see you as more than a *freind*?"

"Because men never take me seriously. I've spent my life watching Salina and Christiana get dates and have men pursue them. I used to wonder why I wasn't *gut* enough, and then one of Christiana's boyfriends told me that I was cute, perky Bethany, but not someone he'd want to date. I realized then that men don't notice me because they think I'm just a joke."

Micah gasped as his expression turned stony. "That is not true. I noticed you right away."

She waved off his comment as if it didn't meant anything. "You don't have to lie to me. I also know you don't feel comfortable with my family. We're too loud for you. And I understand. Like I said, as long as we can still be *freinden*—"

"Whoa." He held his hand up. "Who told you that?"

"Laverne told Simply Sara Ann—I mean, Sara Ann King—and she told me. Apparently they had talked at church, and Laverne shared that you had told your family that supper with us was too much for you. You were overwhelmed by how loud we are." She held up her hands as his expression twisted into something that looked like embarrassment or regret. "Don't worry about it. I can't say I blame you! I understand we're too different. You prefer a quiet dinner instead of people talking over each other."

Saying the words aloud hurt her heart, but she had to be honest with him. Clearing the air was the only way they could truly be friends.

He shook his head as contrition seemed to flicker over his handsome face. "I'm so sorry, Bethany. I did tell Laverne that, but I never meant to hurt you. Your family is amazing, and I can't thank you all enough for how kind and helpful you've been to me. I think the world of you, Anthony, and your parents. In fact, you've all become like my family since I'm estranged from my parents, *mei schweschder*, and her family."

He hesitated. "*Mei dat* came to see me the same day Neil did."

"He did?" She gasped.

Micah nodded and frowned. "He said *mei mamm* told him to check on me. After a month." He snorted. "The entire conversation was strange. I told him I was going to be shunned and he shouldn't have been surprised since I've always been a failure. Then I told him about the debts and how I had planned to sell everything and move. He asked why I hadn't come to him for help, and I said he would be the last person I'd ask for help. Then he did the strangest thing. He got up to leave, and he said he never felt I was a failure or a disappointment. He also told me he would miss me if I moved to Ohio. Then he left, and I haven't heard from him since. I'm still trying to figure that one out."

"Perhaps he's had a change of heart since he lost his *daed*, and he wants to start over with you and fix your relationship. Maybe he misses you."

"Maybe." Micah looked down at his lap. Then he met her gaze again. "All I know for sure is I never could have made it through this past month without you and your family. Please accept my apology. I'm truly honored to be welcome at your table."

"You don't have to apologize." Her voice wavered as he shifted closer to her. "Like I said, I'll be fine as long as you're still *mei freind*."

"But that's the whole problem, Bethany. I can't be just your *freind*." He cupped his hand to her cheek. "That would never be enough for me."

"I don't understand," she whispered as tears escaped her eyes.

"I want to be so much more." He paused, and his lips compressed. "The truth is that when I came to Bird-in-Hand, I wanted to start over after losing Dawn. I was convinced I would never fall in love again or find a *maedel* I could care for as much as I loved her. I thought she'd been my one chance at a *froh* future. I tried to keep a cover over my heart and guard it from more hurt."

He moved his fingers down her cheeks, swiping away her tears, and she quivered at the intimate touch. "But then I met you. As much as I tried to stop myself from caring for you, I felt this invisible force pulling me to you." He paused for a moment. "Bethany, you're *schee*, sweet, funny, and thoughtful. You're a ray of sunshine when the world is gray and lonely."

He gave a little laugh. "You're the opposite of me. You're talkative and you've never met a stranger. You're never afraid to greet a new customer or talk to a guest at church. I'm shy, and sometimes I need a quiet space to recharge my batteries. But I love that we're different. You bring excitement and unpredictability to my life. You always bring me out of my shell. You've taught me what's important in life, and you've taught me I'm never alone. But most important, you've taught me that I can love again, and you've shown me that I'm *ready* to love again."

"What are you saying?" she whispered.

"I'm saying I'm in love with you, Bethany. And I'm saying I want to stay in Bird-in-Hand, but I want you to be a part of my life here. I want you by my side as I rebuild my business. I want to share everything with you because you make me a better man. And if you can forgive my past mistakes, I promise I will do everything in my power to build us a bright future."

A small gasp escaped from her mouth as she stared up at him. Was she dreaming?

His expression clouded with something that looked like worry. "Do you care about me too? Do you want a future with me?"

"*Ya*, I do. *Ich liebe dich*, Micah."

A relieved smile turned up his lips. "*Gut*." Leaning down, he kissed her cheek, and heat hummed through her veins. "I would like to ask your *daed*'s permission to date you after I face my shunning and make myself right with the church."

She smiled as happiness buzzed through her body. "I would like that. Let's go inside. You can stay for supper."

Bethany climbed out of the buggy and started up the porch steps feeling as if she were walking on a cloud. Micah followed her, carrying her box of leftover donuts. When they entered the kitchen, she found her mother setting a platter of fried chicken on the table. She looked up and beamed at Bethany and Micah.

"Hello, Micah," *Mamm* announced. "What a nice surprise! Are you staying for supper?"

Micah's smile was equally as bright. "I'd like to, if that would be okay."

"Of course it is." *Mamm* turned toward the doorway. "Harvey! Anthony! Come on for supper! *Dummle!* We have company!"

Bethany cringed at her mother's loud volume. But when she peeked over at Micah, she found him still grinning, and she felt her body relax. Perhaps they could be a couple despite their differences. She took the box of donuts from him and set it on the counter beside her tote bag and purse.

Dat and Anthony walked into the kitchen and greeted Micah, shaking his hand.

"It's great to see you again," *Dat* said. He gestured to the table. "Let's eat."

After washing their hands, Bethany and Micah sat next to each other at the table. They bowed their heads for a silent prayer and then began filling their plates with fried chicken, buttered noodles, green beans, and rolls.

"What brings you here today, Micah?" *Dat* asked as he buttered his roll.

Micah set down his fork as he looked at *Dat*. "I wanted to discuss your business proposal with you."

"Really?" Anthony asked, looking excited.

"I'd like to accept it." Micah said.

Bethany's heartbeat raced as she shared a smile with her mother.

"I just can't exchange any money with you until after I've

completed my shunning." Micah expression became embarrassed. "If you remember, the deacon came to see me."

Dat nodded, his expression grave. "I do remember that, and we can work around it."

"Micah," Bethany said. "I want you to know I never told Neil or *Onkel* Lamar about your drinking." She glanced over at Anthony. "*Mei bruder* didn't either, but I think Sara Ann may have overheard me talking to Salina in my booth." She frowned. "I wasn't gossiping about you. I was just upset, and I shared what happened with Salina. But she wasn't the one who told either. She makes it a point to stay out of church business."

Micah's expression remained serene. "It's okay. I made the mistake, and I need to face the consequences. I'm not upset with anyone."

Bethany breathed a sigh of relief.

Micah looked at *Dat* again. "Until my shunning is complete, I won't be able to eat at the same table as you or do any business with you. But maybe we can talk about your plans before I go to see Neil and Lamar. Then we can work out the details later."

He explained that he'd gone to Brandon earlier in the day. "I told him to give me a final figure on what I owe him so we can work that out. And I'll get final figures from the other suppliers."

"Don't worry about any of that." *Dat*'s expression was warm. "I can go talk to Brandon and work it out while you're under the *Ban*. Right now we'll just need to make things right with the bank so that your farm doesn't go into foreclosure. We can talk about that before you speak to the deacon and bishop about your shunning."

Micah paused, and his expression became emotional. "I can't thank you enough for all you're doing for me."

Bethany touched his arm. "We're called to take care of each other. Like I've been trying to tell you, your community cares for you."

"*Ya*, that's true," *Mamm* said.

"Exactly," Anthony added.

Micah glanced around the table and nodded. "*Danki*. I can't thank you all enough for what you've done for me. You're a blessing to me. I'm so glad God led me to stay here in Bird-in-Hand."

Bethany's heart warmed. She was glad too.

After supper, Micah enjoyed a delicious dessert of chocolate cheesecake and a cup of Bethany's special peppermint patty coffee. He laughed with Harvey and Anthony as they shared stories of their fishing adventures. When the meal was over, Bethany and Darlene began cleaning up the kitchen while Harvey and Anthony invited Micah out to the workshop with them to discuss the business plan.

Excitement and a little bit of anxiety filled Micah as they discussed how they would combine their businesses and work on new advertising and distribution. Yet the more they talked, the calmer Micah began to feel. By the end of the conversation, he could sense contentment deep in his bones. This was the path God had chosen for him, and he suddenly felt sure that his grandfather would approve.

"I'm so glad you decided to accept our offer," Harvey said as they walked back toward the house together while Anthony went into the barn to check on the horses.

"I'm grateful you offered it to me."

Harvey's smile became sheepish. "It was Bethany's idea."

"She told me."

Micah looked toward the house as his palms began to sweat. Now was the time for him ask permission to date her. "Harvey, I care about your *dochder*. She's very important to me. I know I've had some challenges, and I've made some mistakes. However, I'm on the right path now. I've disposed of the alcohol, and I won't touch it again. I would like to ask your permission to date Bethany after I finish my shunning and I'm made right with the church."

Harvey smiled. "Of course you have my permission. I can tell my Bethany cares for you, and I think you will make her very *froh*."

"*Danki*." Micah shook his hand. "I won't let you down."

"I know you won't, *sohn*."

Hearing Harvey call him "son" was almost too much for Micah's heart to handle. Bethany's family had become his surrogate family, and he was so grateful to have them in his life now that his grandparents were gone.

As Micah walked beside Harvey toward the house, excitement coursed through him. He was walking toward his future, and his future would include Bethany.

Thank you, God, for bringing the Gingerich family into my life. And thank you for giving me the chance to make things right with them. All the glory to you.

༺࿇༻

Bethany set the last pot in the cabinet as Micah and *Dat* walked into the kitchen. She could tell by the expression on Micah's face that their conversation had gone well. She smiled at him as excitement poured through her.

Soon she would call him her boyfriend. Oh, she couldn't wait!

"*Danki* for supper," Micah said as he smiled at *Mamm*.

"We're so glad you joined us tonight," *Mamm* told him as she wiped down the table.

Then Micah turned to *Dat*. "We'll talk soon."

"*Ya*, we will," *Dat* said.

When Micah looked at Bethany, she felt heat crawl up her cheeks.

"Would you please walk me out?" he asked her.

"*Ya*. Just let me get my coat."

Bethany's heart thumped as she rushed to the mudroom, pulled on her coat, and walked with Micah toward his waiting horse and buggy. She stood beside him and looked up into eyes that reminded her of her favorite dark-roast coffee. His eyes had become so familiar lately that she felt as if she had gotten to know him to the depth of his soul.

"Bethany," he began, his voice thick. "You are *schee*, wonderful, and sweet. You've been an angel to me, helping save me from a dark path. You've been *mei freind* and confidante, and you've stood by me even after I've shared my darkest secrets with you. You didn't reject me when I told you about my estranged relationship with my family, and you were my strength when I lost *mei daadi* and I told you about losing Dawn."

He took her hands in his. "I can't tell you how much you mean to me, but I'm hoping someday I can find a way to show you. I'm sorry for losing my way and hurting you. I'm so grateful you helped me find my way back to God, the community, and you. Your *dat* has given me permission, so I want to ask you now. I would be honored for you to be my girlfriend. Would you please date me?"

"I'd love to."

"*Gut.*" He cupped his hand to her cheek. "I love you, and I can't stand to spend another day without you by my side. I didn't realize a piece of me was missing until I saw you smile and I suddenly realized what it felt like to be whole."

He leaned down, and when he brushed his lips across hers, the contact sent her stomach fluttering with the wings of a thousand butterflies. She closed her eyes and savored the taste of his mouth against hers.

This was her first kiss, and it was from the love of her life. Joy blossomed inside of her.

When he broke the embrace, he leaned his forehead against hers. "*Ich liebe dich,* Bethany."

"I love you, too, with my whole heart," she whispered. Then she closed her eyes as he kissed her again.

Epilogue

"*Gude mariye*," Bethany chirped as Micah walked into her booth. "Welcome to the Coffee Corner."

"And good morning to you." Micah's smile was wide as he approached her.

"You're here early."

"I was able to convince the security guard to let me in before the doors were unlocked. I told him I needed to speak to you immediately."

She laughed. "That was awfully sneaky."

He looked up at the chalkboard listing her specials for the day. "What do you recommend for this sunny morning in June?"

"Hmm." She gave him her best coy smile. "I would recommend the orange-creamsicle *kaffi*."

"Sounds amazing." He leaned across the counter and kissed her cheek.

Bethany's face seemed to ache permanently from all of the smiling she'd done since Micah told her he loved her in March.

Soon after that night, he and her father had arranged to refinance the loan on his farm so that Micah could keep it. Then Micah had gone to visit her cousin Neil and told him that he wanted to make himself right with the church. The following Sunday he had confessed his sins to the baptized members of the congregation at a church members–only meeting after the service and then started his six weeks of shunning. During those weeks he met with the bishop before church began and sat up front during the services. He left right afterward since he wasn't permitted to eat with the congregation. He was also not allowed to do business with any members of the church.

Once Micah's shunning was completed, he was again able to eat with the congregation after the services. He also started running the combined business with Bethany's father and brother, which they named Bird-in-Hand Custom Gazebos and Patio Furniture. And, best of all, Bethany and Micah were able to start officially dating.

Bethany was grateful and excited when the shunning was over and the pieces of her life began to fit together. Now she was dating Micah, and his new business was thriving. Everything seemed to be perfect, and she was so grateful.

"Hi there," Micah said as he bent down and gave Lily and Daisy a soft rub. "You two seem *froh* this morning." He looked up at Bethany. "They're purring away."

"They just had their breakfast, so their bellies are full. Where are you headed today?" She handed him his cup of coffee and a chocolate-glazed donut.

"I'm going to see your *dat* and *bruder* at their shop. We're meeting with a new vendor today."

"That's exciting."

"It is." He added creamer and sweetener and sipped the coffee. "Oh, perfect as always, *mei liewe*."

"*Danki.*"

"I'll pick you up the regular time when the market closes?"

"That would be perfect." She reached over and touched his hand. "Will you stay for supper tonight?"

"Of course." He glanced behind him and then slipped behind the counter. "No one is here yet. I don't think the doors have opened."

He leaned down, and her breath hitched in her lungs. When he brushed his lips across hers, it sent the blood singing in her veins, pumping with excitement. She closed her eyes and savored the sensation of his warm mouth against hers.

When they parted, the intensity in his eyes sent more heat palpitating through her. "I need to run, but I'll see you later." He ran the tip of his finger down her cheek. "Don't forget I love you with my whole heart. I've never been this *froh*. I'm so glad God brought you into my life. You and your family have become the family I've never had, and I can't tell you how much it means to me. I feel as if I have all I need."

He paused. "I've decided to reach out to *mei daed*."

"Oh, Micah." Bethany knew how important those words were. She beamed up at him and gave his arms a squeeze but let him continue.

Micah nodded. "I can't instantaneously fix the problems he and I have, but I'm not angry anymore. I'm forgiving him from a distance, but I'm also hoping there's a possibility for more. I feel like he was reaching out to me when he came to see me the day Neil had stopped by. Hearing *mei dat* say he didn't think I was a disappointment or a failure was huge. I believe that was his way of trying to start to make things right. Also, I'm learning what it really means to be a family and to care for each other. I have you to thank for that."

"I'm so thrilled to hear you say that. And I want to thank you for showing me that I am worthy of love." She touched his chin as happiness expanded in her chest. "*Ich liebe dich.*"

As Micah pulled her close for a hug, Bethany felt overwhelming gratitude—and silently thanked God for giving her and Micah a chance to find each other and to find love.

Acknowledgments

As always, I'm thankful for my loving family, including my mother, Lola Goebelbecker; my husband, Joe; and my sons, Zac and Matt. I'm blessed to have such an awesome and amazing family that puts up with me when I'm stressed out on a book deadline.

An extra thank-you to my mother, who graciously read the draft of this book to check for typos. I'm sure you had some giggles due to my hilarious mistakes!

I'm also grateful to my special Amish friend who patiently answers my endless stream of questions.

Thank you to my wonderful church family at Morning Star Lutheran in Matthews, North Carolina, for your encouragement, prayers, love, and friendship. You all mean so much to my family and me.

Thank you to Zac Weikal and the fabulous members of my Bakery Bunch. I'm so thankful for your friendship and your excitement about my books. You all are amazing!

To my agent, Natasha Kern—I can't thank you enough for your guidance, advice, and friendship. You are a tremendous blessing in my life.

Thank you to my amazing editor, Jocelyn Bailey, for your friendship and guidance. I appreciate how you push me to dig deeper with each book and improve my writing. I've learned so much from you, and I look forward to our future projects together.

I'm grateful to editor Leslie Peterson, who helped me polish and refine the story. Thank you so much for your hard work on this book!

I'm grateful to each and every person at HarperCollins Christian Publishing who helped make this book a reality.

To my readers—thank you for choosing my novels. My books are a blessing in my life for many reasons, including the special friendships I've formed with my readers. Thank you for your email messages, Facebook notes, and letters.

Thank you most of all to God for giving me the inspiration and the words to glorify You. I'm grateful and humbled You've chosen this path for me.

Discussion Questions

1. Bethany enjoys spending time with her three favorite cousins. Do you have a special family member with whom you like to spend time? If so, who is that family member, and why are you close to him or her?

2. When her two cousins are married and not spending as much time at the market, Bethany feels like she's being left behind. Have you ever encountered a season when you felt like life was changing too fast? If so, how did you handle the changes?

3. Bethany and Micah are different in nearly every way, yet they fall in love. Do you believe that opposites attract?

4. Micah knows his behavior will cause him to be shunned. What is your opinion of the Amish community's practice of shunning?

5. Bethany is convinced men don't take her seriously. She always felt as if she was passed over for her cousins. Have you ever felt like you were misunderstood or ignored? If so, how did you handle that?

6. Micah decides to stay in Bird-in-Hand despite all of his challenges after his grandfather dies. Why do you think he felt he belonged in Bird-in-Hand?

7. Bethany and her cousins consider Sara Ann King to be the marketplace's gossip. Gossip, even in a community that is supposed to be Christlike, can hurt and lead to misunderstanding. Do we do this in our own church communities—judge and gossip about our fellow Christians without considering the consequences?

8. Which character can you identify with the most? Which character seemed to carry the most emotional stake in the story? Was it Bethany, Micah, or someone else?

9. Micah is devastated after his grandfather passes away, and he starts down a destructive path. Think of a time when you felt lost and alone. Where did you find your strength? What Bible verses helped?

10. What did you know about the Amish before reading this book? What did you learn?